E NG IN THE GARDEN

EVERYTHING IN THE GARDEN

by

JO VERITY

HONNO MODERN FICTION

Published by Honno
'Ailsa Craig', Heol y Cawl, Dinas Powys
South Glamorgan, Wales, CF6 4AH

The author would like to stress that
this is a work of fiction and no resemblance
to any actual individual or institution
is intended or implied.

ISBN 1 870206 70 3

Published with the financial support of the Welsh Books Council

Cover design by Chris Lee Design
Cover photograph by Nicola Schumacher

Printed in Wales by Gomer

For my father
Ken Evans

1909 - 2003

Acknowledgements

Thanks to Honno and the Welsh Books Council
for their confidence and support;
Elin ap Hywel, my gentle editor;
Cardiff Writers' Circle for listening and advising;
And my family for making me feel like a proper writer.

1

Anna took the letters from Len. He hovered, waiting for her to open them. She glanced at the hand-written envelopes and pushed them deep into the pocket of her overalls. The postman, disappointed, climbed back into his battered van and, with a blast on the horn, disappeared down the drive. She had planned to spend the morning working in the vegetable garden and didn't want anything to spoil it. The trouble was, it had already been spoiled. Seeing the envelopes had done that.

She walked across the yard to the outbuildings. Anna and Tom had claimed the one on the end. Inside it was gloomy and smelled of uncured concrete and white spirit; a masculine smell. The one small window, set deep in the thick wall, allowed a shaft of sunlight to paint a rhombus on the uneven floor. Tom had concocted a wooden rack from a floorboard, salvaged when the builders were in, doing the conversion work on the old farmhouse. He'd fixed this board to the rough stone wall, then inserted pairs of wooden pegs to hold his tools, head up, dangling. He graded them by length of handle so that they looked like a family standing to attention in the shadows. She lifted down a rake and took a trowel, a line and a pair of leather gardening gloves from the smaller items neatly stacked on open shelves, dropping them into a black bucket.

Leaving the outhouse, she skirted the swimming pool. A couple of inches of water stood in the deep end, where it had rained a few days earlier. Through the winter, a tarpaulin had kept the rain and leaves out but now it lay, like a beached whale, at the side of the pool.

The vegetable garden was divided into four equal plots, three of which were covered with grass and dandelions. Here and there a currant bush or rhubarb crown hinted at what had once been. Tom had double-dug their quadrant last autumn. While the others were inside, painting and decorating, he'd been getting ahead of the weather. Then the winter frosts had played their part, breaking the clods down to a fine tilth. The purple sprouting broccoli plants, although planted later than Anna would have liked, had flourished, giving the first indication that the soil was fertile.

She worked down the rows, nipping off the purple florets and dropping them into the bucket. The crop was tailing off now. The scruffy, wind-scorched plants leaned at crazy angles but there was plenty for everyone. If their section of the garden could produce such abundance, they could all be self sufficient in organic vegetables within twelve months. The snag was that the others were showing little interest. They thanked her for the greens each time she distributed them but, on the last occasion, she was sure she heard Jenny groan. She had checked, once or twice, to see whether they were finding their way straight into the dustbin. Tom had pointed out that there were plenty of other ways of disposing of unwanted broccoli. Anna wasn't always sure where Tom stood.

She stretched the line across the dark soil and made a shallow trench with the corner of the rake head. From the pocket not containing the letters, she took a packet of seeds. The picture on the front showed a bunch of carrots, straight and unblemished, unlike any carrots that she'd ever grown.

Every year she was taken in by such promises of perfection and every year she harvested misshapen vegetables, pockmarked with insect nibblings. But they were tasty and free from chemicals and they set her firmly in the season, something she missed when she bought her vegetables from a supermarket. She shook the packet, hearing the rattle of the seeds, each bearing its blueprint of colour, taste and smell. The very essence of carrot. She didn't dare think too hard about such things or gardening became a religious experience and she was, on the whole, anti-religion.

This was the best moment of all – trickling the dry seeds into the soil. She abandoned the gloves. They put a thick skin between her and real life. People often commented on her 'capable hands' and she took this to be a compliment. She wore her square nails, often harbouring traces of soil or clay, as a badge of honour. In her book, manicured nails were evidence of inactivity.

She tore the corner off the packet and tipped the seeds into the palm of her hand. Bending low over the soil, she moved along the row, sprinkling them evenly into the shallow drill. Some of her hair had escaped from the tortoiseshell combs which pulled the tangle of curls back from her face. She was hot and beginning to sweat. Wisps of hair corkscrewed, dampened by the moisture on her neck and forehead, and her nose started to run. When she fished in her pocket for a tissue, the letters were there, waiting to invade her meditation. Two time bombs, bearing her name. She folded the soil over the seeds and tamped it down with the flat of the rake and, as she did so, the smell of leaf mould rose from the disturbed soil. She found a stout twig to mark the row and jammed the empty seed packet onto it. By the time the picture had faded, they would be eating the real thing.

It was not yet eleven o'clock. She'd left Tom at his drawing board, working on a barn conversion for one of the farmers who lived further down the valley and he had made it clear that he didn't want to be disturbed. There were several cars in the yard but little sign of life, apart from the washing on one of the rotary clothes-lines. Celia must have pegged out those towels after breakfast.

She collected the tools, dumping them in the corner of the plot alongside the bucket of greens. Beyond the vegetable garden the land rose towards the wood and she followed the footpath up through the two fields, where fresh spring grass was pushing up through last season's matted layer. She still felt slightly uncomfortable with their recently acquired status as landowners but it was wonderful to wander without fear of trespass. She tried to be magnanimous towards ramblers who walked the footpaths criss-crossing Pen Craig but it wasn't always easy. Some of them, intent on demonstrating their right to roam, brandished elaborate compasses or made a big deal of peering at maps in see-through holders, slung around their necks. Sally had confronted a group of them the weekend before, pointing out that there were two options available to them. They could either carry on down the footpath or retrace their footsteps up the hill, neither of which called for advanced orienteering skills. Anna was relieved that she hadn't been there.

At the top of the field, there was a stone wall and a stile giving access to the wood. Years ago, one of the oak trees had fallen, crashing down across the wall. Whoever owned the land at the time had more pressing matters to deal with and the tree had been left to form part of the landscape. The winter winds and snows had stripped it of small twigs and lesser branches and now it resembled the skeleton of a woolly mammoth.

Anna perched on one of the huge limbs, wiped her nose on the sleeve of her shirt, and took both letters from her pocket. One was from her father, the other from Madeleine. She held one in each hand, trying to decide. She liked to know what was in a letter before opening it and, whilst she sat guessing, Tom would tell her how ridiculous this was. 'Just open it and find out, woman'. These days the mail consisted of bills and advertising junk. Very few hand-written envelopes came through the letterbox, apart from Christmas and birthday cards. The family communicated by telephone or e-mail. There were only two reasons to put pen to paper. Either the writer needed to consider carefully what they had to say or they didn't want to be diverted from their message. With a sigh, she slid a muddy finger under the flap of her father's letter. In a few seconds this perfect day was going to be ruined.

The writing on the single sheet of thin paper was so familiar. In his late seventies, his handwriting was the one thing about him that never changed. It slanted to the right, the descenders looping and bold. She had read somewhere that this indicated a deep-rooted sexuality. Reason told her that handwriting was a result of schooling but, ever since reading the article, she made sure that the tails of her g's and y's were generous and executed with a flourish.

Her father's letter had been posted the previous day but was dated almost a week earlier. She'd spoken to him since then but he hadn't mentioned anything out of the ordinary.

Anna,
I met someone at Christmas. Her name is Dorothy Holton. We get on very well. We will be getting married. I have been very lonely since your mother died. I think she would want me to be happy.
I hope the family is well. I never hear from the girls.
Love, Dad
I have written to your brother.

She read it twice, marvelling at the way her father had combined his momentous news with a criticism of her lack of attention, a side-swipe at Flora and Madeleine and an implied blessing from his first wife, all in fifty-nine well-chosen words. And she understood now why he'd opted to write. If he were here with her now, they would be having a row. She would be crying. He would be shouting. As it was, her stomach turned over, as though she'd missed the bottom tread of the stairs.

It was six years since her mother had died but, whilst her father was alive, Anna felt Nancy Hill was still with them. How could this continue if he were to marry this Dorothy person? Where would her mother go then? She knew that he wasn't happy but that was the price he must expect to pay for fifty years of a wonderful marriage. It was part of the deal. To make things worse, he had revealed nothing at all about this woman. There were ramifications when people embarked on a second marriage. Complications.

Anna looked down at Pen Craig. She watched a figure in the yard (probably Bill - it was difficult to tell at this distance) throwing bricks into a wheelbarrow. The bricks landed, the sound reaching her a split second later, like a film with the sound-track out of synch. A chain-saw across the valley screeched through a tree stump. A dog barked. A tractor toiled up a slope. None of these noises shattered her peace as her father's letter had.

When they moved from Bristol, he had been her main concern. She'd made sure that there was a full range of support systems in place. Cleaner, gardener, window cleaner. Tom had checked the house and done all the outstanding odd jobs and always took a complete set of tools, whenever they went to visit. They gave Frank Hill a Rail Card for his birthday and assured him that he was welcome to turn up at Pen Craig whenever he wanted to. He'd visited only once in the eight months since they had moved in and that was only because Steven had offered to drive him, door to door. His life was never going to be perfect but was anyone's? Now he had taken up with this Dorothy Holton and thrown everything out of kilter. He was behaving like a schoolboy, up to no good as soon as the teacher was out of sight. And why hadn't Steven spotted what was going on? He lived less than ten miles away. Men were astute enough when it came to assimilating details of cars or football teams. How could he have failed to notice that their father had a girlfriend?

Celia came out into the yard and went to her car. The sun glinted on the glass as she opened the door to take something from the back seat. Bill wandered across to join her. It didn't look as though Len had brought letters to spoil their lives.

She folded the paper and put it back in its envelope.

Madeleine's letter had been written and posted two days ago. The writing was big and sprawling. There were crossings out.

Dear Mum and Dad,
Everything is fine, so don't worry. In fact I hope that my news will make you happy and excited (once you have time to think about it!) I'm pregnant - due in July. I didn't tell you at Christmas because I wasn't sure myself. I'm doing all the right things – going to clinics and I've stopped smoking and drinking (well, cut down).
I'll ring when I'm sure you've had this. At the moment we're in Dorset. There are lots of women with babies here so I have plenty of help and advice.
Can you tell whoever you think ought to know? I'll write to Flora myself and let her know that she's going to be an auntie.
Love you xx Maddy
P.S. You'll be the first grandparents at Pen Craig!

The letter started 'Dear Mum and Dad' but the envelope was addressed to her. Some things never changed. Once again she was supposed to be the go-between. Maddy expected her to pave the way, lay the foundation, cushion the blow.

Anna had always known that, sooner or later, she would receive a letter like this and she'd been pretty sure it would come from Maddy, not Flora. At least Maddy had reached the age of nineteen before she needed to write it. Pregnancy seemed almost benign compared with some of the problems she'd thrust upon them. Her adolescence had included all the classic crises - and a few more. Whilst Flora was spotty, moody and insolent, her younger sister found more extreme ways to rebel. She smoked, drank and dabbled with drugs. She came home with tattoos, shaven head and body-piercing. She was suspended from school for leading a protest against the incompetence of the staff. At sixteen she left school to live in a squat, until the apparent lack of parental disapproval and real lack of hot water drove her home. She helped run a soup kitchen for the homeless and taught literacy to the hopeless. The down-and-outs loved her. She may have looked odd but those not directly concerned for her welfare saw her as a crusader for justice, prepared to put her family last and help the disadvantaged. At the moment she was with a group of travellers, living in a bender and she was expecting a baby. It wasn't easy, being Madeleine's mother.

Why had these letters both arrived on the same day? A solitary magpie had perched on the chimney-pot that morning but she didn't want to start blaming birds for her problems. She wondered if there was a divine edict, stating that Anna Wren had become too complacent and needed a shot of reality. So. Her father was remarrying and her daughter was about to become a single parent. Perhaps it was as well that the two pieces of news had arrived together. She had only so much capacity for anxiety.

She closed her eyes. The very first time they'd seen Pen Craig had been on a spring day, just like this, two years ago. On the journey from Bristol, with Bill and Sally, they'd agreed to be absolutely objective. 'We mustn't allow ourselves to be seduced by a pretty view and a big garden,' Tom had insisted. But as they drove up the sunny valley and caught a glimpse of the old house, nestled half way up the hillside, it was easy to convince themselves that Pen Craig met all their criteria.

'The perfect place to grow old with my dearest friends,' Bill had said as they tucked in to fish and chips on the way home. 'And it'll be such a laugh.'

Tom emerged from the house and the brick-into-wheelbarrow noise stopped as Bill raised his hand in greeting. They talked for a while, accompanied by lots of pointing and gesturing which probably signified that they were discussing important issues, then Bill returned to his bricks and Tom walked towards the garden.

She knew he was looking for her. He put his hand up, shielding his eyes from the sun as he scanned the hillside. She sat motionless, listening to him whistle through his fingers, the shrillness ricocheting back and forth across the valley. He waited for her to come to his side as he might wait for a faithful dog. She didn't move. After a few minutes he gave up and went back to the house.

She closed her eyes again. The warm, still air and the repetitive sounds of distant activity were calming. There was nothing at all she could do about her father or her daughter. No matter how much she worried, events would run their course. It was so, so simple. There was no need to get involved with any of it. They were adults and had made their choices without consulting her. She was perfectly at liberty to write back, congratulate them both, wish them well and her involvement could end there. But she was Anna Wren, so there would be sleepless nights, frantic phone calls, arguments, coolnesses, stormings out, apologies, discussions and so on and so on and so on. In the coming weeks, as she planted bean seed or pulled radishes her mind would wrestle with thoughts of family heirlooms and foetal defects, wicked stepmothers and infant mortality. The prospect was exhausting.

The odd thing was that it was her father's remarriage that was upsetting her. To most people, a bastard grandchild would be the more troubling issue but Anna had rehearsed this so many times that the sting had gone out of it. Dorothy Holton, on the other hand, was a bolt from the blue.

It was getting on for lunchtime. She started down the field, her feet sweating in wellington boots and her knees aching as she braced them, stopping herself from hurtling towards the house. She returned the tools to the shed and, carrying the bucket of greens, she crossed the yard to Number Four. The back door was open and, standing on the step, she shucked off her muddy boots then walked through the utility room, her feet leaving damp prints on the cold slate floor. Music came from upstairs. Paul Simon. 'Graceland.'

'Hi,' she shouted, dumping the bucket next to the sink. Tom wouldn't be able to hear her above the music. She went into the hall and called again, 'Hi, love.'

He appeared, looking over the banister. 'Where were you?'

She pretended not to hear and returned to the kitchen. The unwashed breakfast things were still on the draining board. When they'd eaten their toast and drunk their tea, the day stretched ahead, dotted with achievable goals. There were seeds to plant, drawings to prepare, ironing to do, a bill to pay. She filled the kettle and began putting things out for lunch. Salad and milk from the fridge. Rolls from the bread bin. Butter. Salad cream. Two knives. Two mugs. At the same time she attempted to organise her undisciplined thoughts.

She could tell Tom, 'I planted two rows of carrots. And by the way, Maddy's pregnant and Dad's getting married.'

Or she could give him the letters to read and make no comment.

Or she could not say anything at all and carry on as though there had been no mail.

Or she could destroy the letters.

Or she could run away.

Whoa.

Or she could bury her head in Tom's chest and let out the sob that was blocking her throat and making it ache. He would hold her and rock her and wait for her to tell him what was wrong. Then they would talk it through and the world would get back on track.

2

'How exciting.' Sally grinned when Anna told her about Madeleine's pregnancy and added, 'Dirty old sod,' when she heard about Dorothy Holton.

Sally's kitchen, where they now sat drinking strong coffee, reminded Anna of a show home on a new-build estate. Nothing cluttered the draining board or worktops. The wooden spoons were unstained. The toaster didn't sit in a sea of crumbs and the saucepans were stacked in ascending size on the pot stand. Sally kept a tight rein on Bill and his possessions, too. If he left anything lying around for more than a few minutes, it went in the bin. In the early days of their marriage, several of his O.S. maps and countless vital bits of this and that had made the one-way trip and, having done such a good job on her husband, she had no problem in maintaining standards when the children came along.

They discussed Anna's concerns for her daughter. 'I wish she'd come and talk to us. Or at least phone.'

'And how's poor old Tom dealing with it?' asked Sally.

'You know Tom. Throwing himself into work. And today he's not speaking to me. As if it's all my fault.'

'Well, I think she'll be fine. She's a sensible girl,' said Sally. 'Despite the tattoos.'

'And I didn't get round to showing him Dad's letter.'

She hadn't told Sally the whole story. Tom had cuddled

and rocked her, as she had anticipated but, when he read his daughter's letter, he'd started to cry. She found herself reassuring him with the platitudes that he was supposed to trot out to her. But he'd taken no comfort from them, accusing her of encouraging Maddy by meekly accepting whatever the girl threw at them. He rambled on, as if she were lost to them forever. He would not have been more distraught if Maddy had announced that she was terminally ill or had murdered someone. Anna hadn't foreseen his extreme reaction and kept silent, hoping he would calm down, but he didn't. He refused lunch and took a sandwich to his office for supper. Then he'd spent the night in the spare room and had been up since seven o'clock, digging.

The Webbers' kitchen was pink and tentative. Celia couldn't resist tea-towels covered with sentimental slogans. China mugs, with curlicued handles, dangled from a mug tree. A tiny vase held a modest bunch of pinks. She made coffee too weak and tea too milky.

'Will she keep the baby?' asked Celia. And 'When are we going to meet your father's lady friend?'

Anna had asked herself neither of these questions. From what Madeleine had written in her note – the mention of 'grandparents' and 'auntie' – she assumed that her daughter was intending to keep the child. But if she did give it up for adoption, what would her own position be? Would she have any rights? Genetically, she would always be the child's grandmother but there must be thousands of grandmothers who had never cradled their grandchild. Who didn't even know they were grandmothers. How sad. And how odd that she'd never thought of this before. Perhaps she and Tom were already grandparents. Had Maddy ever been absent long enough to have gone through pregnancy and given birth? She thought back through the three years since their daughter left home. No. The longest spell of non-contact had been when she was working in Greece, and that had only lasted three months. Although the possibility of being a grandmother to a child she'd never know only occupied her for a matter of minutes, it was a weight lifted when she could dismiss it.

Of her three women friends at Pen Craig, Celia was the sweetest and from Anna's point of view, was proving to be the least interesting. She looked like a Sindy doll which, in itself, would not have caused Anna's thoughts to wander when she was in Celia's company. If Sindy-Celia had discussed the French Revolution or deep-sea diving, it would have been intriguing, but she didn't. She talked recipes, medical symptoms and hairstyles. OK, these matters deserved consideration but not to the exclusion of everything else. Sometimes Anna hid when she spotted Celia coming towards the house, then, overcome by guilt, invited her round for coffee and a chat about pencil-pleats.

It was only as she was leaving Number Two that the penny dropped. The Webbers had one child, Judith, whom they'd adopted as a six-week-old baby. They had been beneficiaries of an unwanted pregnancy and Celia was looking at it from another perspective.

At first glance the Redwoods were an exception to Tom Wren's Rule of Style-Consistency: 'Once you find a style that suits you, why change it?' Jenny and Peter chopped and changed constantly and, to guide them, they employed Giles (pronounced 'Jeels') de Courcey, Design Guru. Over the years their kitchens had been French Provincial, Swedish Cool, hi-tech Minimalist and now back to Provincial (Spanish this time). So, although their homes had all looked very different, their design rationale was consistent – every room must be eligible for the current edition of 'Homes and

Gardens'.

'Will they marry before the baby arrives?' and 'You'll have to make sure that this Holton person doesn't do you out of your inheritance,' were Jenny's responses to the two items of news.

Appearances meant everything to Jenny Redwood. As Peter climbed his professional ladder, Jenny saw to it that both his family and home befitted his status. From House Officer to Senior Consultant, each step up triggered a move, a makeover and a change of school. Anna was still surprised that the Redwoods had wanted to join the Pen Craig experiment. After all, with Peter's money it was unlikely they would end their days, with other lonely strangers, in a third-rate geriatric home. But, after overhearing Jenny telling a friend that they were living in a 'huge house in the country, with its own grounds,' she understood a little better.

Madeleine's letter had not mentioned marriage, or even a putative father but, these days, neither were a pre-requisite to parenthood. She (the baby was certainly a girl) would surely look like Maddy or Flora. She and Tom would be closely involved in decisions about names, clothes, the books she read and the school she went to. But now Jenny had confused things by raising the spectre of a stranger in the family group. A man (Young? Old? Blonde? Dark? Tall? Short? Fat?) loomed up, waiting to usurp Tom's position in the child's life. And what's more he would have a father and a mother, with equal claim to this grandchild. The baby had started to become part of the family in Anna's calculations but already the family portrait needed a larger frame.

Now there were three more people to fret about. Dorothy Holton, who was hell-bent on depriving her and her brother of their inheritance. Maddy's lover, who wanted to muscle in on the child's upbringing. And Tom, who was treating her as if she'd put Maddy up to the whole thing.

Jenny was keen to turn the conversation to a function that she and Peter had attended in London, where they had been introduced to Lord Someone-or-Another. Anna wasn't very good at the Royal Family, or the aristocracy, or the military if it came to that. She knew that the Duchess of Kent was the one who went to Wimbledon and that was as far as it went. Jenny's preoccupation with the Establishment had long been cause for amusement. Mark Webber was convinced that the Redwoods were fully paid up members of the Tory Party. 'They read The Telegraph and wear a lot of blue,' he said, tapping his forefinger to the side of his nose.

Sally had laughed 'That's not unusual if you've been brought up on a council estate and are desperate to bury your working-class roots. You might be the same if your father had been a milkman.'

All those years ago, when they met and got to know each other at the school gate, differences in politics and philosophies had been unimportant. Children were the focus of their lives. Their own careers were a backdrop to achievements in the classroom or on the sports field and discussions were about reading ages and swimming without armbands, graded music exams and nits. As they advanced in their professions, aspirations for their families diverged but, by then, friendships were established and they tolerated each other's views. Most of the time.

Anna had dropped a large pebble in the gossip-pool and the news was already rippling out. Sally, Celia and Jenny would be telling Bill, Mark and Peter. Then all their children would find out. Relieved that there had been no hint of disapproval of Maddy's condition, she detected in herself stirrings of anticipation.

Dorothy Holton was of less interest to them. Several of her friends' parents had found new partners in later life. In theory this had to be a good thing and she'd spent part of the previous sleepless night analysing her own reaction. Frank Hill had been a lonely, sad man for six years, but that was as it should be because he was the guardian of the jagged hole in their lives which her mother had left when she died. If he married this Dorothy person, he could no longer be trusted to guard that hole. Indeed, it might start to seal up and leave no indication that Nancy Hill had ever been there.

And, to be honest, it was embarrassing. Did these two old people find each other physically attractive? Were they having a sexual relationship? She thought of her father's scrawny arms and the hair that burst out of his ears. She loved him despite these unlovely details but found it impossible to imagine that a stranger could find them anything less than repulsive. Her thoughts strayed to the woman. Did she have false teeth? Varicose veins? Thick, corrugated toenails? Shuddering, she'd gone downstairs to make a cup of cocoa.

She began preparing lunch and switched on Radio Four as a distraction but it was hard to concentrate on Harris tweed manufacture when Tom kept pushing his way into her thoughts. She was useless at having rows and this wasn't even a row, more a moat, filling with icy water. After years of practise, she knew what had to be done. She must cast a small fly, something innocent but tasty, and wait for him to bite. Then, ever so slowly, reel him in. It was a ridiculous charade but it was the surest way to get back to normal. This still left her with Maddy and her father to sort out but it wouldn't be so bad if Tom were here, not off, sulking in the garden.

From habit, she prepared enough lunch for two. She had no appetite and struggled her way through one sandwich, putting the rest in the fridge for later, then went outside. The hum and buzz of agricultural noises had stopped. Since they'd moved here, she'd learned that farmers are sticklers for routine and they would all be at home, eating their dinners. The sun beat down on her head and her scalp prickled with the heat. She should find a sun-hat then check the garden, but before anything else she needed to make friends with Tom.

Voices came from behind the outbuildings. Tom and Bill were sitting on the edge of the empty swimming pool, legs dangling in the deep end. Bill, large in every dimension and with a huge head, made Tom appear undernourished. Between them stood a tray, bearing the remnants of a substantial meal and several empty beer bottles. Engaged in boisterous discussion, they didn't notice her watching them from the shadows. They looked like a couple of schoolboys, up to no good and having such a nice time. This was going to be easier than she had imagined.

They spotted her and Bill beckoned. 'Anna. There you are.'

'Were you looking for me, then?'

'I thought I'd better get my own lunch,' Tom confessed, pointing at the tray.

'That's fine. How did you get on with the digging?'

'Almost finished.'

'I'm afraid I lured him away,' said Bill. 'But we've not been wasting our time, have we?'

Anna sat down next to Tom and he offered her a piece of the apple which he'd cut into quarters. She took it and kissed his cheek. Inclining his head towards her, no more than an inch or so, he let her know that they were friends again.

Tom and Bill had been engaged in a favourite pastime. The disused swimming pool, a reminder of Pen Craig's brief spell as a hotel, gave everyone hours of amusement. Bill, Tom and Mark had various hair-brained schemes for the redundant hole in the ground, while the Redwoods insisted that it be reinstated as a swimming pool.

'Of course they'd consult Giles about the tiles,' said Tom.

'Don't you mean Jeels about the teels,' Bill corrected him and they yelped with helpless laughter.

She couldn't help smiling. 'I expect you've told Bill our news.'

'News?' asked Bill.

'I thought you must be celebrating.' She indicated the bottles. 'We're going to be grandparents.' She put her hand on Tom's knee and rested her head on his shoulder. 'Aren't we, love?'

Bill, with bruising enthusiasm, slapped Tom on the back. 'Congratulations. Brilliant. Flora or Maddy?'

Tom, with no alternative but to fill in the details, relaxed a little, as if the act of speaking about it lanced a suppurating boil. In no time at all, Bill was anticipating the fun they would have with train sets, Meccano, tree houses and go-carts. (No mention of dolls' houses, tea parties and dressing up, but Anna let it go). Tom didn't say a great deal but they were making some progress if he was able to contemplate grandparenthood without crying or digging.

Bill opened another bottle and raised it in the air. 'Here's to the first Pen Craig baby.' Then he held it out towards her. 'D'you know, I never thought I'd envy a man who was sleeping with a granny?'

She stared at him. Already flushed from the beer and the sun, he turned a deeper shade of red. His eyes held hers for longer than they should and she looked away. Tom, tidying up the debris from their picnic, didn't seem to notice.

Mumbling something about ironing, she hurried back to the house, her anger mounting with each step she took. How dare he look at her like that? They'd known each other for twenty years and she really didn't need him to start looking at her.

By the time she reached the kitchen she was furious and Bill replaced Tom on her list of 'bloody men'. But it was complicated. It was possible for her to discuss her concerns about Maddy and her father with Tom. (Well, she would be able to talk to him about her father once she had told him about her father.) But there was no way she could tell him about Bill's lingering look. Bill was his best mate. They had been easy with each other from the day they first met, at the school carol concert. Peter was proving to be a social climber and Mark was, perhaps, a little too straightforward but Bill was a satisfying combination of anarchist and softy, with enough of the dreamer about him to balance the scientist. Now, out of the blue, he had given her one of those looks.

Anna had never gone in for flirting, preferring to earn a man's admiration by engaging him on equal terms. Politics, music and the arts – she could hold her own. And as for sport, she knew more about cricket than most of her male acquaintances. Her father had seen to that. While her female friends fluttered eyelashes and giggled, she discussed the merits of the squad selected to tour Australia.

So when Bill had given her that lingering stare, she was shocked. Casting her mind back, she wondered whether she had overlooked any signs of his increasing attention. Through the endless meetings and discussions as the plans for Pen Craig reached fruition, had she done anything to give him the impression that she might welcome his advances? Definitely not. No. Bill was out of order.

She stood in the utility room, folding the towels for the umpteenth time, holding them to her nose. The worst thing about the winter was the need to dry laundry in the house. People became recognisable by the smell of the detergent clinging to their clothes. When washing dried in the open air it smelled of nothing, the best smell of all.

Tom came in and caught her with her nose in his boxer shorts. 'I won't ask.' He bent to take off his boots and, while he was doubled up, mumbled an apology. She fondled the back of his head in a kind of benediction.

'Let's go for a walk,' she suggested, wanting to have him to herself for a couple of hours. Talking would be easier while they walked and she needed to gauge how he was coping with the baby bombshell. Then, at the right moment, she would tell him about her father.

She pushed Bill Davis to the back of her mind.

3

They walked up to the wood and along the ridge, taking the footpath back down through the trees and into the valley. They stopped for a drink at 'The Lion' in Cwm Bont and here she showed him her father's letter. He assumed that it had arrived in the morning mail and she didn't disabuse him.

After his wife's death Frank Hill, whom Tom had always liked and respected, remained in Bath, still living in the house where Anna had grown up. When they were raising their own family it had been ideal. Bristol was near enough to allow frequent and informal visits, yet far enough away to prevent interference from either side. The girls loved going to see Frank and Nancy and, when they were old enough, they had been able to get themselves there by train or bus. In fact, the first time Maddy ran away she'd headed straight for Grandma Nancy.

'He hasn't been happy, love.' Tom squeezed her hand.

She shook her head. Of course he hadn't been happy. What a stupid thing to say. How could he ever be happy again, now the love of his life had died? Yes, he had changed but how could he have stayed the same when half of him was missing? He'd lost his edge and turned into a boring old man but his mundane routine was the very thing that enabled him to function.

'I know, I know. I just feel weird about it. I suppose I'm hurt that he hasn't mentioned her until now. You must admit it's strange. We've been there several times since Christmas. Why didn't he tell us about her then?'

'Perhaps he was waiting to see how things developed. I'm surprised Steven didn't spot it, though. He's at your father's quite often.' He shook his head.

'Dad's obviously been keeping her a secret. But surely she must have found it odd. Would you want to get involved with a man who hides you from his family?'

'Let's not pre-judge her,' he cautioned.

They walked back home along the road. The circuit took two hours and they'd talked about Maddy and her pregnancy for most of that time. Tom wasn't happy with the situation but he was starting to make practical suggestions and they agreed to try and see the positive side of it. They'd always imagined themselves with hordes of grandchildren and the process had to start sooner or later. It was only when the conversation strayed towards the baby's father that he became agitated, but she stopped herself suggesting that they 'shouldn't pre-judge' this man, either.

Back at the house, several telephone messages awaited them. The first was from her father. He'd never got to grips with message technology and spoke with exaggerated clarity, in terse phrases, as if he were speaking to a foreigner who was hard of hearing.

'Message for Anna Wren. Dad here. Everything's fine. Get my letter? Going out now. Speak soon.' If everything was so fine, why had he broken his own golden rule and phoned before six o'clock when the cheaper tariff started?

Flora had called, twice, and said she would try again when she got home from work.

No word from Madeleine or Steven.

'Let's make a pact never to get a mobile phone,' said

Tom. 'Think how the wretched thing would have ruined our walk.'

'Perhaps we should offer to buy Maddy one for her birthday. At least we'd be able to keep in touch with her.'

He ignored her suggestion.

They prepared supper. A persistent stomach-flutter had put her off food all day but now she was ravenous. They were finishing their meal when Flora rang as promised. Anna confirmed that they'd received Maddy's letter and that they were getting used to the idea. Ever since the children were old enough to have their own opinions, they'd treated Anna as a shock-absorber between themselves and their father and Flora slipped easily into the one-sided telephone conversation.

'Dad's there?' asked Flora.

'Yes.'

'Is he in a state?'

'Yes.'

'Has Maddy spoken to you yet?'

'No.'

'I think she might want to come to Pen Craig to have the baby. How would he feel about that? She'd want Taliesin to be with her, though.'

'...'

'Mum? Ring me back when you can talk. I'm around all weekend.'

She replaced the receiver and smiled. Tom looked at her and raised his eyebrows. 'Flora,' she said. 'She's fine.' He never objected to being fed the censored version because he trusted her to tell him what he needed to know.

Taliesin. Mmmm. She accepted that the conception had not been immaculate, so now she could put a name to the father of her grandchild. And what an odd name it was. It rang bells. King Arthur? Frank Lloyd Wright? She would have to look it up.

They washed up, Tom whistling while he dried the plates, staring through the window, as if he expected someone to come across the yard. Whistling was often a sign of good spirits but Tom's whistling indicated a retreat into his own thoughts. After all the good work she had put in on their walk, he was slipping away from her again and, to keep lines of communication open, she talked about their plans to use part of the outbuilding for her wheel and kiln.

Until these were installed there was little she could do apart from make sketches and notes for future projects. She'd attended a few evening classes in Ludlow, to keep her hand in, but she was a far better potter than the teacher, a fact which she'd tried to conceal from the rest of the class. This wasn't through modesty but more a desire to get on with her own work and not to get roped in to coach the beginners. 'Teaching a few classes might be a good way to get your name known,' Tom had ventured.

They took coffee upstairs to the sitting room. It was almost dark. The weather had settled into a pattern of warm clear days and frosty nights. The sky was graded from royal blue to azure where it touched the hilltops, and lights were already glowing in the redbrick farmhouse across the valley. Tom switched on the television and embarked on non-communication. She picked up her book, staring at the page. Why did no one phone? Her brother must be as disturbed by the wedding announcement as she was. Maybe not. Steven and his wife lived ten miles from their father but Elaine didn't get on with Frank and contact was minimal.

She closed her book. 'I think I'll pop and see Dad tomorrow. I haven't been for a while.'

'What if Madeleine phones?' said Tom.

Maddy was 'somewhere in Dorset' without a telephone.

Short of touring around the county, looking for a group of New Age travellers, they had no means of contacting her. 'You'll be here if she does, won't you?'

There was no reply from her father when she rang later that evening but it suited her not to speak to him. He might try to deter her. She left a message, saying that she would be coming the next day. 'If he's not there I can always go to Flora's or drop in on someone else.' She needed, whatever happened, to see Flora and have a proper chat.

Tom glanced at her and smiled. 'Good idea.'

Now she had a plan of action she managed to struggle through two chapters of her book before it was time for bed. While Tom went down to lock up and check that they had switched everything off, she climbed the stairs to the top floor.

Their bedroom was her favourite room. With its daffodil-yellow walls and white woodwork, it felt fresh and welcoming. The planes of the ceiling, tucked up here under the old roof, came together at irregular angles to form interesting spaces without a hint of the fakery prevalent in most farmhouse conversions. Tom had been disappointed when the Webbers managed to get carried away at a local sale of architectural salvage. Consequently, Number Two now boasted 'features' concocted from distressed and stripped timber. Every piece of wood used had already existed in at least one other form, not counting the tree. They had found someone to cobble together tables out of floorboards, cupboards from panelling. Celia said she found it romantic to think of all the things their floorboard-table had witnessed. 'Probably a lot of boots covered in dog shit,' Sally had ventured. It was too easy to wind Celia up.

Anna stood in front of the mirror and brushed her hair. Thick, with a tendency to curl in the wet weather, it was half-and-half, black and white. The first grey hairs had appeared when she was at college and she'd let nature dictate the rate of greying. She pulled it back, catching it with a velvet scrunchy to prevent it irritating Tom during the night.

She crossed the landing to the bathroom, washed her face and cleaned her teeth. She'd once calculated how much time she saved by going without make-up. Its application and removal might take fifteen minutes or more each day and, from observing friends, this was a conservative estimate. Fifteen minutes every day. One and three quarter hours each week. Ninety-one hours a year. And say she'd been not using make-up since she was sixteen. That came to one hundred and forty days. Add to that the time not spent fussing with her hair, and she might have accrued a total of seven or eight months.

What should she do with the seven or eight months of saved time? She looked around the bedroom and the answer was staring her in the face. The room resembled the drum of a washing machine after a fast spin, with clothes, towels and books on every surface. Most belonged to her. The trouble arose when, for instance, she decided to do some gardening. She would shed her tidy clothes and pull on old jeans and shirt. The sun would shine and she would be eager to get outside. Spending five minutes fiddling blouses back on to hangers or folding t-shirts could be done when the light had faded or it was raining. Besides, it was tedious. Apply this logic to the whole house and it explained why it had such a 'homely' look (Celia's generous description). It would be a sin to spend eight months of a precious lifetime, tidying up.

Anna wandered around the room, collecting clothes and shoving them into drawers. She located her book beneath a sweatshirt on the chair, climbed into bed and switched on the bedside lamp.

Tom was taking a long time to come up. She read another chapter before she heard his footsteps on the stairs. He went straight to the bathroom and completed his bedtime routine. When he came into the bedroom, he undressed in silence and put out the light, leaving the room in the mellowness of the bedside lamps.

'I'll go straight after breakfast if that's OK,' she said. 'If you could pop me to the station, there are plenty of trains on a Saturday.'

'No need. I saw Bill just now, when I was putting the rubbish out. They're going down to see Luke tomorrow, so you can have a lift with them. As far as Bristol, anyway. They're leaving about ten.'

There was no plausible reason for refusing this offer. It made perfect sense, but the last thing she wanted was to be trapped in a car with Bill and Sally. One of the attractions of a weekend away from Pen Craig was to put some distance between herself and Bill.

'What's the matter?' he asked when she failed to enthuse.

'Nothing. I suppose I was looking forward to finishing this on the train.' She waved her book in the air.

'Bill wouldn't take no for an answer.' Tom switched off his lamp and adopted his sleeping position.

She marked her place with a dusty receipt for something she'd purchased last summer. It was for a 'dmsn sht slved' and, whatever it was, had cost nineteen pounds ninety-nine. She switched off the lamp and lay in the darkness, trying to fathom out what it could have been. It was a good ten minutes before she remembered the purple short-sleeved shirt.

4

Anna stood back from the window, peering across the yard. It was just past ten o'clock. She had been ready for a quarter of an hour, her overnight bag on the floor next to the back door. Bill was already out there, prowling around the car, wiping the windows with a chamois leather. Sally was nowhere to be seen. Tom had said his goodbyes and stood poker faced whilst Anna issued instructions for his survival during her absence. When she had finished telling him that there was bread in the bread bin and fruit in the fruit bowl, he had smiled, kissed her on the forehead and gone to get on with some work.

Neither her father nor Maddy had been in touch but she had spoken to Flora, agreeing to make the final arrangements for their get-together when she saw how the land lay in Bath.

A tappity-tap on the brick-paved yard heralded Sally's progress to the car. Whenever Anna undertook a journey, she looked on it as an endurance test and wore loose clothes which wouldn't show the dirt, and comfortable footwear, in case she was forced to tramp several miles to safety. With this in mind, she also carried essential rations – bottled water, fruit and muesli bars. Sally took the opposite tack. She travelled in her smartest clothes and her highest heels. If she were hungry or thirsty, she would stop at a service station or restaurant. If the car broke down, she would pay a garage man lots of money to come and sort it out.

'I'm off now,' shouted Anna, grabbing her holdall.

Sally was settling herself in the front seat. Bill raised his hand in greeting and dashed towards her, eager to take her bag and stow it in the boot of the car.

'You're looking as lovely as ever,' he whispered. 'Purple has just become my favourite colour.'

Oh dear, now she would have to discard this shirt and about half the clothes in her wardrobe. He opened the car door and made great show of helping her into the back seat.

'Stop fussing, Bill. Anna can look after herself.' Sally turned and grinned at her friend. 'Sorry about that.'

It was nice to be made a fuss of, now and again, but Anna dared not say this, afraid Bill might take it as encouragement. Instead, she fiddled with her carrier bag.

The journey from Pen Craig to Bristol usually took a little over three hours, but today this extended to more than four by the time they had taken a leisurely brunch-break at a service station on the M5. Anna wanted to treat them to the meal, as a thank you for the lift, but Sally insisted that Bill should spend some of his redundancy money.

The Davises were off to visit their children. Luke, having secured a good law degree, had announced that he no longer wanted to become a solicitor. He was currently working with a charity for the young homeless. And Emily was half way through the second year of a teaching degree, following in her parents' footsteps. Brother and sister shared a flat and kept an eye out for each other.

'Em's going through a bit of a bad patch,' said Sally. 'That's mainly why we're going down this weekend.'

'I still say it's daft to spend four years training if she can't stand teaching,' Bill mumbled.

'And it looks as if Luke's lost his mind,' Sally added, as if

Bill hadn't spoken. 'He's got to pull his socks up and stop all this social conscience rubbish. It's very self-indulgent.'

Anna felt ill-equipped to hand out advice on child-rearing but she did feel that it was unfair to force someone into a job they hated. How could any eighteen-year-old be expected to know what they wanted to spend the rest of their life doing? Her own parents had been disappointed when she chose art college, rather than university, but they didn't stand in her way. She'd always been grateful to Steven for fulfilling their ambitions, which had taken the heat off her.

From the moment they left home, Bill spent too much time checking the rear view mirror. Once or twice, their eyes made contact and she felt her cheeks grow warm. She sank down in the seat and closed her eyes.

After their refreshment stop, Sally offered to drive but Bill wouldn't hear of it. Then she suggested that she and Anna change places. 'There's not much leg room in the back. You must be dreadfully cramped.'

'I'm fine.' Anna edged herself into the corner. Bill immediately realigned the mirror. This improved his view of her, but left him with a serious blind spot. After one or two near misses, she wished she'd accepted Sally's offer.

'I assumed we'd be able to avoid travelling at weekends, now that we've joined the SAGA ranks.' Bill knew how Sally hated his clumsy references to senior citizenship.

'I know,' said Anna. 'I could visit Dad in the week, I suppose, but then I wouldn't catch Flora.'

'Why didn't Tom come?' asked Sally.

'He's got something to finish and I thought it might be better to talk to Dad on his own – try and find out about this Dorothy woman. If Tom's around, they go off and do manly things.'

'I don't envy you,' said Sally. 'It might be tricky. What if she's some bimbo gold-digger?'

31

Anna watched the landscape slipping past. Travelling with her head twisted to the side was making her feel sick and shutting her eyes made it worse. The farmland, greening up after the winter, undulated beyond the motorway verges, bland in comparison with the patchwork of fields which lined their wooded valley. She wondered if Maddy was out there, muddy and smelling of wood smoke, with Taliesin and her New Age friends. At least the April sunshine would keep her warm.

Anna had planned to make the last stage of her journey by bus but the matter was taken out of her hands. Sally concocted an excuse to take a detour to visit a dress shop in Bath, taking them more or less past Frank Hill's door.

'Give us a ring tomorrow, about getting back,' Sally instructed.

'OK. I'll be at Flora's for lunch. I know she'd love to see Luke and Emily, if they've got time to pop over.' This wasn't entirely true. Flora and Luke had always been close. They'd been in the same class when they started school. But Emily, who was the same age as Maddy, had been an inscrutable, self-contained child, inclined to stick to the rules. Maddy had once described her as a 'little mother' which Anna took, from her tone of voice, to be an insult. Even Sally grumbled that she never needed to discipline Emily because she never did anything wrong. While Maddy was running away, shoplifting and getting tattooed, Emily Davis had done nothing worse than paint her fingernails and lose her homework diary. Perhaps her current dissatisfaction marked a turning point in her blinkered progress.

The car pulled up outside the house where Anna had grown up. She gathered her things and was on the pavement before Bill had time to dance attendance. She waved them off, glad to have a few moments to herself.

The brick-built semi and the garden in front of it had barely changed since she and Steven had played there as children. The flowering cherry, planted when they moved in, spread its branches across the drive. A birdbath marked the centre of the lawn. It had been a vital element in their childhood games. It was the place where she had to stand and count to one hundred, while Steven dashed off to hide. It was the lighthouse, marking the dangerous rocks, when pirates invaded. It was the totem pole where Indians danced around the camp-fire. Now it was nothing more than a grey concrete dish balanced on a tapering column, one side green with moss, a pile of crumbled biscuits on its rim.

The garage doors were shut so there was nothing to indicate whether her father was at home. The kitchen, where he spent most of his time these days, overlooked the back garden. She wondered whether to go around to the back door, her habit when she lived in Bristol, but today it seemed important to announce her arrival. She rang the front-door bell and waited.

She still expected her mother to welcome her, wiping floury hands on a jolly apron. Six years hadn't stopped her hoping that there had been a terrible mix up and that the woman in the cemetery, under the marble stone, was someone else. Then she saw her father coming across the hall, his face distorting through the frosted glass, as though surfacing through choppy water, and she composed her mouth into a smile.

At seventy-eight Frank Hill was still a handsome man. Tall and slightly built, with plenty of hair and few wrinkles, his skin was the type that holds its tan through the winter, and although it was only April he looked as though he had already caught the sun. He wore green corduroy trousers and an open-necked shirt, sharp creases down the sleeves.

'You'd better phone Tom,' he said, before she was through

the door. 'He's been fretting about you …'

'Hi, Dad. You're looking well.'

'… and I don't really understand why you've bothered to traipse all the way down here.'

Not a great start. She took a deep breath. Even blindfold, the smell of woollen carpet and toast would have placed her in this house. It was as if the walls exuded their own scent.

Tom picked up the phone before the second ring and she knew he must have been sitting within arm's reach of the receiver. She explained why the journey had taken so long and he told her that now he knew she had arrived safely he was going to spend the afternoon in the garden.

'Anything from Maddy?' she asked but he had received no calls.

She followed her father to the kitchen, glancing around for evidence of cohabitation, but everything looked much as usual. There was washing outside on the line, but she could see that everything hanging there belonged to him. From habit, she washed the plate and mug that stood on the draining board, whilst giving an elaborate justification for her visit – chance of a lift with Bill and Sally; needing to deliver something to Flora; her only free weekend for a while.

'Baloney.'

She gave up. 'You're right. I needed to talk to you, face to face. We never get anywhere on the telephone. The thing is, your letter, or rather the contents of your letter, came as a real shock.'

'Assumed I'd peter out, here on my own, did you?'

'I didn't mean that, Dad.'

'How did you see it going then? Or perhaps you haven't thought much about it. Look, when you moved to Pen Craig, did I do anything to dissuade you? No. But it gave me a clear signal that I'm on my own from here on. OK, Steven isn't far away but he's completely under Elaine's thumb. You know she can't stand me. And it's mutual. He does his filial duty and I'm sure he'd be here like a shot if I were in trouble. But that's as far as it goes.'

'You know you can come and stay with us whenever you like.'

'As long as it's not too often and I don't stay too long.'

He was right. He'd been to visit them just that once and she'd sighed with relief when he left. Tom was very patient with his father-in-law but it had been like having a child around the place. A child, moreover, who needed to be occupied. At one point he'd resorted to asking Frank to sort screws and nails into various sizes and put them in labelled jam jars.

'Fancy a cuppa, Dad?' As ever, she needed a little time to adjust to the house without her mother. She occasionally allowed herself to wonder how it would be now, had Nancy been the survivor. Her mother would certainly have been better equipped to deal with the practicalities of widowhood. Cooking, washing, cleaning, ironing would all have lent a familiar rhythm to her days. Her father had been forced to learn these skills from scratch. There had been times when she had driven away from the place sobbing, after seeing the remnants of an inedible meal in the waste bin or washing pegged chaotically on the line, white vests discoloured by a green towel.

But there were ways around domestic shortcomings. There were restaurants and laundry services. What couldn't be found in Yellow Pages were companionship and a reason to carry on. That's where Nancy Hill would have come to grief. She would have been like a boat without a sail or a rudder, foundering in no time at all without Frank to steer her. Without him, she wouldn't have lasted a year.

Anna had been amazed that her father hadn't died of

a broken heart and she had watched him summon up his determination, as he learned to exist without his soul mate. There had never been any suggestion that he would 'get over' his loss but it became clear that he was going to survive. Now that she had advanced to the front line, as it were, she occasionally allowed herself to contemplate life without Tom and could appreciate that there were benefits to being the first to die. Then she would snap out of it, imagining that they would both live to be a hundred, breathing their final breath together, like synchronised swimmers.

They took their mugs of tea outside and wandered around the garden, spotting the first signs of life in the flowerbeds. Nancy had been the gardener and now Frank worked hard to keep her garden as it had always been. Anna felt more at ease moving about. With spring shoots and foliage to distract them, they became father and daughter again and by the time they went back into the house, they had linked arms.

'Dorothy must be a nice woman.' Anna smiled and waited.

'Well, I think so. She'll be here soon.' From his tone it was clear that he didn't wish to say any more about Dorothy Holton at this stage.

She took her bag upstairs to 'Anna's Room', as it was still known. Decorated and refurbished several times in the thirty-odd years since she had left home, the glass art-deco lampshade, the afternoon sunshine falling across the foot of the bed and the smell, of course, were the only constants but it felt just the same. She ran her finger across the chest of drawers and along the skirting board but found no trace of dust. The cleaning woman was on the ball, or perhaps Dorothy Holton demanded high standards.

The window overlooking the drive and garden was ajar and she heard footsteps crunching on the gravel. An old lady, a neighbour perhaps, was making her way towards the front door. Her white hair was scraped back into a bun at the nape of her neck and her handbag was slung, tourist style, across her chest. She wore a dark green cotton suit and a white blouse. Walking was a huge effort and she leaned heavily on two sticks but her mouth was set in a determined grin. Anna heard her father open the door and the mumble of voices in the hall beneath. Although she couldn't make out what they were saying, from the tone of their conversation she realised that this was Dorothy Holton.

'So how old is she?' asked Flora. They were eating lunch, next day, in the small café around the corner from Flora's flat.

'Eighty-four.' Anna shrugged. 'And don't ask me what it's all about because I haven't got a clue.'

'Did he talk about her at all? After she'd gone?'

'Only in factual terms. Where she lives. Where they met. That sort of thing.'

'Didn't you try and find out a bit more, Mum?'

'I tried but he kept changing the subject. He didn't want to talk about it. It's like he's made up his mind and that's that. End of story. I really need to speak to Steve,' she said, more to herself than to Flora.

'When's the wedding?'

'Don't know. "Soon" was all he would say. "And we don't want a fuss".' She shook her head as if to free it from clinging vegetation. 'He can be so bloody minded, your grandfather. Let's talk about something else.'

'Maddy?' said Flora.

But Anna shook her head again. 'You. How are things with you?' She looked across the table at Flora, neat in white linen shirt and clean jeans. How could her two daughters be so different?

If Flora committed to anything, or anyone, she did not

waver. This didn't mean that she was dull or unadventurous. By no means. She'd back-packed and abseiled. She'd danced and drunk and partied. She'd been on protest marches and sit-ins. At the same time she was a dreamer but, like Tom, she always made sure her dreams were achievable. Sometimes she and Tom worried that they hadn't given Flora enough of their attention because she demanded so little of it. She was a designer, like her parents, and worked for a small graphics firm. Coincidentally, one of her current projects was the inaugural newsletter for Luke Davis's community group.

They couldn't avoid it any longer. 'Have you spoken to Maddy, then?' Anna tried to sound off-hand.

'No. She wrote to me. It's funny but I don't think I've ever had a letter from her before. I was almost scared to open it.' Flora took an envelope from her bag. 'Doesn't tell us much. I expect she'll phone when she thinks we've calmed down.' Anna noticed that Flora included herself with the concerned parents, as she offered her mother the letter. It gave no more information than the one they had received, apart from the P.S. 'Taliesin likes the idea that the baby might be born in Wales.'

Anna knew that the reason she was feeling calm was because she hadn't yet spoken to Maddy. In that respect, her daughter's decision to impart the information by letter had been spot on. There had been no mention of how things might be after the birth of the baby. Childbirth might well be a natural human function but child rearing threw up lots of awkward questions and she suspected that she wasn't going to like some of Maddy's answers.

By the time they were back at the flat, it was four o'clock and Anna needed to ring Sally, to arrange a pick-up time. She'd written Luke's telephone number on a scrap of paper and began turning out her bag to find it. Flora had always possessed a remarkable facility for recalling phone numbers but nevertheless Anna was surprised when she was able to recite Luke's number.

Luke Davis was the nearest thing Anna had to a son. At difficult moments through his growing up, he had turned up in the Wrens' kitchen to moan about his parents or elicit a little sympathy and she was sure Flora had made similar journeys to the Davises' house.

Luke answered the phone and they exchanged pleasantries. She could hear Sally, twittering in the background. 'Is that Anna? Let me talk to her.'

'I'm ready, whenever you want to head back,' Anna said.

'Could you shut the door?' Sally shouted to someone. There was a pause and Anna heard a door bang. 'Sorry about that. I'll fill you in when I see you but I've decided to hang on for a day or two. Emily's stressed out and needs a bit of support.'

'That's fine. No problem. I'll get a train.'

'No need. *I'm* staying but Bill's driving back. Emily wants girlie chats, so there's no point in his hanging around. Actually, it would make it more difficult. He'll be with you in about an hour. Got to go.' Sally put the phone down.

5

Amidst a flurry of farewells and promises, Anna and Flora made their way out to the waiting car. For a second Anna, spotting someone in the passenger seat and assuming it to be Sally, sent up a little 'thank you, God'. Her atheism was confirmed, alas, when Luke emerged asking whether Flora fancied a walk on the Downs.

'That'd be lovely. It'll be a chance to sort out a few things on the newsletter,' she said.

Bill beamed as Anna settled into the seat, still warm from occupancy. Flora and Luke waved them off. She watched them miniaturise in the wing mirror, thinking that a stroll on the Downs with the children seemed the most desirable thing in the world.

The first thing that she noticed was Bill's aftershave. It caught in her throat like the fumes from oven cleaner and she checked his chin, convinced it would be lifting his skin. He turned, gazing straight into her eyes, and she blushed. But today she felt guilt without a hint of excitement. Faking a fit of coughing, she concentrated on unearthing a tissue from her bag and sneaked a look at her watch. They had been travelling for less than four minutes.

For a while the conversation revolved around the visit. She told him about the meeting with her father's fiancée.

'I'd sort of assumed he'd found himself a dolly-bird. Your

dad's a very dapper sort of a chap,' said Bill. 'I can see how he might be attractive to women. Perhaps Dorothy Whatsit's filthy rich.'

This had crossed her mind. Her father might not have set out to land himself a rich widow, but it was possible that Dorothy Holton was comfortably off. Anna hadn't learned much during her visit but he did mention that Dorothy had been widowed for twenty years. Whether her dead husband had been a wealthy man was still undisclosed but her jewellery, clothes and general demeanour indicated taste and breeding.

'I don't think I should be held responsible for my children's actions any more so it seems a bit unfair that I've got to start making excuses for my father's behaviour.'

They left Bristol through the familiar suburbs. The houses huddled together, cramped and shabby, front gardens grimy with the dust and fumes spewed out by the traffic. Anna pictured Pen Craig, big and bright and clean. She imagined Tom getting himself something to eat after a day in the garden and the carrot seeds starting to stir in the dark soil.

They joined the motorway and the volume of traffic increased. Even on a Sunday the lorries and trucks pounded along at an alarming speed. The first few caravans of the season toiled in the slow lane, an irritation to everyone. If Tom had been driving he would have lapsed into silent concentration but Bill chatted away and she held her breath as he nipped in and out of the fast lane, the needle never dipping below seventy. He did most of the talking, her response becoming more and more cursory as she tried to deflect his attention to the road.

Bill talked about Emily. They were worried that her new boyfriend, Dominic, was playing Svengali. She was talking about leaving her course and travelling the world. 'Finding herself. You know the sort of claptrap.'

'Sally always said that she wanted Emily to live a little,' Anna reminded him but a near miss with a bread van increased her resolve to remain silent.

Ticking off the passing motorway junctions was more effective than counting sheep and the drone of the engine, combined with last night's lack of sleep, lulled her. She drifted. Bill, assuming that she was sleeping, stopped talking and sang along with the tape. '…down at the end of Lonely Street, at Heartbreak Hotel…' Like many large men, he had a pleasing, baritone voice.

Her head dipped and she savoured the retreat from consciousness. Now and again she dragged herself back, like an angler reeling in a line and then letting it run. Each time she was carried a little further downstream. The traffic noise became the sound of insects buzzing in a summer meadow. Her hands rested on her thighs but she had no sense of the connecting arms. It was an interesting state but a difficult one to maintain and, just after Junction 11, she abandoned herself to sleep.

A jolt and the rasp of the handbrake woke her from a dream of covered wagons and the search for a new watch-strap. For a second or two, she thought she was in the chair at home then Bill's voice broke through. 'Let's take a break.'

She would have preferred to keep going but he was the driver. 'Fine.' She was queasy from the nap and the motion of the car. There was a metallic taste in her mouth and she fished in her pocket for a Polo mint. 'Where are we?'

'Strensham. Just past the M50. About half way.'

As they walked across the car park to the cafeteria they passed a rank of phone boxes. The booths were all empty, a spin-off from mobile phone ownership. Tom maintained that soon there would be no public payphones and eventually everyone would have a telecommunications port implanted in their brain.

'I'll ring Tom and let him know we're on our way,' she said. She had two reasons for doing this. First, it would remind Bill that she had a husband called Tom – his best friend. Secondly, it would ensure that they didn't spend too long over their break.

'Here,' said Bill, pulling a phone from his jacket pocket, but she pretended not to notice and made for the privacy of the kiosk. She fed her money into the slot and dialled. It rang ten times, then the machine cut in. Bill was waiting for her at the entrance to the café and she turned her back to him. She left a short message for Tom but kept the receiver to her ear, as if involved in conversation. It wouldn't do to give Bill a chance to linger.

The shops and the café were busy and it was a while before they collected their food and found a seat. She was impressed at the sanguine way Bill parted with ten pounds for two coffees and two Danish pastries. Tom never stopped at motorway service stations, preferring to go without than to be 'ripped off'.

For a while they talked about Madeleine's baby. 'I can't wait to be a grandfather,' he said. 'It'll give me a valid excuse to regress. At the moment, if I want to be childish, or should I say child-like, I have to pretend I'm carrying out some sort of scientific experiment. I've always thought that childhood was one long sequence of scientific and social experiments.'

That was rather a clever way of looking at it and she reminded herself that Bill was rather a clever man – when he wasn't being stupid. 'Can't you persuade Tom to see the positive side of it? He just wants to hit someone.'

'He'll come round.' He reached across the table and patted her hand. 'And the baby's going to have the most wonderful grandmother. Beautiful, intelligent, funny...'

She shoved the last piece of cake into her mouth and downed the rest of her coffee. 'When's Sally coming back?' she mumbled through a mouthful of pastry.

'When she's sorted Emily out. A day or two, I should think. I told her to take as long as she needs. It's good for us to spend time apart, once in a while.'

She never thought that she would hear Bill Davis voice such a sentiment. He and Sally were inseparable. He followed her around like a faithful dog, reluctant to let her out of his sight. Sally pretended that she found this tedious but did nothing to shake him off and everyone assumed that this was how they liked it.

When Bill took early retirement, a few months before the move, Sally continued working. It was possible for a writer to write anywhere. She needed to make occasional sorties to a decent reference library and sometimes she visited a castle or a battle site, to get a feel of the place. Now that she had become a minor celebrity in the world of educational books, she was often invited to give talks at schools. Bill usually accompanied her on these jaunts, as minder and bag-carrier.

Anna assembled the crockery in two neat piles and stood up. Bill made no move. He stared at his huge hands resting, clasped together, on the table. 'To tell you the truth, things haven't been too good between us recently.'

She started to laugh. 'Don't tell me Sally doesn't understand you. If ever a woman understood a man …' She faltered, horrified to see him pull out a hanky and blow his nose.

'I don't know so much about that. It's not straightforward. It may look like it from the outside, but she treats me a like a child. Keeps bossing me about. Belittles me in front of people.'

'But she's always done that, Bill. The first time I met you she was telling you off for wearing the wrong tie. She doesn't mean it. And you love it. You know you do.'

'Not all the time, though. She must see that it's getting to me but she doesn't stop doing it. Sometimes I think she can't bear to have me around. That's why she does all this lecturing. It gives her an excuse to get away from me.' Anna could see that they weren't going anywhere for a while and sat down again. 'I couldn't wait to finish teaching so that we could spend more time together. Now I spend most of the time on my own.'

He was crying in earnest now, his face blotchy and wet. She would have put her arm around him but she was wary of physical contact. He trumpeted into his hanky and several people turned to stare at the sobbing man. It was an unusual sight and they shifted their gaze to her, no doubt wondering why a wife was doing so little to console her distraught husband.

The muzak and the smell of stale food were overpowering. 'Fresh air, that's what you need.' Hauling him to his feet, she piloted him through the maze of tables. He stumbled past the shops and out through the automatic doors. They found a seat next to an overflowing litter-bin, surrounded by cigarette ends, but the breeze was cooling and they were less conspicuous here. He stopped crying and took deep breaths to calm himself.

His face started to return to its proper colour and he sniffed occasionally. 'Sorry. Sorry. I didn't mean that to happen. Can't think what came over me. It's just that you're so...so...'

'You're probably overtired.' When things became difficult, Anna's instinct had always been to go to sleep, or advise someone else to. 'Look, why don't I drive the rest of the way? You have a nap. We'll be home in no time.'

Without any show of resistance, he slipped into the role that she had seen him adopt so often. He became a small boy. She guided him to the car, as if he were a sleepwalker. It took her back to times when the girls, beside themselves with exhaustion, needed to be coaxed and cajoled into bed.

Roughly, to avoid misinterpretation, she fished in his trouser pocket for the car keys and eased him into the passenger seat. Once he was strapped in, she reclined the seat until he was almost horizontal. He didn't argue or attempt to touch her. There was a tartan rug on the back seat which she tucked firmly around him, pinning his arms against his sides. His compliance surprised her.

She drove out of the service station and joined the motorway. It was dusk and the traffic had thinned. Because of the reclining angle of the passenger seat, she was sitting abreast the mountain of Bill's stomach and his head was almost on the back seat. She was thankful that it was too dark for overtaking traffic to catch a glimpse of what appeared to be the Scottish mummy alongside her. Before long, to her great relief, he began to snore and she reflected on what he'd told her. Had she noticed a change in Sally's behaviour? Had there been any indication that all was not well? Or was he playing for her sympathy? Apart from the physical upheaval of the move, they had all made changes to their working lives. She couldn't be sure if, amongst it all, she would have spotted cracks appearing in the Davises' relationship. Or the Webbers' or the Redwoods', come to that.

But there *had* been changes in her relationship with Tom. Insignificant things, if taken in isolation, and she had pushed these misgivings into the corner of her mind. Family concerns and this recent problem with her snoozing passenger created distractions but the car headlights, cutting through the darkness, seemed to illuminate this growing mound of uneasiness.

She wondered about the time Tom spent in his office. In the beginning he'd been as keen as she was on growing their own food but he now was spending less and less time working with her in the garden. When they had house meetings to discuss the running of Pen Craig, he was contributing little to the debate and giving in without a fight on matters which had once been important to him.

Insulated from the world, they covered the motorway miles. In the darkness nothing looked familiar and, at one point, she thought that she had missed her exit. She drove for ten minutes before reaching the next junction and then felt a twinge of disappointment that it was, in fact, the one she needed. Her chance of adventure evaporated as she left the motorway and joined the winding road that led home.

The sounds of a middle-aged human male, rousing from sleep, came from the bundle alongside her. Her women friends all agreed that men make an alarming amount of noise when they do almost anything. Waking up, washing, nose-blowing, sneezing. 'Perhaps Peter should put it forward as a research topic at his next conference,' Jenny had suggested, after they had listened in awe to Mark blowing his nose.

Bill grunted and coughed into wakefulness, embarrassing her with the intimacy of the moment. His vulnerability was something that should only be witnessed by a wife, or lover, and she fixed her eyes firmly on the road.

The wrapped torso rose from the darkness, yawning. 'I must have dozed off.'

She was anxious to keep conversation to a minimum, not wanting to risk any further confidences. It appeared that he, too, was happy to travel in silence. Perhaps he was regretting his outpouring at the service station. They were in the middle of nowhere, but a roadside pub, its eaves decorated with fairy lights, loomed to her rescue. Without discussion she pulled off the road, into the pot-holed car park. It would not do to arrive home with Bill in the passenger seat of his own car. 'It's only about half an hour from here, as far as I remember,' she said.

He stood in the car park, tidying his clothing. He ran his fingers through his ruffled hair, pushing it back. She handed him the keys.

'Fancy a drink?' he asked, pointing at the door of the pub.

'I think we should get home. I'm quite tired.'

He didn't try to persuade her.

They started the last lap of their journey. Apart from a word here or there, they spoke little. He exuded a hangdog aura. Poor Bill. If he wanted to lay his soul bare, he would have to find another listener. She would not become his confidante.

Tom was in the yard, bent over the recycling bins, sorting cans and bottles. He straightened up, watching Bill park the car. The bright security-light leached the colour from his face and he looked tired. She hurried across and kissed him, holding on to him longer than she might have done, explaining why Sally wasn't with them. Bill followed with her holdall.

'Bad traffic?' asked Tom.

They hastened to justify their extended journey time. 'Dreadful.' 'Nose to tail.'

'Tea?'

Making eye contact with Bill, she shook her head slightly and he gave the right answer. 'No thanks, mate. Few things to do.'

'Thanks for the lift.' Linking arms with Tom, they crossed the yard and went into the house.

The kitchen smelled of burnt bacon and oranges. Tom had tidied the surface clutter into piles, pushing them into corners of the windowsills and worktops. There was a plate of sandwiches, inexpertly covered with cling film, on the table. Sinking onto the shabby sofa, she kicked off her shoes while he made tea in the brown pot. She leaned her head back and shut her eyes.

'You OK?' said Tom.

'Mmmm.'

'You needn't eat them.' He waved the plate towards her. 'I wasn't sure if you'd be hungry.'

She wasn't but she ate three sandwiches and drank two cups of tea. He watched her as a parent watches a convalescent child taking solids for the first time after a long illness.

She told him about Dorothy and her father's determination to marry. 'I didn't get much out of him but he seems to be happy enough.'

'Are you feeling any better about it?' was his only question.

He sat next to her and she relayed snippets of Flora's news. He nodded and smiled as he listened to the latest details of job and flat. This daughter made sense to him. The ups and downs in her life resulted from outside influences and, consequently, could be solved by conventional methods. She avoided taking on the woes of the world and concentrated on sorting out her own difficulties. It was easy to talk about Flora.

'Maddy wrote *her* a letter, too,' said Anna. 'Oh, she hasn't phoned, has she? Maddy, I mean?'

'I know who you mean. No.' The ticking clock and the carrumph of the central heating boiler, cutting in, were the only sounds to break the silence. Now she should tell him about Bill and Sally. Explain that their friends were having difficulties. Expand this to justify Bill's need to talk to a sympathetic friend. Talk about his state of mind. And, if Tom looked as though he was ready for it, go that final step and let him know that his best friend appeared to have a crush on her.

6

When they moved, Tom had decided to forgo his daily newspaper. There was no means of getting one delivered and the radio gave him the all the news he needed. Occasionally, however, the craving for good editorial or informed comment was irresistible and he would succumb. The nearest place to get a paper or a magazine was in Cwm Bont, where the post office doubled as general store. The village also boasted a pub (The Lion), a hardware store-cum-gift shop, a chapel and the village hall. Finally, there was a garage with a couple of pumps. By no means the cutting edge of retailing but a godsend when there was no time to drive the twelve miles to Ludlow.

After breakfast, Tom announced that he was planning to stroll down for a paper. Anna was surprised that he hadn't left Pen Craig, at all, over the weekend. He'd spent most of the time working in the outhouse, preparing the floor for her wheel and kiln. He looked delighted when she offered to keep him company and they decided to make a decent walk of it, going the long way round.

The utility room was crammed with coats, jackets and overalls. A mountain of muddy wellingtons and walking boots rose in the corner. Hats and gloves littered the top of the freezer, as though several snowmen had crept in here to melt. It was obvious that country folk lived in this house.

'It's blowing in from the west,' said Tom as they pulled on waterproofs. They had become weather experts, too.

Before setting off, Tom took her to inspect his handiwork. It had been too late last evening when she arrived home, but now, in the daylight, she could see what a wonderful job he was making of the floor. He had salvaged bricks from what must once have been a walled garden, cleaned off the mortar and was setting them in a herringbone pattern. While she was away, he had completed about two square metres of floor. Slow progress but the result was stunning.

'What d'you think?' he asked.

'It's beautiful.' She was entranced by the colour of the old bricks and their satisfying geometry.

'Remind you of anything?'

'Of course. The square in Siena. Remember sitting there, by the Gaia Fountain, watching those boys showing off on their scooters?'

He grinned and everything between them was fine. The drive home last night had been exceedingly stressful and she'd allowed herself to become fanciful.

Crouching, she ran the palm of her hand across the brickwork. He'd started in the corner where she would be working, and had created a terracotta island in a rough sea of concrete. 'It's a dreadful shame to cover it up,' she said.

'Now I've perfected a method for setting it out, the rest will be much quicker, and it's very rewarding, watching it grow. I think I'll have enough bricks to do the whole floor.'

She hugged herself as she imagined working in this peaceful place, filling shelves with interesting pots. She had it in mind to make mugs, plates and bowls for everyone, each piece unique, to remind them of their reasons for coming to Pen Craig. 'Thanks, love. It's the nicest present I've ever had.' She kissed him.

They left the buildings and crossed the patch of rough

grass towards the swimming pool. A detached stone building faced the pool; Tom suggested it had probably started life as a cowshed, or perhaps a dairy. In the brief period when the house had been a hotel, it had been done out as a kind of summerhouse, where guests could shelter from the weather and read or watch the swimmers. Although the fate of the pool remained undecided, there was unanimous support for retaining this summerhouse. It made a perfect meeting place, large enough to accommodate them all, and it had taken on the ambience of a common-room. They'd never planned to live communally (although that was the impression family and friends were determined to have) but this communal space was a great asset. They had installed a wood-burning stove, a refectory table, some well-worn leather sofas and an upright piano, donated by the Redwoods. Here they'd eaten their Christmas meal with the depleted complement of guests who had managed to reach Pen Craig before a foot of snow fell, making the place unbearably beautiful but infuriatingly inaccessible. Jenny had taken it personally, as if some Welsh witch had summoned up the blizzard to foil the upstart incomers. Her 'Country Life' event had been thwarted by power cuts and unfinished shopping. Everyone else had taken it in their stride, even those, Flora amongst them, who had failed to negotiate the last few miles and been forced to spend a couple of days in the Travel Lodge, out on the Ludlow bypass. (By all accounts, they'd had the time of their lives and were planning to reconvene on the A49 next Christmas.)

As they passed the summerhouse, she spotted Bill peering out of the window. She suspected that he'd heard them talking and stationed himself on their route. He opened the French windows and came out to join them. She thanked him again for the lift. 'Any news from Sally? When's she coming back?'

'Emily's being a bit prima-donna-ish so Sal's going to hang on. Play it by ear. I'm on my own for a couple of days at least.' He sighed. 'Flippin' quiet without her, as you can imagine. Still the old boy scout training's paying off. I can still incinerate a few sausages.'

Tom fell for it. 'You're eating with us tonight, isn't he, Anna?'

Bill needed no persuading and beamed his acceptance.

A threesome with Bill did not appeal to her. 'How about inviting the others? We haven't had a get together for ages. Nothing elaborate.'

Tom nodded agreement. 'Couple of bottles of wine. Just the job.'

'Where are you two gadding off?' asked Bill. She had to admire his persistence. Tom took the bait, again, and invited him to join them on their expedition. Bill had the decency to mumble a few words about 'not wanting to muscle in' but he was already zipping up his jacket.

'Look. Why don't you two go down to Cwm Bont and I'll see if Celia and Jenny are around.' She watched Bill's face. Either he was an accomplished actor or she was getting steamed up about nothing.

Anna's culinary forte was peasant fare – basic and tasty. She left the fancy stuff to Sally or Celia and the really fancy stuff to Jenny. After a few minutes' consideration, she plumped for beef casserole followed by rice pudding. And maybe a fruit salad for the faint-hearted. That would do. She preferred impromptu invitations. They removed any expectation of perfection. To cater for the extra mouths, her fortnightly supermarket session would need topping up and she wrote a list of things for Tom and Bill to get from the village.

She surveyed the cars in the yard. When everyone was at home, there were seven. Theirs was the only one-car household. They'd agreed that they could manage with a single reliable vehicle and a small trailer. Tom had always hankered after a trailer to transport the fruits of his skip raids and this one had already paid for itself in scavenged materials. 'Recycling. It's recycling, love,' he would say, stacking his booty of bricks or timber in the corner of the outhouse.

There were six cars today. Peter's Jag was missing. She knocked at the back door of Number Three, which was no longer called 'Number Three'. Within two months of occupancy, it had been re-named 'High Trees' and had a nasty cast-iron plate, screwed to the wall, to that effect.

Jenny invited her in. 'Coffee?' she asked, going over to the chrome machine. The Redwoods had machines for doing most things. Coffee maker, juicer, toaster, bread maker – all top of the range models, pristine and unscratched, as though they were fresh out of the box. Copper pans, graded by size, hung from a rack above the Aga. Bunches of dried lavender scented the air. A huge turquoise bowl, piled high with lemons, limes and aubergines, stood on the table. (What sort of a meal could Jenny make with those?)

'It's not a dinner party – just a meal. Bill's on his own and it sort of went from there,' Anna explained while the machine hissed and gurgled.

Jenny, too, was on her own. Peter had left early to do his regular 'list' in Reading and she had nothing planned. 'Shall I bring dessert?' she asked.

'It's all under control, thanks.' Anna was determined that the evening should not be railroaded into an 'event', which tended to happen when Jenny was involved.

'Did you meet your father's girlfriend when you were down there?'

Anna gave her a brief rundown on Dorothy Holton. 'I rather liked her but it's early days.' It surprised her to realise that she meant what she said.

'And when's Maddy coming home? I told Sophie about the baby. She's very excited.' Jenny's expression was one of sympathy, if not outright pity.

'Next week.' Why did she lie? She had no idea when they would be seeing Madeleine. She hadn't intended to play cover-up games with Jenny or anyone else, but over the years they'd all indulged in face-saving exercises. Bill's disclosure of his personal problems might make *him* feel better but it put her in an embarrassing position. Sharing practical problems, or even money worries, was one thing but the internal workings of the family were a private matter. Wrens were allowed to criticise Wrens but she was damned if Jenny could.

When she knocked at the Webbers' back door, Mark opened it wearing an open-necked, brushed cotton shirt with yellow cravat, lemon lambswool cardigan and baggy cavalry twills. It all went wrong around his feet. He was standing on two dead animals. In fact they were slippers, in the form of furry rabbits with lop-ears and pink noses at the toe. He grimaced. 'Celia gave them to me for my birthday. They're very warm. Come on in.' He turned to lead the way, white tails bobbing at his heels. 'There's a knack to them. I have to keep my feet apart or the fur locks up and I fall over.'

Celia was setting the table. In pink angora sweater and grey pleated skirt, it appeared as if she had just popped home from the office for a bite to eat.

'Don't let me hold you up,' said Anna, quickly explaining her reason for calling. 'Nothing special. Just something to eat and a chat. Bring a bottle, if you like.'

Mark escorted her to the door and glanced back into the kitchen before confiding, 'Celia's a bit down at the moment. An evening out would do her good.'

There were two messages on the machine. Madeleine had phoned about an hour earlier. 'Hi, you two. Out gallivanting again? Just saying hello and letting you know that I'm – we're – fine. I expect Mum's worrying as usual. I'll phone again soon. Byeeee.'

The second caller left no message, just the sound of distant voices. Anna one-four-seven-one-d. It was a local payphone, probably Tom calling from the village, but it had eliminated the chance of getting Maddy's number. It irritated her that his pointless, message-less call had done this but she was cross, too, that she'd been lingering in Jenny's kitchen when Maddy telephoned.

As she made herself a sandwich, the frustration of the missed phone call welled up and she started to cry. Crying felt good. While the tears were streaming, she took a wet mug from the draining board, and as she carried it over to the kettle it slipped from her fingers and smashed on the flagstone floor. That felt good, too. She took another and held this one high above her head before letting it drop. It bounced three times before breaking, the noise ringing out like a bell. Two plates next, then another mug. She looked about her, through a blur of tears. Broken crockery covered the floor. It appeared that mugs were more robust than plates. Whilst their handles sheared off, the rest remained intact, just cracking or chipping at the rim. 'Because they are three-dimensional', Tom's voice explained inside her head. Sobbing amongst the debris, she watched a red stain spreading out from the underside of her foot. She felt no pain but knew that she must have stepped on a piece of plate. Damn. All she wanted was to have a good cry and smash a few things. Was that too much to ask? Now, bleeding profusely, she grabbed a tea towel from the back of the chair, using it to blow her nose and wipe her eyes. If she hopped to the sink, it was more than likely she would step on another piece of pottery and injure her other foot. It was all Tom's fault. Why was he always off doing something stupid when she needed him?

She ran her hand under the instep of her bleeding, throbbing foot. The sock was sticky with blood and, through the knitted cotton, she could feel the place where the splintered china protruded from the flesh. It was possible to walk, as long as she put only the toes of her injured foot to the ground, so, flicking the pieces of crockery out of the way with the tea towel, she cleared a route to the sink.

Anna pulled off her sock and immersed her foot in a washing-up bowl of cold water. This eased the throbbing but failed to slow the blood, seeping out in tiny swirls, turning the water crimson. The image of a slashed-wristed suicide, lying in a bath, flashed up and she pulled her foot from the bowl.

There was a broom leaning in the corner and she swept a path to the sofa. She flopped down, pulling her foot up and twisting it towards her. There was a tiny puncture on the sole but no sign of what had caused it. The offending sliver must have come out when she removed her sock. She twisted the tea-towel around her foot and, lying back on the sofa, hoisted it up onto the padded arm. After a few minutes the bleeding slowed to a trickle but she gave it a few more, to be on the safe side, before hopping to the dresser where they kept the Savlon and sticking plasters.

Her foot twinged when she put it to the ground and she limped upstairs to get clean socks and comfortable shoes. While she was there she took a couple of Paracetamol tablets to combat the throbbing and the headache which had developed. Exhausted from crying and physical exertion, it took all her willpower to resist the lure of their unmade bed. There were too many things to be done.

She was gathering up pieces of broken crockery when the phone rang. She let the machine take the call, standing next to it, ready to pick up if it was Maddy. But it was Tom again. 'Anna? Hi. It's me. You OK? Bill's treating me to lunch in The Lion. So you carry on. OK? Oh, we've got the shopping. I assume you wanted button mushrooms.'

This message might have re-activated the crying and plate smashing, but she lacked the necessary energy. With supper scheduled for seven o'clock, she had less than five hours to prepare the meal and clean the areas of the house (kitchen, dining room, sitting room, bathroom and stairs) where guests (or more precisely, Jenny) might stray. She also had to bathe and wash her hair. Really speaking she should have a tetanus booster but there wasn't enough time for a trip to the surgery.

By six o'clock, she had abandoned several of the things on her list. They would eat in the kitchen now that the floor was sparkling clean. No one would spot the dust or grimy windows in the sitting room, if they kept the lighting low and lit a welcoming fire. The stairs weren't too bad. And if she plaited her hair, she could get away without washing it.

Tom, eager to please after his extended and obviously liquid lunch, was detailed to clean the bathroom while she concentrated on the food. The kitchen was already fragrant with the smell of simmering casserole and a golden skin was forming on the rice pudding. Detritus from sills and surfaces was hidden in drawers and cupboards. The yellow tulips which Tom had brought back from the village stood in one of her pots on the scrubbed table. There were fresh candles in the holders and two bottles of red wine 'breathing' on the mantelpiece.

Her foot was swollen and sore but she didn't mind. It had been worth it for that exquisite moment when the mugs bounced across the stone slabs. Was it pure luck that she'd only smashed items that she didn't care for?

7

'**M**mmm. Smells wonderful.' Bill wrinkled his nose and advanced across the kitchen towards her, arms outstretched. It was on the dot of seven.

She pressed a bundle of cutlery into each of his hands. 'Could you put these on the table, Bill? I'm a bit behind.' Escaping to the hall, she called up the stairs to Tom, who was lighting the fire in the sitting room. 'Bill's here, love.'

Celia and Mark were next. Despite the understanding that it was to be an informal supper, Celia was dressed for The Palace. Her hair, rigid with hairspray, sat on her head like a yellow hard-hat. Bright pink lipstick and nail varnish accentuated the paleness of her skin. The kitchen was hot but she shivered, pulling her jacket around her. Anna shut the window and resigned herself to sweating for the sake of her guest. Tom poured everyone a drink. 'We might as well stay down here. We'll eat as soon as Jenny arrives.'

'Shall I go and jolly her up a bit?' Bill appeared to have had a drink or two already and brimmed with enthusiasm. 'We don't want Anna's delicious meal to spoil, do we?' Anna dissuaded him and found a few unnecessary tasks for him to perform.

They were on their second glass of wine when Jenny knocked at the front door. Anna went to let her in, pressing the backs of her hands to her cheeks, knowing they were flushed from cooking. Her white shirt, clean at six-thirty, was already splashed with gravy from the casserole and Jenny, every shining hair in place, made her feel like the hired hand.

'Am I last? Sorry.' As Jenny bent forward to kiss her, the subtlest hint of exotic scent reached Anna and she wished that her own hands didn't smell of onions. 'Family crisis.'

The Redwoods were perpetually in crisis. Jenny lost more credit cards, car keys and passports than anyone in the whole wide world. The children cost them more money than anyone else's did. Peter was more stressed than anyone in the medical profession. In short, the Redwoods had cornered the market in crises.

'Peter forgot his laptop. I had to get it couriered to Reading. He's presenting a paper tomorrow.'

Anna would never have admitted to being so disorganised. 'The Redwood Phenomenon', first noted when Jenny and Peter moved Alex and Sophie away from the local primary school, had become legend and they wore it like a badge of honour. It defined them and provided an unending stream of anecdotes. Tardiness, loss or mishap had become more interesting than the event it affected. After all, only important people could get in such tangles.

She was relieved that she'd chosen a meal that couldn't spoil with overcooking. No collapsing soufflés or leathery steaks to worry about, thank goodness. But she wasn't so sure about eating in the kitchen. It put her centre-stage, transforming things she did every day, without thinking, into a performance. She had never been comfortable with an audience.

That wasn't quite true. When she was nine or ten, she'd been first to volunteer to sing or dance in school concerts, never suffering from the slightest flutter of nerves. This had come to an abrupt end when, after a few months of violin lessons, she'd offered to play 'Brahms' Lullaby' in a school concert. Within the first few bars it started to go dreadfully wrong. Her sweaty fingers slid about and sometimes her bow scraped the wrong string. Things deteriorated, and before the first repeat she was conscious of a titter running along the cross-legged rows. It spread like a forest fire, flaring into snorts and guffaws, until one of the teachers helped her off the stage in tears, the piece unfinished.

Celia and Jenny offered to help but remained at a safe distance, leaving her to wrestle with the dishes of hot food. Once she had manoeuvred everything to the table and Tom had topped up the glasses, she sank onto her seat and gave up. From here on, the evening would have to run itself.

'I do love this kitchen.' Bill waved a laden fork in the air. 'It's just like a kitchen should be. The nerve centre, the heart, of the house. Jeels would make a fortune if he could reproduce this.' Jenny smiled but ignored the bait.

'It's not intentional,' said Anna. 'It just happens.'

'I think it's amazing how all our homes here are the same, yet so different,' said Celia. 'And so lovely, of course.'

It was customary at gatherings like this to toast Tom in appreciation of his role in planning the refurbishment. 'Well done, mate,' Mark raised a glass towards his host. They all drank to Tom.

Through mouthfuls of food, they exchanged news about the children. Anna wondered whether the time would ever come when they didn't. The children weren't sitting around talking about *them*, that was for sure. They would only be topics for discussion when, like Frank Hill, they became a problem for the younger generation. Anyway, if everything went to plan, the move to Pen Craig would spare them the loneliness and indignity that, all too often, accompanied growing old.

'It'll be lovely to see Maddy, next week,' said Jenny.

'How far on is she? Five months? She should be through the sickness by now but you never know. I remember how ill I felt the whole time I was carrying Alex. You'd think Peter would have been able to give me something but doctors are like plumbers, so busy sorting out everyone else's leaks that they don't get round to fixing their own.'

'Were you leaking, then?' Bill was having difficulty in keeping up with the conversation.

Anna avoided Tom's questioning glance when Jenny mentioned Maddy's visit.

'Does she want a boy or a girl?' asked Celia.

Tom concentrated on his food, as though cutting it up and getting it to his mouth demanded his undivided attention. Anna muttered the usual things about it not mattering, as long as the child was healthy. She'd hoped that the discussion about the baby wouldn't crop up this early in the evening. Unless she diverted the conversation it could run on and on, raising a lot of questions which she wasn't in a position to answer. She sent a telepathic SOS to Tom. Help. Help. Talk about something else.

It was Bill who came to her rescue. 'Is it me, or is that man in the Post Office some sort of psychopath? Tom and I called in for a few things today and there he was, brooding about like a ruddy Russian tragedy.'

'The Welsh are a very soulful nation,' said Mark.

'I don't know about soulful. But I do know that he's got it in for me. Whatever I ask for, he either doesn't have or doesn't want to sell it to me.'

'That makes no sense, Bill. The man's a shopkeeper. Of course he wants to sell you things.' Mark paused. 'What sort of "things" are you talking about, anyway?'

'He's talking about the *Guardian*.' Tom looked up from his plate. 'Bill is convinced that Prosser is prejudiced against *Guardian* readers.'

'He's always been happy enough to sell Peter the *Telegraph*,' said Jenny. Bill let out a strangled yelp. 'What? What have I said?' She looked around the table. 'Well his wife's very pleasant, anyway. And she's an excellent cleaner.'

'Didn't somebody, Len probably, mention that Prosser was connected with Pen Craig in some way? Something to do with his grandfather. What was the name of the farmer who used to own the place? Before it was a hotel.' Anna shook her head, the details eluding her.

'Richards. Roberts. Something beginning with R.' For once, Tom was vague.

'I've bumped into him a couple of times, when I've been walking in the woods,' said Mark. 'Didn't even pass the time of day. He was carrying a shotgun, so I assumed he was hunting vermin.'

'He probably doesn't like incomers, darling,' Celia joined in.

'He'd be rather stupid, then. Between us, we buy quite a bit from his shop and Mrs. P. comes to Jenny several mornings a week.' Anna passed around the dish of carrots.

'Isn't that the thing about psychopaths, though? They're not rational.' Mark pulled the paper napkin from the v-neck of his sweater. 'I must admit, I haven't really taken to the man. Anyone carrying a gun gives me the willies.'

'They all have guns out here.' Anna, with this sweeping generalisation, attempted to reassure Celia that there was no particular cause for concern.

Tom raised his eyebrows. 'Really? I can't say I've noticed Len riding shotgun on the post van but maybe I've missed something.'

'Perhaps Mr Prosser's shy.' Celia did not appreciate irony.

'Let's forget Prosser and have pudding.' Anna brought

the dish to the table and the conversation switched to the attributes of the perfect rice pudding. The colour, the density and the skin were the critical factors and the men tucked in, reminiscing about rice puddings that their mothers and grandmothers had made. She was already full but took a small portion to allay any suggestion that she was watching her weight. Jenny, who did nothing but watch her weight, opted for the fruit salad, refusing cream. Celia had eaten next to nothing of the main course and declined dessert.

From rice pudding they moved on to recycling. Celia excused herself to go to the 'little girls' room' and Anna took the opportunity to ask Mark if his wife was feeling unwell. Mark was incapable of telling a lie, an unusual trait in an accountant, and his face told her that something was amiss but, before she could question him, Celia had rejoined them.

She looked dreadful. Her face was pale and the two patches of blusher across her cheekbones stood out like bruises. Her mascara was smudged and she was shivering. It was impossible to pretend that there was nothing wrong and Mark hurried to put his arm around her. 'Come on, love, you're bushed. Let's get you to bed.' He led her to the back door and called a quick 'Goodnight. Thanks for the meal.'

As soon as they had disappeared, Jenny broke the silence. 'Should I go after them? See if I can help.'

'Let's give them a bit of time. Mark will let us know if he needs anything.' Anna cleared away the pudding plates.

The foursome sipped coffee and speculated on the cause of Celia's distress. 'Perhaps she's starting a cold,' suggested Anna, but she hadn't mentioned feeling out of sorts when she'd called at lunchtime. Neither had Mark dropped any hint of a problem to Tom or Bill.

They cleared the table. Anna refused Bill's offer to help wash the dishes and they trooped upstairs with a second pot of coffee. It was a frosty evening after a day of April sunshine and Tom's fire had caused condensation to form on the windowpanes. Anna lighted the candles and pulled the heavy curtains around the bay, drawing the focus of the room inside. She waited to see where Bill would sit and made sure she was well out of reach, perching on the wide arm of Tom's chair.

'Poor Celia never seems quite a hundred percent,' said Bill. 'Come to think of it, Sally saw them at the hospital the other week. Coming out of Outpatients. She was visiting a friend. Sally was, I mean.'

'Didn't she ask them why they were there?' said Jenny.

'Said they didn't seem to want to chat.'

'I feel terrible,' said Anna. 'Sometimes I can see Celia wants to talk but she takes so long getting to the point that I give up.'

'Mark could be the one who has the problem. Wives can make themselves ill worrying about their husbands, you know.' Tom stared at her and she felt as if she'd been chastised.

'Whatever it is, she knows we're here if she needs us.' Jenny shook her head then smiled, signalling the end of the Celia discussion.

Tom leaned forward to stir the fire with the iron poker. A storm of sparks raced up the chimney. Some caught on the sooty sides and glowed for a few seconds before fading. 'When I was a child, my grandmother used to look after us occasionally. My Dad's mother. We were living in Swansea then. She was the most wonderful grandmother any kid could have. Game for anything. On this particular day, she told us some tale about a wizard who lived up the chimney. It must have been in the winter because I remember the curtains were shut and we were sitting in the dark. Anyway, she had us writing messages to this wizard, on sheets of toilet paper

– that scratchy Izal stuff, you know? – and floating them up the chimney. They rose with the heat and, of course, some of them caught alight. Set the chimney on fire. Mum and Dad got back to find a fire engine outside the house. It was one of the best days of my life.' He threw another log onto the glowing embers, sending a shower of sparks skittering upwards.

While Bill reminisced about his grandparents, Anna's mind remained fixed on Tom's story. If that had been the best day of his life, why had he never mentioned it to her? It was hurtful that Bill and Jenny should hear it at the same time as she did. Bill's voice, trained to reach the back of a restless physics class, irritated her as he droned on. Jenny, too, was getting louder, her BBC English slipping into its natural West Country cadence. She wanted them both to go home. She wanted Tom to herself.

The phone rang in the office next door. It was almost eleven o'clock, the time of night when phone calls were made for a reason and she hurried to answer it. It was cold in here after the cosy sitting room and the bright light hurt her eyes.

'Mum?' It was Madeleine.

'Maddy? Are you OK? Hello. Hello.' For a second she thought her daughter had hung up.

'We're at Ludlow station. Could you bear to come and pick us up?'

We? Who was she talking about? 'Yes, of course. No, hang on. We can't. We've both drunk too much.' It sounded dreadful. 'We've had everyone round for supper. Can you get a taxi? We'll pay.' She gave Maddy the number of the local firm.

'Mum? Dad's going to be OK about it, isn't he? He'll want to see me?'

'Don't be silly. You make him sound like an ogre.' She wanted to convince herself, too, that Tom could handle it.

'See you in an hour or so.'

She paused on the landing, listening to the voices in the sitting room. They were arguing about something but stopped and looked up when she entered the room. 'That was Maddy. They're at Ludlow. I told them to get a taxi.' She hoped that her use of the plural would prepare Tom for … what?

'Right,' he said getting up from the chair and collecting the coffee cups on a tray. He was renowned for signalling when guests should leave. On one occasion, he'd put the milk bottles out and gone to bed, leaving Anna and the visitors to get on with it. She had been mortified but no one else seemed at all bothered. It was just Tom's way.

'Come on, Bill.' Jenny poked the large body, slumped next to her. 'These people have things to do.'

Bill, disappointed that the evening was coming to such an abrupt close, hoisted himself off the sofa and followed the others downstairs. The kitchen was a chaotic muddle of dirty pots and dishes.

'Lovely meal, Anna. Much nicer than a stuffy dinner party. Shall we help with the washing up? I don't often get the chance to put my hands in soapy water.' Jenny took the opportunity to criticise the Wrens' decision not to install a dishwasher.

'We'll manage, thanks,' Tom replied.

At the last moment, Bill caught Anna in a goodnight hug, pulling her face against his scratchy sweater. How different he smelt from Tom. Not unpleasant – just different.

Before they were out of the door, Tom was running hot water into the sink. 'We could leave that until tomorrow,' she said. He didn't answer. 'I'd better sort out the room.'

'Are you going to put them in together?'

'It's a bit late to separate them now.'

He leant over the sink, scrubbing violently at a pan. She went up behind him and put her arms around his waist, resting her head against his shoulder blades. 'Lets not make up our minds until we've met him.'

'You obviously think he's OK.'

Madeleine and Taliesin were within half an hour's drive and she didn't want to start a conversation which would end in sulky stalemate. Tired, her foot throbbing, she hobbled upstairs. The smell of cooked food had filtered up to the top of the house and lingered in the bedrooms. She opened the windows for a few minutes, shivering as the frosty air caught her damp skin. The twinkling stars looked unreal.

There were two spare rooms. One had twin beds and the other, a double. Despite what she'd said to Tom, she was undecided which room to prepare. First she opted for the double bed, thinking to prove to Madeleine that they were prepared to accept her physical relationship with this man, this Taliesin. Then, to be on the safe side, she put sheets on the twin beds, too, piling towels in both rooms. At least the bathroom had been cleaned for their supper guests. Finally she took another two tablets as a precaution against the headache which surely lay ahead.

Tom was still sloshing water about in the sink. He disliked cleaning saucepans and casseroles. Remnants of rice pudding, such a delight a few hours ago, clung to the sides of the Pyrex dish. It would be easier to shift if it were left to soak overnight but she knew he wouldn't appreciate her advice. Her aim was to keep busy so she went into the utility room to track down the hot water bottles, stowed away in the pre-supper tidy up.

Now the working day was done, the tractors and chainsaws put away and the dogs locked in their kennels, the valley fell silent. Standing in the yard, she strained her ears. The road to Cwm Bont lay below and the sound of an occasional vehicle rumbled on the breeze. The light was still on in the Webbers' bedroom but the other houses were in darkness. She looked at her watch. Almost midnight. A car changed gear as it turned into the gate and laboured up the lane, breaking the silence. Not wanting to be caught waiting, she hurried back into the kitchen. Tom had finished at the sink and was collecting empty wine bottles in a cardboard box.

'I think they're here,' she said. 'You won't start anything will you, Tom? Not tonight.'

'I'll say whatever I think needs to be said.' He gave her a defiant stare.

8

Anna hugged her daughter, breathing in her familiar smell. Vanilla and baby lotion.

'I'll put the kettle on.' Tom needed to do something.

'Hi, Dad.' Maddy caught his cheek with a kiss as he turned away.

Anna looked at this girl who, beneath the trappings of New Age-dom, looked so much like her. The loose jacket, covering several layers of clothes, made the bump invisible but she'd felt it when they hugged. Maddy had last visited them at Christmas, flaunting a tangle of dreadlocks and multiple body-piercings. Whatever had happened since had caused her to tone it down. Flora complained that, having been fortunate enough to inherit Anna's wild curls, Maddy had done her best to ruin them but today her hair was brushed out and drawn back in a topknot. She had lost the metal that had protruded from her lower lip, nose and eyebrow and her ears had only three earrings apiece.

'I thought you were bringing…what's-his-name,' Tom turned the tap too far and cold water splashed out of the kettle.

'His name's Taliesin, Dad. Tal-ie-es-in. It's not difficult to say. He's outside, waiting with the taxi.'

'I'll get my purse,' said Anna.

As they walked across the yard, Maddy touched her

mother's arm. 'Mum. There's something I didn't mention on the phone. It's not just me and Tal.'

For a second Anna imagined that Maddy had invited the whole troupe of travellers to come with her. It wouldn't have been out of character.

'Arthur's with us. But it won't be a problem.'

'Arthur?'

'Tal's son. He's five. He's very sweet.'

She was sure he was. Most five-year-olds are. She took some money from her purse and pushed it into Maddy's hand. 'You pay the taxi, I'll go and pave the way.'

'Thanks, Mum. You're a star.' Maddy kissed her.

Within minutes of her arrival Madeleine was counting on her to mediate. First, she had to break the news to Tom that Arthur, whoever he might be, was in the taxi, too. Next, she would need to make sure that he would at least be civil to this stranger and his son. And she had two minutes to do it.

Tom listened without comment, then he took a fifth mug from the shelf and slammed it down on the table, alongside the others.

Maddy came in first, her finger to her lips. 'Art's asleep. Can we try and put him straight to bed? Which room, Mum?'

A tall, thin man, older than Anna had anticipated, ducked through the door. He carried a sleeping child over his shoulder, one hand behind the boy's head to prevent it from lolling backwards. 'This way,' she whispered and guided him upstairs. 'Second floor, I'm afraid.'

She followed him up the stairs and noticed that he was in his socks. He must have taken his shoes off in the utility room. The socks weren't a matching pair and were worn thin on the heels. It was difficult to demonise a man who had been thoughtful enough to remove his muddy shoes.

When they reached the top floor, Anna showed him the

bedrooms and let him choose. 'If it's OK with you, I'll pop him in the double bed. I'll sleep in with him, then if he wakes in the night he won't be frightened.'

She flipped the duvet back and they manoeuvred the boy onto the bed. The man removed his son's shoes and gently peeled off his anorak. Arthur barely stirred. 'He's exhausted,' said Taliesin. 'It's been a bit of a day.' He paused. 'I suppose I should wake him for a pee.'

'Don't you dare,' said Anna. 'That was my only rule of parenting. "Never wake a sleeping child."' She drew the duvet up to the boy's chin and watched as he snuggled further into his dreams, only just stopping herself from bending down and kissing the pale cheek. They left the door ajar and the landing light on. It felt so familiar to put a child to bed and creep downstairs.

Tom and Maddy appeared to be on speaking terms. They had brought the bags in from the utility room. From the size of the pile, she tried to calculate how long they might be staying, determined not to raise the question this early in the visit. Maddy made the introductions and they concealed the discomfort of those first minutes with talk about trains and taxis. Anna offered them food, which they declined, and compensated for Tom's silence by chattering about the supper party. Taliesin seemed content to sit and listen, his eyes fixed on Maddy's face.

When he had drained his mug, Tom started switching plugs off and checking window catches. 'It's late and I'm tired, even if no one else is.'

They sent their visitors up to the bathroom, whilst they made do in the downstairs cloakroom. Standing side by side, they cleaned their teeth. 'What's it all about then?' Tom asked, through a froth of toothpaste. 'Did he say anything? About the baby? Or about Maddy?'

'We just settled Arthur in the double bed and came down.

73

I wasn't going to start interrogating the poor man the second he arrived. Did you notice that he'd taken his shoes off?'

'That's fine then. He took his shoes off, so he must be OK.'

'Tom, you're not being fair. All I know is that he really loves that little boy. Anyone could tell that, from the way he put him to bed.'

'What's that got to do with us? You should be asking whether he loves Madeleine. And what happened to the boy's mother?'

'I just need to go to bed now,' said Anna. 'We'll start again tomorrow. Or is it today?'

By the time they made their way upstairs, there was no sound from either room. In their own bedroom, relief that Maddy was well and safe under their roof brought on a feeling of euphoria and Anna started to laugh. Exhaustion compounded her loss of control and within seconds she was helpless. She buried her face in the pillow to stifle the sound. Tom watched her, waiting until she had calmed down and had wiped away the tears of laughter. He often admitted that she was a complete mystery to him. She liked this idea. It made her feel exotic. On the other hand, Tom had always been an open book to her. Until recently.

'I'm sorry. I'm sorry,' she said. 'It's me. I know it's not funny. I'm just feeling all pent up.'

Tom stared miserably at her, as if she were in a freak show. It wasn't kind of him to stand watching her like that. She started to strip off her clothes, tossing them on the floor and twisting this way and that. He made no move to undress.

Naked now, she climbed on to the bed and walked across to Tom's side. The mattress sank beneath her weight, bringing her breasts level with his face. Still he didn't move. The bedside lamps cast shadows of her onto the ceiling, tilting them at crazy angles across the sloping eaves. She clasped his head and pulled it into her breasts, expecting him to nuzzle into her and laugh. But he stood, rigid and motionless.

'Stop it. It won't work, Anna,' he said, pulling his head away. She bent to kiss him but he twisted his face to the side. 'No.'

'What's wrong?'

'You can't divert me with a quick fuck. You're skimming over life, avoiding anything that's remotely serious. Aren't you concerned that Madeleine's having an illegitimate child? D'you think it's acceptable that she turns up with some ageing hippy, who's already sown wild oats God knows where? You can handle this how you like but please don't expect me to take it so lightly.'

Still standing on the bed, she struggled to hold back the tears of frustration and anger. Snatching up the t-shirt that she used as a nightdress, she dragged it over her head.

He turned away from her and began undressing. She flung herself down and pulled the duvet over her head. He climbed into bed and she lay facing away from him, hanging on to the edge of the mattress, keeping as far away from him as she could. Hating him. Jibes and justifications jangled around in her head, formless and unstructured.

She shivered. Her feet were almost numb with cold. Tom was always warm when he came to bed and most nights she fell asleep in his arms, the heat from his body spreading through her. Tonight there was a draughty chasm separating them.

She listened to his breathing, recognising the moment when he slipped into sleep. Within minutes he was snoring and she edged herself back a few inches, feeling the air warmer as she neared his body. How dare he accuse her of taking things lightly? How come he could fall asleep, if he were so anxious? She composed responses to his criticisms, time and again losing the thread of her argument in its convolutions.

If there had been a spare bed she would have gone to it.

Across the valley a dog barked, persistent and urgent. Perhaps a fox was after the poultry. She moved a little nearer to Tom's warm hulk, trying not to look at the clock on the bedside table but it caught her eye. It was gone half-past two.

The landing light went on and she heard the mumble of a man's voice. Taliesin was taking Arthur to the lavatory. Poor little soul. What sort of a childhood was he having? What was it like to be five years old, waking up in a strange bed in a strange house? Maybe he was used to being dragged from pillar to post.

The flush sounded and the light went out. Tom rolled over and put his arm around her. She pressed her back into his chest, feeling warm from top to toe, as they fitted together like spoons in the drawer.

'I love you,' he whispered, kissing the nape of her neck.

9

She half heard Tom get up but sank back into her dream. Those first seconds of wakefulness were blessedly untroubled; then, whatever was currently topping her worry list would come crashing in, like a wave demolishing a sandcastle. This morning it was Tom who had displaced Madeleine and her father at the top of her list. And she wasn't sure whether Arthur's name should be added to it somewhere.

It was after nine by the time she went downstairs. The doors of the other bedrooms were shut. She paused at the window on the first floor landing. It gave a view across the garden and up the hill to the wood. The trees were about to burst their buds and the faintest cast of green skimmed the tips of their branches. The blossom was still on the blackthorn, a splatter of white along the hedgerows and through the woodland. She opened the window, the breeze stirring the curtains, bringing the spring morning into the house.

Remnants of breakfast covered the table and worktops – two cereal bowls, several plates, sticky with marmalade or honey, and a clutch of mugs – but it was impossible to calculate how many people had eaten. She made herself toast and a cup of tea, then condensed the crockery into tidier piles next to the sink.

Light-headed, as though she had been to an all-night party, she closed her eyes and rotated her head, hearing the bones click at the base of her skull. There was the suggestion of a headache behind her eyes but at least her foot was no longer painful. She drank a glass of orange juice to flush down two painkillers. One glance in the cloakroom mirror confirmed her suspicions. Puffy eyes. Pasty face. She pinched her cheeks and then went to track down Tom.

Mrs Prosser was pegging out the Redwoods' laundry on one of the rotary clothes-lines, singing as she went. Anna preferred high lines of washing, flapping like bunting in the breeze, but they had taken a vote and rotaries had won – five votes to two. (Celia had abstained).

Beryl Prosser was younger than Anna. A short, bouncy woman who looked as though she enjoyed her food, she came to Pen Craig dressed for action, in clothes both sporty and protective. Today she was wearing leggings, a polo shirt and white Nike trainers, topped off with a paisley wrap-around pinafore. Her dark hair was scraped back from her wide face and caught in a yellow plastic bulldog clip.

She smiled when she saw Anna coming across the yard. 'Good drying weather, Mrs Wren, isn't it? Still a bit nippy, though.'

'You make me feel lazy, Mrs Prosser.' Anna wasn't sure how to be with cleaning ladies. The possibility of *not* doing the household chores was very appealing but the idea of paying someone to do them made her feel uneasy. They chatted about the weather and the garden and Anna enquired after her husband, intrigued by the partnership of this bustling, cheery little woman and the gloomy Postmaster.

'He's up and down, you know. He was very close to his Mam.'

From this she assumed that Prosser's mother had died recently but couldn't remember Jenny mentioning it. It might explain why he was so morose. She nodded sympathetically. 'Did she live locally?'

'She was a Roberts,' Mrs Prosser replied, as if that made everything clear. She nodded towards the house. 'I see you've got visitors.'

How did she know this? There was no strange car parked in the yard and no sign of anyone in the garden. 'Yes. My daughter and her ... some friends. I'm on duty, so I'd better get back.'

The door to the outhouse was open. The sun hadn't yet had a chance to warm it and was chilly inside. A mug half full of hot tea stood on the windowsill. Tom couldn't be far away. She went through to the garden beyond, walking on tip-toe, but her socks were soon damp through her thin shoes. Low sun was catching the droplets of dew on the grass, creating a carpet of tiny rainbows.

Tom was in the summerhouse, cleaning out the stove. She scraped her feet noisily on the plastic matting, ridding them of the dew and strands of grass and warning him that she was there.

He turned. 'I thought you could do with a lie in.'

The room smelled of wood smoke and motes of dust hung in the shafts of sunlight. While he continued with his task, she wandered around, plumping cushions and tidying the books which they'd all donated to start the Pen Craig library.

'I'm sorry about last night,' said Tom.

'Me too. We were both tired. And it was a weird evening.'

'Can I take you up on your offer some time?'

Over the years, Anna and Tom had developed their own system of communication. If she sensed that he was anxious, she would hold him and stroke him, like an animal. If he felt her disapproval, he would be extra considerate. It meant that they had become lazy about talking things through and sometimes the silent process failed. When it did, the hurts they inflicted upon each other accumulated like layers of dust on top of a wardrobe.

Tom had breakfasted with Taliesin and Arthur. 'Funny little boy.' He had nothing to say about his father.

'Where are they now?' she asked.

'I left them in the kitchen.'

He went to get on with work on the paving and she returned to the house to prepare a breakfast tray for Madeleine.

The bedroom door was still shut and she stood outside, listening for signs of life. A muffled 'Come in, Mum,' answered her gentle knock.

'How did you know it was me?'

Maddy pulled herself up from beneath the quilt. 'Well, Dad wouldn't come to see me in bed and Taliesin wouldn't knock. It's a novelty having doors, actually.'

'Oh dear.'

'Don't worry, Mum. It's fine. Benders are really cosy. You'd love it. Nothing to dust or hoover.' She looked at the tray. 'Breakfast in bed. Wow. It's not even my birthday.'

'How are you feeling?'

'Pretty good. I'm over the sickness. I just feel like I'm going around in slow motion. And by nine o'clock I'm ready for bed. Pathetic.'

'Nature's way of telling you to slow down.'

'That's what Tal says.'

There were so many things that she wanted to ask her daughter but she knew she must proceed carefully, gathering bits of information as best she could.

'Have you seen Tal and Art this morning, Mum?'

Anna explained that they must have gone out before she got up.

Maddy nodded. 'I think he's leaving us on our own, so we can have a chat. He's brilliant like that.'

'He seems very nice.'

'Mmmm. Too nice sometimes.'

'And he's marvellous with the little boy.'

Maddy patted the bed, inviting her mother to sit down. 'I know it's not really fair, asking you to be piggy-in-the-middle, but Dad flies off the handle so easily. He's so uptight.'

Maddy, knees pulled up to her chin, began talking. They wanted to stay for a couple of days, then they planned to visit Taliesin's father. 'He's a writer. Lives near Brecon.' She mentioned his name and Anna was taken aback. The man was a celebrity and had written several successful books, at least one of which had been made into a film. 'It's different, isn't it, now you know his father's rich and famous?'

It was true. Taliesin with a pedigree presented a very different proposition.

'You haven't asked about Art. Aren't you dying to know?' Maddy paused to ensure maximum impact. 'Tal and Sarah were together for a long time. Ten years, I think. When Arthur was born, they were living in Spain. She wasn't Spanish. Anyway, they came back to this country. Then, about two years ago she was killed. Hit and run as she was walking back from the shop.'

Anna pictured a broken body lying on the roadside, Arthur standing crying beside his mother, and shuddered. But dreadful as it was, Madeleine must be her priority. She needed to talk to her about money, antenatal care and where the baby would be born. Where did her daughter see herself in five years time? But today things were going so well. Maybe she would leave it for a while before rocking the boat.

While Maddy finished her breakfast, Anna gave her the latest news of family and friends. Maddy was intrigued to hear that her grandfather planned to remarry. 'It must be weird for you, but it's not as if he's trying to replace Grandma Nancy. He and Grandma were one person. When she died, he had to become another person or he couldn't have gone on.' She reached her arm around her mother's shoulder. 'You have to let him get on with it, Mum. Anyway, do you like her?'

'I don't know. We were being very polite with each other when we met. I was surprised that she was quite so old. But I liked her clothes.'

'That's a start. And I think it's good that she's old. It rules out all that money stuff. It'll be different when you meet her next time. You'll be able to see whether she really cares about him.'

Maddy got out of bed and Anna could see, through the thin nightdress, that her waistline had disappeared and there was a heaviness about her breasts. Her little girl's beautiful body was about to inflate and distort and she felt a little of Tom's regret.

With visitors in the house, she wasn't sure what she was supposed to be doing. Tom, visitors or no, carried on with the floor. There was no sign of Taliesin or Arthur. Maddy was enjoying the luxury of a bathroom. It left her in limbo. Obliged to hang around, in case she was required to cook something or fetch something or entertain someone, she decided to do some baking and was up to her elbows in flour when Taliesin and Arthur returned from their walk. The boy was carrying a posy of bluebells and primroses. He held them out to her. 'It's nice here. Thank you for having us.'

It was the first chance she'd had to look at him. The night before he'd been slumped over his father's shoulder or buried beneath a quilt.

Arthur resembled a miniature adult. Gangling and lean, like his father, without a trace of chubbiness, he had the face of a grown-up. But whereas Taliesin might be mistaken for an Italian, Arthur had mousey brown hair and a pale face. His bright eyes, green and fringed with dark lashes, redeemed his plainness.

'We only picked a few.' He laid the flowers gently on the worktop.

She rinsed the flour from her hands and took a purplish-blue vase, the same colour as the bluebells, from the cupboard. She had made the pot thirty years ago and had used it whenever the girls brought her their offerings of violets or snowdrops. 'I'll put them here,' she said, placing them on the windowsill next to the sink. 'They'll cheer me up when I'm doing the dishes.'

She finished making the pie and chatted to them about their walk. There was a small piece of pastry left when she trimmed the pie and she offered it to Arthur. 'Would you like to make something?'

'Jam tarts?' he suggested and, without instruction, set about rolling and cutting out the pastry.

'I can see you've done this before.'

He smiled and nodded. 'We share the cooking.'

She knew nothing of Maddy's life with these people but this phrase conjured up an Indian encampment. Benders in place of tepees. Communal meals around the campfire. 'Do you go to school, Arthur?'

'Art. I prefer Art. No, but I learn lots of things.'

Taliesin let his son explain how the adults in the group taught the children whatever skills they needed, when they needed them. 'And what does Dad teach you?' she asked, glancing up to see if she was overstepping the mark.

'How to mend things and make things. And the Latin names for plants and animals.' He handed her the tray of jam tarts. 'And Maddy teaches us about the stars.'

'And what else?' Madeleine came into the kitchen, dressed in tie-dyed dungarees, her hair twisted in a towel. She looked younger than her twenty years. 'Not only about the stars. We do a bit of reading too, don't we?'

'Reading is jolly useful,' said Anna, wanting to encourage

the child. He looked at her and said nothing, making her feel that she was the five-year-old.

'I've been keeping out of the way, so you could talk about me,' said Madeleine. 'Where's Dad? Can we have cheese on toast for lunch?'

Anna wanted to get Tom on his own and fill him in on what she had gleaned from the morning's chats. Before she reached the other side of the yard, she sensed that someone was watching her. It was Prosser. He was sitting on the wall outside the Redwoods' house, presumably waiting for his wife. Occasionally she had seen him collecting her in his battered white van after she'd finished her cleaning stint at 'High Trees'. She waved in his direction and shouted an overly cheery 'good morning'. He nodded but did not smile.

By the time she found Tom and they returned to the house, Prosser had disappeared. 'Don't worry about him. He's OK,' said Tom. 'I bet he thinks we're the nutters.'

In the few minutes that she had been out of the house, Steven had phoned. Maddy had taken the call. 'He's been to see Grandpa.' She held up her hands, watching panic flash across her mother's face. 'No problems. He'll ring again tonight.'

They ate lunch and had Art's jam tarts for pudding. He carried the plate proudly around the table, enjoying the plaudits. During the meal the boy had entranced them with visions of the world through a child's eye, whilst his father seemed content to take a back seat. She watched Tom to see whether he, too, was falling under Arthur's spell.

They talked, again, about family and friends. Madeleine was always interested to hear news of Flora. 'I wasn't sure how she'd be about the baby but she was really nice when I phoned her yesterday. Really mellow. I think there must be a new man in her life.'

They moved to ongoing projects at Pen Craig. At Christmas there had been much talk of a wind-generator, sheep, hens and, of course, the swimming pool. 'The trouble is, everyone's too busy working,' said Anna. 'Ridiculous, considering we came here to wind down.'

'So, are you in gainful employment?' Tom asked Taliesin. The ceasefire had been too good to last.

'Dad, don't.'

'It's OK. It's a fair question,' said Taliesin, laying a hand on Madeleine's arm.

'D'you think this is an appropriate time?' Anna nodded towards Arthur.

'Art, could you go outside and play for a while? We've got grown up stuff to discuss,' Taliesin said quietly. The boy nodded and they waited until he was out of earshot.

'I don't take handouts from the state, if that's what you're hinting at. Neither do I have what you would probably term a 'proper job'. But I've managed fine for fifteen years and I can't see any reason to change.'

'Isn't this baby a reason?' asked Tom. 'It costs a lot to rear a child. Children need security and certainty. Are you intending to stick around?'

'I can't believe I'm hearing this.' Madeleine jumped up, her chair crashing over onto the flagstones.

'It's OK. It's OK,' said Taliesin.

Anna felt sick. It was happening again. Tom was digging in and Maddy was storming out.

'Yes, I do plan to stick around, as it happens. And I don't mean to be impolite, but I think Maddy's the one I have to convince.' He joined Maddy, who was standing by the door. 'Go and lie down for a bit. Stress is the last thing you need.'

Maddy ran upstairs and they heard a door slam at the top

of the house. Tom shook his head and hurried out. Anna didn't know which of them to go after.

Taliesin picked up the chair and checked that it hadn't been damaged. She wanted to kick him for being so calm. Outside the back door, Arthur was singing to himself. 'London's burning, London's burning. Fetch the engine...'

She wished she were five years old again, when the very worst thing that happened was being forced, every Sunday, to drink cold cabbage water.

10

Arthur was playing with the Webbers' cat, Blackie, a stupid animal without charm or character. How typical of Celia to choose the undistinguished kitten from the litter and then to give it an equally undistinguished name.

If she stayed talking to Taliesin, she would be seen as disloyal by Tom and prying by Madeleine. Displaced from the kitchen, Anna needed something to occupy her.

'Shall we go for a walk?' she asked the boy.

'Yep. I'd better tell Dad and put my wellies on.'

She would have preferred to leave without explanations but the child was right. While he went to find his father, she took two apples and some chocolate biscuits from the larder, then followed his example and pulled on her boots.

The cat shadowed them for a while, then gave up and sat on the wall, watching them climb up the fields to the wood. At first she walked quickly. Arthur didn't complain but was forced to trot to keep pace with her. She slowed when the incline steepened, a 'stitch' jabbing under her ribcage. When they reached the fallen tree, they stopped to catch their breath.

'This is where Dad and I came.'

His voice surprised her. Caught up in her own resentments, she'd forgotten he was there. None of this muddle was his fault and she tried to make amends. 'You can be the navigator and decide which way we go. How does that sound?'

They climbed over the wall, into the wood. 'This way.' He pointed up the track towards the ridge, then ran ahead to make sure that the way was safe.

The trees up here were mainly ash, hazel and oak, spindly or bent where they crowded each other and strained up to the light. An ash tree, blown down by the winter gales, leaned against its neighbours, inching its way down to rot on the woodland floor. The sun permeated the leafless branches, falling on the matted grass. A few tangled holly bushes without a single berry formed dense, dark clumps. The ground was soft with season upon season of decaying leaves and it gave slightly, like a padded insole, beneath her boots.

It was ages since she'd spent time with a small child. At first she played the part of teacher on a nature ramble, but she soon discovered that he knew as much as she did about woodland matters. He lived in a wood, for goodness' sake. He could distinguish between a crow and a jackdaw. He could name the early wild flowers. He pointed out a badger's sett, showing her the tufts of brown hair caught on a snarl of brambles. 'It's called *meles meles* in Latin,' he announced and she knew he was right.

The breeze stirred the treetops as they climbed higher, sounding like running water coursing between the upper branches. They sang as they went, songs that she'd sung with Flora and Madeleine when they needed encouragement on a long walk. 'If you're happy and you know it…'. Their clapping hands sounded like the snap of Christmas crackers.

Then the path emerged from the wood and they were on a rough stone road, wide enough to take a car. She and Tom had walked up here, once or twice, but had always looped back down to Cwm Bont. Arthur found a sturdy stick. He used it to point along the track. 'This way.'

'Aren't you tired? We've come quite a long way.'

'Nope. I'm skinny but Dad says it's all muscle.' He held out his arm for her to feel his soft bicep.

They came to a fallen oak, much bigger than the others they had passed. It lay a little way off the path, the tangle of its root ball poking crazily into the air, like a massive tooth pulled from its socket by a giant dentist. She took the biscuits and apples from her pocket and they found a place on its ridged trunk to perch and eat their snack. The sun was warming and Arthur took off his fleece, tying it around his shoulders like a cloak. He stood on the stump and held his stick aloft.

'You're King Arthur with Excalibur,' she said. 'D'you know that story?'

'Of course I do. That's why I'm called Arthur.'

'What are they thinking of calling the new baby?' She felt guilty but it was a chance she couldn't miss.

'Don't know.'

'Your Dad's got an unusual name. Taliesin. Is it a family name?'

'It's not his real name. His real name's Rupert.' The boy thought for a moment then took a deep breath 'His great, great, great, grandfather was called Taliesin. It's Welsh.'

They resumed their walk, Arthur skipping along swiping at the dead bracken with Excalibur. Rupert Leighton, son of Charles Leighton. It started to make sense. He wouldn't be the first son who felt the need to shrug off a famous father. It would make things much simpler, though, if Maddy would just tell them all this. She shouldn't have to prise the facts from a child.

As they swung round a bend in the track, she saw four men walking towards them and caught Arthur's hand. These were the first people they'd seen since they left home. Wearing shabby waxed jacket and battered caps, they were not at all like the county set who shopped in Ludlow on a Saturday morning. Two black dogs walked to heel and each of the men carried a shotgun, the stock under his arm and the barrel, broken, across his forearm. As they came closer, she recognised one of them. It was Prosser.

'Afternoon, Mrs Wren,' muttered Prosser, touching his finger to his cap. He ignored the boy.

'Hello, Mr Prosser.' She could think of nothing more to say and they passed, their boots crunching on the loose stones. Her heart raced and she was cross that she had allowed herself to be intimidated by the guns. She could feel them looking back at her but she would not allow herself to turn her head, fixing her eyes on the winding track, glad to be holding the small hand in hers.

Two shots rang out from the wood behind them. The noise ricocheted between the valley sides and was soon followed by another volley. She glanced down at Arthur. ''Spect they're shooting crows,' he said.

They had been walking for an hour. The boy had stopped chatting and she knew that he must be tired. They should turn back and retrace their steps but she didn't want to go into the wood, where Prosser and his mates were skulking about, shooting things. She pictured the Ordnance Survey map which Tom had pinned on the board in the utility room. The ridge that they were following was the high point separating their valley from the next. If she could find a route down into the adjacent valley, there was certain to be a phone box somewhere along the road, and she could ring Tom to come and pick them up. She asked Arthur to keep his eye open for a footpath and within minutes he was pulling her towards a gap in the trees.

They turned off the ridge road and followed the path. Sometimes the leggy hazels and hawthorn trees on either side met overhead, cutting out the sunlight. The stones here were covered with moss and dangerously slippery. Arthur looked anxious when she missed her footing and she laughed to reassure him, but a fall here could be disastrous. It had been irresponsible to drag the child so far and now she was anxious to get him home safely.

The descent was quick. The hedges became more defined and the lane led them past a farmhouse where the footpath became pitted tarmac, broadening to a car's width. The house was drab and rendered with pebbledash. Net curtains obscured the windows. The woodwork was warped and rotten and flaking paint made it impossible to identify the colour of the front door. A ramshackle sprawl of sheds and outhouses surrounded the house and several vehicles stood, rusting, in the farmyard.

'Look,' Arthur pointed to the fence running up to the house. Strung along it, like a necklace of voodoo charms, hung a selection of dead birds and small animals. Crows, squirrels, magpies and a stoat or two dangled by the neck. Some had been there for months but some looked fresh. 'What's it for?'

'I don't know. Perhaps it's to scare other animals away.'

'Or people.'

If she were inclined to fancy, she might have thought someone was watching her. She turned quickly, peering back at the farmhouse, expecting to see a curtain twitch, but there was no sign of life, not even a dog barking in the buildings.

And then they were down at the road. It felt gloomier here than in their own valley. The orientation must be different, the valley sides steeper. She looked back from the road but there was no sign of the house, nothing at all to indicate that it existed.

She took over the navigation, walking down the narrow road where she was sure it would join the main road to Ludlow. Arthur looked pale but wasn't grumbling. He was trailing Excalibur behind him now. She checked her pockets but she had no coins to make a call even if she found a phone box.

Ahead she heard the sound of a vehicle, toiling up the road in a low gear. Arthur caught her hand and dragged her to the side of the lane, pulling her tight in against the quickthorn. The spiked twigs punctured her jeans and dug into her legs. She remembered how his mother had died and realised why he was so concerned. 'It's OK, Art,' she said as she saw Len's van grinding towards them. 'It's the postman.'

Len drew alongside and stopped the van. 'Afternoon. I haven't seen you up this way before, Mrs Wren.'

Anna explained how they came to be here. She wanted to ask him about the house. The postman would be bound to know all about it but something stopped her. 'Is there a phone box along this road?'

Len, revelling in the drama, said that there was but it was out of order. 'I'd offer you a lift ... but it's against Post Office policy.' He let this statement settle and then held his finger aloft, as if he'd had an astounding revelation. 'You can use my mobile if you like.'

She phoned Tom. It rang ten times before the machine cut in. If Arthur and Len had not been there she would have sworn. The only other number she could recall was Sally's, so she tried that. Bill answered before the third ring, as though he were waiting for her call. 'Hi, Bill. Could you pass a message to Tom? He'll be in the outhouse or the garden. Just tell him we'll keep walking towards the main road, if he could come and collect us.'

'It'll be quicker if I come,' said Bill. 'No arguments. I'm on my way.'

Before she could protest he had put the phone down.

Len drove off, up the valley, and they started walking again. Arthur insisted that they walk on the right 'to face the oncoming traffic'. She remembered her father drumming this into her head when she was a child and having no idea what he was talking about. There had been so many things that she had accepted without questioning and, if there ever had been questions to ask, she always went to her mother.

Her socks were too thin and her boots were starting to rub. The boy dragged his feet and she knew he must be exhausted. 'Won't be long. You are such a good navigator. I never would have seen that little path.'

'Is Tom coming for us?'

'No. Bill. He lives in the house across the yard. You'll like him. He's fun.'

There was a wall lining this stretch of the road and she decided to wait here for Bill. Arthur allowed her to lift him up onto the top of the rough stones, then she scrambled up after him, putting her arm around his shoulder, pulling him against her. Almost immediately his eyes closed and he slumped down to rest his head in her lap. She stroked his hair.

Within five minutes Bill turned up. Tom would have told her off for dragging the child so far and gone through a whole list of 'what if's' but Bill just helped her lift him, still clutching his stick, into the back of the car. They took his boots off and she could see the holes in the heels of both socks, a puffy blister evident through one of them.

'Who's this?' whispered Bill.

She told him.

'Must be a tough little kid.'

'Mmmm. Maybe. When's Sally coming back?'

'Tonight, I think.'

'I hope you're going to cook her a nice meal. Bottle of wine. Flowers. Or at least hoover around.'

'Is that what women like? Is that what Tom does?'

'No,' she said.

'What's his secret then?'

It had been kind of him to come for them but she was tired and didn't feel up to coping with Bill's advances. 'Tom's secret? He knows how to pleasure me.' It was a phrase she'd heard Germaine Greer use, in a lecture, and had all but given up hope of using it herself.

'Ahhh.' Bill flushed. 'Good old Tom.'

They arrived back at the house to find the yard full of people. Maddy and Taliesin were talking to Celia and Mark. Peter was lifting a suitcase out of his car. There was no sign of Tom. Taliesin smiled when he saw his son, asleep on the back seat. 'Everything OK?' he said.

'Fine. I'm afraid I walked him too far, poor little soul. I phoned but nobody answered, so Bill very kindly came to rescue us.'

Arthur woke, as children often do when movement stops. The short nap had revived him and Anna suggested that they go in for a drink and a piece of cake.

Maddy followed them in. 'You were away for ages. Where did you go?'

Anna told her.

'Dad went down to the village, looking for you. He's still not speaking to me. Now he's upstairs, pretending he's working.'

'I'd better go and see him.'

'I've been thinking, Mum. Perhaps we should leave. Dad just has to be in control, doesn't he? Can't he accept that I'm not like his beloved Flora?' She put her arms around her mother. 'You can see we're fine, can't you, Mum?'

'You can't leave tonight. I'll go and talk to your father. You see to Art. He must be famished.'

She ran upstairs. Glancing out of the landing window, she saw Taliesin laughing and talking with the Webbers. That was the way civilised people behaved.

She tapped on the door of Tom's workroom. He was sitting at his drawing board but she could see that he hadn't been working. A doodle wandered across the tracing paper, its meanderings covering it from the bottom right hand corner to the middle of the sheet. 'Hi,' she said.

'Hi. I couldn't find you.'

'I rang but there was no answer.'

'I'm sorry. I must have been outside.' The formality and coolness had returned.

'Have you talked to Maddy since lunchtime?'

'No. I've been working.'

'She thinks you want her to leave. That you don't want to see her any more.'

'That's rubbish. Of course I want to see her. She's so melodramatic. I can't bear to watch her heading for another disaster, that's all. We don't know a thing about this man.'

'We do, actually.' She recounted what Arthur had told her. 'I don't think he's quite as alternative as she'd like us to think. And if they're on their way to visit Charles Leighton, it must be to tell him about the baby. That seems a pretty reasonable thing for a young couple to do.' She went for broke. 'I rather like him. And the little boy is amazing.'

'Oh well, I'm obviously the villain of the piece.'

'Don't be silly. Why don't you come down and have a glass of wine before supper? It's chicken and mushroom pie. Can't we just have a nice meal together and take things as they come? Please. For me.'

By the time supper was ready, Arthur had flaked out. 'He's really good company,' said Anna as she passed the dishes around. 'I kept forgetting he's a little boy.'

'He probably spends too much time with adults,' said Taliesin.

They were civil to each other during the meal. Tom was

allowed to make dogmatic statements. Madeleine restricted her conversation to gossip about the Pen Craig inhabitants and their families. Taliesin said very little. Anna, unable to relax, waited for the evening to founder. The danger was that after a few glasses of wine people might be less guarded, but they reached the end of the meal without conflict.

They were finishing the washing up when Steven rang. He sounded agitated. 'Is Dad trying to wind us up, or something? What's he playing at? We can rule out all the obvious things – sex, housekeeper, money. She's eighty-bloody-four for God's sake.'

'Why don't you just ask him?' said Anna. 'That seems a reasonable thing to do. We know how lonely he's been. Maybe he chose her so that no one could possibly accuse him of trying to replace Mum. I was hoping that you'd figured it out. You see him more often than we do.'

'To tell you the truth, I don't go there that often. I'm knackered by the time I get home from work and you know he doesn't get on with Elaine.'

She heard footsteps climbing the stairs and the sound of a running tap. Steven was getting around to his favourite subject, his relationship with Elaine. She cut him short, reminding him that they had visitors. They arranged to speak again soon but, after she'd put the phone down, she realised she had no idea why he'd called.

Tom was already in bed, the duvet drawn up around his neck, but she could see that his pyjamas were neatly folded on the chair.

11

There was a bus leaving Ludlow for Brecon at mid-day, and Anna was to give them a lift, then carry on to the supermarket. She'd become accustomed to catering for two and the visitors had, in less than two days, cleared the fridge and made inroads into their emergency rations. On her way to the dustbin she had bumped into Celia, who was also planning to go shopping, and Anna had offered her a lift too. Before the move, Mark had made calculations of the savings in petrol and car depreciation if they doubled up on this sort of journey. They had made a real effort for the first few weeks, but the organisation required and inconvenience caused outweighed the benefits and enthusiasm petered out.

Everyone was still on best behaviour, with Tom trying particularly hard. Anna had seen him laughing with Maddy over some photographs which had come to light during the move. Then he took Taliesin off to show him his handiwork in the outhouse. Not much, but it was a start. Arthur was quiet and she wondered whether he was suffering from yesterday's walk. Her own legs were still stiff and they were a lot longer than his. She checked the map and saw that they had covered over four miles, which wasn't bad going for a five-year-old. 'I'm nearly six,' he protested when she traced their route with her finger.

'When is your birthday?'

He looked across to his father and frowned, putting his head on one side. 'Dad?'

'September 21st,' said Taliesin. 'That's almost half a year away, Art.'

'And, d'you know, that's the very date we moved here,' said Anna, 'so we'll never forget to send you a card.'

The boy smiled and his plain face lit up. 'Will you come to my birthday party?'

The room fell silent. Arthur wasn't the only one waiting to hear how she would respond. 'September's a long way away, but if it's at all possible, and if you still want me to, I promise I'll come.'

They went around the house, collecting their bits and pieces. Arthur had a small blue backpack which contained his treasures. When he tipped the contents onto the bed, she was intrigued to see what he had chosen to bring on his visit. A magnifying glass. Some marbles. A pencil and a notebook. A necklace of glass beads. A tennis ball. And a photograph in a plastic wallet. It showed a woman standing with Taliesin on a beach. 'That's my Mum and Dad,' he said.

Anna looked at the laughing girl, her hand brought up to shield her eyes from the sun. 'She's very beautiful.'

'She's dead.'

She could attempt to soften death with a litany of perhaps-es or maybe-s but children craved certainties. She'd tried the 'some people think this, some people think that' approach with her own daughters, but they had stared her in the eye and asked 'But what do you think, Mum?' However Taliesin had explained the tragedy to his son, she felt sure that conventional religion was not involved. How could any divine master plan demand that his beautiful mother be mown down by a joy-rider?

The boy touched her hand. 'It's OK, Anna.'

'I think I'm going to give you a birthday present now, a

98

sort of five-and-a-half-years-old present. Wait right there.' She ran down to Tom's office and searched out the box of coloured pencils which she had bought a few weeks earlier. She'd barely used them and they looked brand new. Folding them in a scrap of gift-wrap, she took them back upstairs.

Arthur was standing exactly where she had left him and he quivered with anticipation when he saw the parcel. 'When can I open it?'

'Save it 'til you're on the bus.'

He placed the package in the front pocket of his bag and took out the string of beads, holding them out to her. 'I made this. Maddy helped me. It's for you.'

She put the necklace on and went to the mirror. 'Thank you. They're the prettiest beads I've ever had.'

He gave her a sweet smile.

Tom found farewells hard. He mumbled a few words to Taliesin and shook his hand, patted Arthur on the head and hugged Madeleine, pressing a roll of notes into her hand. She started to refuse but Anna shook her head and pushed them into her pocket.

'Poor Dad,' said Maddy, watching Tom retreat to the house, blowing his nose.

Before they reached the bottom of the drive Anna was wishing that Celia wasn't with them. She had squeezed into the back seat with Art and Taliesin, to allow Maddy 'plenty of room for her bump', then for the whole journey she enthused about babies and motherhood. Celia was a mother by adoption so what did she know about it? But Maddy took it all on the chin, smiling and nodding. It was impressive how tolerant her daughter could be of someone *else's* mother.

She watched Arthur in the rear view mirror. He sat stiffly, avoiding contact with Celia. It was doubtful whether he'd met anyone quite like her before. It was unlikely that female Travellers applied lipstick, or dabbed perfume behind their ears, before they went shopping.

Had she been on her own, she would have waited with them but because Celia was with her it was impossible. Double-parked near the bus stop, they made their garbled farewells, promising to keep in touch and to visit again soon. She drove on to the supermarket, miserable with all the things she hadn't been able to say.

They loaded the bags of shopping into the car. Anna was more than ready to get back but Celia suggested that they have lunch in the town. 'Let's try the new place on the corner. Jenny says the food's excellent.' Anna had the impression that it wasn't a spontaneous suggestion.

As they walked up the wide street, past the Tudor splendour of The Feathers Hotel, she glimpsed their reflection in the dusty shop windows. They made an odd couple. Celia, dressed for a day at the office, wore court shoes, American tan tights, grey pleated skirt and pink fleece. On the other hand she, in dungarees, rainbow-striped cardigan and boots looked as if she'd wandered out of the garden. Had she brushed her hair that morning?

'Bistro B' was trendy and expensive. Just the sort of place that Jenny would approve of. The waitress made a great show of finding them a table, although there were only half a dozen other people eating. She plonked them in the far corner, as though they weren't glamorous enough to deserve a window seat. The chairs were made of brushed aluminium, cold to the touch and uncomfortable. Cutlery clattered on the plastic-topped tables, bouncing sharp sounds off the reflective surfaces.

Whenever Anna ate out, she used a bowl of home-made soup as a 'value-for-money' indicator. At 'Bistro B' it was the cheapest thing on the menu at over five pounds. She could make gallons of the stuff for that. Celia dithered for five minutes then chose soup, too. Eventually, when it came, it was over-salted, with a metallic aftertaste. The waitress bullied Celia into ordering a glass of white wine but Anna held out for a glass of tap water.

As soon as Celia started talking Anna's mind began wandering, following the bus to Brecon. Arthur had probably opened his parcel and maybe Maddy and Taliesin ('Rupert' would be so much easier) were discussing their visit. She would call in at the library and look for something by Charles Leighton. Don't they always say that novels invariably have an autobiographical element? It might be very informative. She must speak to Flora this evening and tell her all about Arthur.

Celia's face came back into focus. Her mouth was no longer moving but her eyebrows were raised, in anticipation of a reply. Anna, desperate to conceal her inattention, peered over to the far corner of the room and craned her neck. 'Sorry, Celia. I thought I recognised someone. Carry on.'

'That's it really. I go back for the results next week. But Mark doesn't think it can be diabetes. His mother had it and her symptoms were completely different.'

How could she sit there daydreaming while poor Celia poured out her troubles? She was appalled at herself and overcompensated with a volley of questions, asking how long she'd been unwell and about her symptoms. When Celia repeated it all, she was amazed that anyone would bother the doctor with such a vague list. Headache, restlessness, weight loss, insomnia. She almost asked, 'Is that all?' Throughout the twenty years of their friendship Celia had worried about her health, often with good reason. Her stomach-ache had been appendicitis. The lump in her leg had been a thrombosis. The stabbing pains had been gallstones. Perhaps she shouldn't dismiss her fears too flippantly.

Celia started to cry. 'And another thing, I keep crying all the time.'

Anna patted her hand. 'Come on, let's have something else to eat. A bit of a treat.'

They ordered a cappuccino and large slice of chocolate cake, each. 'I love being with you, Anna, you always cheer me up.' As she spoke, her narrow fingers shredded a tissue into small twists.

Anna wanted to apologise for all the times that she'd cut her friend's conversation short or taken avoiding action. 'Well, you've eaten all your lunch. That's a good sign, isn't it?' She sounded like an encouraging nanny.

Celia gave a watery smile. 'The trouble is, it's raised … issues.'

'Issues?'

'With Judith. They suggested that she should be tested too, in case it's something hereditary.'

Anna waited a moment, trying to understand Celia's logic. 'But surely…'

'I told them she's adopted. They said it is possible that Judith's inherited some medical condition. Not from us, of course. Anyway, it's unsettled her. She's talking about contacting her mother. Her birth mother.'

Anna wasn't sure whether this announcement called for her sympathy. 'Judith's such a sensible girl, Cee. And she adores you and Mark. It won't make a blind bit of difference, whatever she finds out.' But how could that be true? What if Judith were to discover that her birth mother was a painter or a prostitute? Or a woman who detested pink.

Celia shook her head. 'It'll change things. I know it will.'

The café was busier now and the harsh acoustics were making conversation uncomfortable. Her eardrums flexed with the pressure of the reverberating sounds. The waitress cleared the plates and cups from the table, removing their excuse to linger. They paid the bill and left.

On the way back to the car Celia apologised for monopolising the conversation. 'I haven't even asked about you,' she said. 'Madeleine looked well. And her young man seems very nice.'

'Yes. They're fine,' she said. 'We're all fine.'

They came to Anna's favourite shop. 'Can we have a quick look around? I love their stuff.'

The shop smelled of incense and unwashed wool and the sound of pan-pipes filled the air. There were shelves of crudely fashioned pottery, cases of chunky silver jewellery. Wind chimes jangled softly in the draught from the open door. She glanced back at Celia, who stood in the middle of the shop looking nervous, as if evil spirits were abroad and she was in mortal danger. The Peruvian jumpers would make her itch. The heavy bracelets and necklaces would weigh her down. The incense would bring on her asthma. And weren't those pagan images on the pottery?

Anna spotted a crushed-velvet jacket on the rail, light catching the nap of the fabric, bringing it to life like a field of long grass when the wind riffles through it. There was a geometric pattern embroidered in darker green at the cuffs and across the yoke, and it flared out around the hem. One huge button at the base of the lapels fastened it. And it was reduced to half price.

She held it out to Celia. 'Isn't it fantastic? Try it on, Cee. It would look wonderful with your skin colour.'

Celia retreated. 'I never wear green. It's unlucky.'

The woman behind the counter, who had been quietly polishing the silver bangles, leant across and confided in a strong West-Midlands accent, 'I used to be like that until one day I thought, "How can a colour change your luck, you stupid cow". It's the same with Friday the thirteenth.

Everyone in the whole world can't be unlucky on the same day, can they?

Celia looked uncertain.

'Go on. Try it,' Anna cajoled, helping her out of the pink fleece and into the jacket. The flare of the hem emphasised Celia's trim figure. If she had put weight on, it was hard to detect. The pine-forest green complimented her pale skin and blonde hair. The garment had transformed her from a pink rabbit into a Scandinavian princess. Celia stared at herself in the long mirror, turning this way and that, the folds of the fabric swinging from side to side.

'It is nice ... but I'm not sure.'

'You look fantastic. Tell you what,' said Anna. 'You take it and if you change your mind, or Mark doesn't approve, I'll buy it off you.'

While she put away the groceries, she told Tom about Celia's troubles. 'Poor Celia,' he said. 'She does have rotten luck.'

Then she went on to tell him about the jacket. 'She wears such frumpy clothes. They remind me of stuff from a catalogue. I thought it would do her good to break away from polyester. She looked almost up to date.'

'Not everyone wants to look like a refugee from a jumble sale, Anna. Anyway, I always think Celia looks fine just as she is. Nice and feminine. Don't bully her.' Tom turned back to his library book.

12

The men were planning a trip to the Centre for Alternative Technology at Machynlleth. When they lived in Bristol Tom had experimented, on a very small scale, with solar panels. They had always composted their kitchen waste but at Pen Craig there was an opportunity to take sustainability a great deal further. He was evangelistic about it and saw this trip as an opportunity to convert the others.

'Saving the planet is a "man thing" then?' Sally asked, when they met in the summerhouse to discuss their route.

'We could all go, if you girls are keen. Take a couple of cars. Make a day of it.' Mark looked enthusiastic.

Sally shook her head. 'You are joking. If I'm taking a day off, I'd rather sit in the sun with a book.'

'I think they're looking forward to a lads' day out.' Anna had noticed the look of dismay cross Tom's face.

What was this 'day off' Sally was on about? She was self-employed and it was entirely up to her how much work she did and when she did it. Underlying her remark was the implication that the rest of the women had nothing meaningful to do. Anna didn't feel non-employed. Keeping the garden in trim took several hours each day, and now that her wheel and kiln were installed she intended to make up for the lost months.

Anna was the only one of 'the girls' up and about when the expedition left. It had rained earlier, purifying the May morning. A day-moon hung, a translucent silvery ghost in the cloudless sky. She shut her eyes and took a deep breath and, catching the faintest hint of wood-smoke, shivered at the terrifying perfection.

To make the most of the early start she would blitz the household chores and be in the vegetable garden by nine o'clock. Then, when it grew too hot and she'd had enough physical exercise, she could retreat to the outhouse and get on with her project.

Madeleine had contacted them several times since her visit. She'd phoned the other evening to tell them that Taliesin's father had invited them to move in with him. His house was far too big for one and they could have a whole wing of the place to themselves. Arthur would have a huge garden to play in and could start, immediately, at the local school.

Tom was affronted that his daughter was prepared to live under another man's roof. Anna reminded him, gently, that they didn't have room for three (soon to be four) additional people at Number Four. They should be relieved that Maddy was going to be safe and comfortable during the latter stages of her pregnancy.

'I don't like to think of a child of mine sponging off anyone,' he said. 'She's our responsibility.'

But she wasn't, was she? She was over eighteen and Tom was no longer the man in her life.

She put away the vacuum cleaner and headed for the garden. At this time of year plants were capable of growing six inches overnight, and each morning something new had sprung up. Today it was a fine crop of dandelions. She picked one, milky sap oozing from its hollow stem. Dandelion. Dentes du lion. As a child she'd pictured a ferocious lion with bright yellow teeth and had been perplexed when her know-all cousin had explained that the jagged-edged leaves were actually the teeth.

As she pushed the hoe between the rows, Eric joined her. The unkempt plot and the untidy borders near the 'High Trees' front door had irritated Jenny, so the Redwoods had taken on a gardener – Eric. The physicality of the work lent it intimacy and, at first, she had been uncomfortable when he was there, working so close to her. Now, after a month or so, they were getting used to each other and tended the gardens in companionable silence. He was a reserved man, with a fund of horticultural knowledge which he was happy to share but only when consulted.

Bill, too, was showing an interest in horticulture and had thrown himself into clearing the adjacent plot. Sally was mystified, but nevertheless delighted, that he had found something to get him out from under her feet. Anna wasn't so pleased. But today, with Bill off to look at windmills, she could relax.

Sally waylaid her outside the summerhouse as she was returning the tools. 'Hi there. Elevenses?'

'Wouldn't want to stop you *reading*.' Anna's dig went unnoticed.

'You look very rosy-cheeked.'

'I'm sweating. A couple of hours in the sun and I'm pooped.'

'Perhaps we *should* reinstate the pool.'

'Please, not the pool.'

They took deckchairs outside and sat down to drink their coffee.

'Where did you say Emily is now?'

'Sydney. At least that's where she was on Sunday night. I'm trying not to think about it. I can't believe she chucked it all up for that Dominic person. And now he's dumped her.

It's so predictable.'

'Is she on her own?'

'No, thank God. She's teamed up with a couple of Dutch girls, or so she says.'

This particular corner of the garden was a sun-trap and Sally put up the huge canvas parasol, dragging her chair into its shade. Her face and plump arms were already a mass of freckles. Anna stayed in the sun, taking off her boots and socks and rolling up the legs of her trousers. They recalled teenage days, when it was *de rigeur* to have an even tan.

'We got it into our heads that the best stuff to use was olive oil. We used to baste ourselves, set my mother's kitchen timer and turn over every ten minutes, like meat roasting on a spit.' Sally wrinkled her nose. 'We smelled disgusting and the oil left a yellow tide mark around the bath.'

Anna hadn't seen much of Sally since the trip to Bristol. It would be useful to discover how things stood between her and Bill, but after an hour of chat she was none the wiser. Sally was perfectly friendly and, if anything, slightly less acerbic than usual. Perhaps she, too, was relieved that Bill was a hundred miles away.

In the early days there had been regular meetings to discuss communal issues. From the outset they had foresworn rotas but there were certain practical issues which needed to be sorted out, if things were to run smoothly. Recycling. Care of boundary fences. What to do with the two fields. These meetings soon became a forum for grumbling discord and they were abandoned.

Anna was disappointed to see how her friends appeared to be replicating their former suburban lifestyles. They might as well be living on the outskirts of Manchester or Nottingham. Her current pottery project was intended as a gentle reminder of the reasons for the move to Wales.

'Mum, what you lot need is a logo. Or an acronym,' Flora had said when she told her about it. Flora loved to play with words and in a few minutes came up with a suggestion. 'How about PARADISE? People At Retirement Age Delighting In Supporting Eachother. You can cheat on the "eachother".'

'It's not strictly accurate though, is it? Only Bill's completely retired.'

'But that's what you all hope lies ahead and you did say that these pots are intended as heirlooms.'

The acronym grew on her. All the mugs, plates, bowls and jugs would carry the inscription 'PARADISE' and the name of the recipient. When she let Tom in on her secret, he'd not been very keen. 'Sounds a bit contrived to me. They probably won't appreciate it.'

But she decided to press ahead and, within a couple of weeks, had finished the complete set of mugs. Each one was unique, colour and shape reflecting the essence of its recipient. She felt most satisfied with Celia's. As part of the anti-pink campaign, she'd plumped for pale turquoise with dark greenish-grey decoration. Strangely enough, Tom's had given her the most problems. It had come out black and straight-sided. Sombre and pure. She wasn't sure she liked it.

An afternoon of doing what she loved best stretched ahead. She took out her clay-spattered sketches, turning to the pages covered with drawings of bowls. They should be the right size to hold cereal or soup. Useful, beautiful and singular.

Folding back the thick plastic which held the clay and kept it from drying out, she saw a small object wrapped in a piece of black bin liner pressed lightly into the clay. It might have been an explosive device but, without a second thought, she opened it. The black plastic concealed a velvet-covered box. The box contained a pair of earrings made from Venetian glass beads. Even in the gloom, she could see that they were exquisite and exactly what she would have chosen for herself. How did Bill know that she loved Venetian glass? Because they *had* to be from Bill.

She re-sealed the pack of clay and returned to the house. It was impossible to work now. Simply by holding the earrings in her hand, she felt herself in league with Bill. How had he imagined she would explain them to Tom? They were obviously too expensive for her to have bought for herself, on the spur of the moment. She locked the back door and ran up to the bedroom before taking the earrings from her pocket. The sunlight, shining through them, revealed the blues and greens of the Adriatic. She held them high, allowing them to swing on the gold wire as they might swing from her ears.

She filled the bath and sank into it, looking down at her body lapped by the soft Welsh water. Her skin tanned easily and a white shadow marked where her watch circled her wrist. When she lay in bath, she came nearest to a state of transcendental meditation. Maddy was into that sort of thing and had once tried to describe the process. 'When you stop thinking about one thing and start thinking about another, there's a split second when your mind is completely empty of thought. All you have to do is enlarge that emptiness and hang on to it.' But the flotsam of life jostled in to fill the space faster than she could extend it. In it all crowded, babies, fathers, guns and earrings.

When she woke, her fingers were wrinkled and the water was cool. In her dream she had been delivering leaflets, door to door, down a street of terraced houses. Then a lorry had passed and shed its load of empty milk bottles on top of her. It hadn't hurt a bit.

Wrapped in a towel, she returned to the bedroom and checked the time. She'd been asleep for forty minutes. Even with the window ajar, the sun had warmed the bedroom and it smelled of dust and lavender. The earrings lay on her bedside table and she couldn't resist hooking them into her ears. Then, standing before the long mirror, she let the bath towel drop to the floor. Where her hair escaped from the combs, it rioted into curls. Her skin graded through the colours of eggshells, from the nut brown of her hands to the creamy white of her breasts. The fuzz of pubic hair matched her curls, grey and black. Silvery stretch marks wandered like snail trails across her thighs. Her hips were broader and her breasts hung lower than they had, but she was fifty-one, after all, and looked considerably more voluptuous than she did thirty years earlier.

The air, moving over her flesh, roused her. At first she walked on tip-toe, as if to make herself less conspicuous. Then she became bolder, planting her heels down firmly. She went down the stairs and wandered from the living room to Tom's office, sitting at his drawing board and leaning her breasts on the cool tracing paper.

The kitchen flagstones were cold beneath her feet. She crossed to the window, recklessly leaning forward to peer into the yard, disappointed that there was no one to catch a glimpse of her. There was half a bottle of red wine on the sill, left from last night's supper, and she filled a wine-glass. The earrings tapped, cold and heavy, against her cheeks. She went back upstairs, taking the bottle with her.

There was enough for two more glasses and she drank them down quickly, like medicine, standing in front of the mirror. She scrutinised herself, pulling her hair this way and that, twisting it up on top of her head or dropping it down on her shoulders.

Taking 'Gymnopedie' from the CDs on the chest of drawers, she put it in the machine. With the volume at maximum, she lay back on the bed, spreading her arms and legs. The breeze from the window played across her flesh, cool, soft fingers, exploring her. She wished that Tom were there. Or even Bill.

She got up too quickly and grabbed the chair to steady herself. Before pulling on her clothes, she removed the earrings and laid them in their box. She chose a faded tee-shirt of Tom's and a pair of shapeless cotton trousers, scraping her hair back into a ponytail. Gathering up the empty bottle and glass she went downstairs, the velvet box rattling in her pocket.

She could think of nowhere in the house to hide them. If she put them with her other jewellery, she might be tempted to wear them. If she pushed them into the back of a drawer or behind some books, anyone coming across them would know that they had been deliberately hidden. If she put them back where she had found them, she couldn't get on with her work. And they were too beautiful to throw away.

Back in the studio, she re-wrapped the box in its black plastic covering and went into the garden. Behind the outhouses, running alongside the path to the pool, there was a dry stone wall which had probably been part of the original stock enclosure. She searched the irregular face of the wall until she found a hole about the size of a grapefruit, where one of the stones had been dislodged. Making sure that the package could not drop down inside, she placed it in the cavity, wedging it with a small stone. This would have to do, until she thought of something better.

She spent the rest of the afternoon cleaning the house. The only interruption was a phone call from Tom, letting her know that they were on their way home.

13

Anna was reorganising the recycling bins when the car came up the drive. The travellers spilled out, shouting and laughing.

'How was Machynlleth?' she asked.

'Very Welsh,' said Peter, 'and quite interesting, in an earnest kind of way. I'm afraid Tom may be overstimulated, though. He's collected a carrier bag full of leaflets, so look out.'

'A lot of it made sense. To me, anyway,' Mark said. 'Back to first principles. Makes you think. Question a few things.'

Jenny, with Celia a few paces behind, appeared from the Redwoods' back door. They had become inseparable over the past few weeks. It reminded Anna of shifting playground alliances. Still, if Jenny wanted to become Celia's best friend, good luck to her.

The men were in high spirits and reluctant to break up the party. The sun had set behind the hill but the air was still warm. They decided it was the moment to sample the cider which they had made last autumn and they arranged to assemble in the summerhouse in half an hour.

Tom went to change his clothes and Anna followed. 'Was it worth going?'

She thought how handsome he was, as she watched him sorting through his pockets, piling the contents on his bedside table. Not quite tall enough but very trim, with a shock of iron-grey hair. On that very first day it had been his hair, black then, and dreaming grey eyes which had drawn her. 'What did I just say, Tom?'

He turned towards her, as if surprised to hear her voice breaking into his thoughts. 'What?'

'Tell me about the trip. What did you talk about all day? I can't believe that it was just about windmills. Was Peter OK? He does like to be leader of the gang.'

'Wind generators, not windmills, love. Pete was fine. Playing the devil's advocate, as usual, but that's no bad thing. Mark was very enthusiastic. He loves the mechanical side of things. Bill was a bit odd, though. I thought he'd be my main ally but he seemed rather detached. Didn't contribute much.'

'Any gossip?'

'Like what?'

'I don't know. Judith. Pete's career plans. Why Bill's a bit off.'

'No. Nothing.' He shook his head, looking like a small boy as he stood in his underpants and socks. 'How was your day? Did you make any progress on the bowls?' He kissed her nose. 'You've caught the sun.'

She pulled him to her and kissed him full on the mouth. He tasted of toothpaste. She pushed her hips against him and brought her hand up between his thighs.

'I must go away more often,' he said, but his body did not respond and the kiss turned into a hug. 'Come on. We'd better join the others.'

The doors of the summerhouse were wide open and the table was heaped with food. A demi-john of cider, shoulders dusty after standing all winter in the outhouse, took pride of place. Anna added her contribution – some rolls, a wedge of cheese and a jar of pickled damsons. The Wrens had always been good at rustling up picnics. Even a couple of jam sandwiches and an apple, eaten out of doors, could drive the children into a frenzy of excitement. A picnic followed by a never-ending game of Monopoly was an abiding memory of those endless summer holidays, when the girls still belonged to her.

Bill returned, alone and empty handed. 'Sally's gone to bed. One of her migraines.'

Anna remembered how bright and breezy she'd been earlier. 'Shall I go and see if I can do anything?'

'She's asleep. Best leave her. Thanks, anyway.'

They gathered around the table and Mark eased the bung from the cider jar. 'We must appease the gods.' He tilted the heavy container, pouring a splash onto the ground but the golden liquid dribbled back, spattering his pale slacks.

'Gods obviously not impressed,' laughed Bill.

Opinions on the cider were divided. Jenny and Peter found it undrinkable and went in search of a bottle of Cava. Tom and Mark, prime movers in the production, maintained it was spot on and getting better with each glass. Celia made herself a shandy with a few drops of cider in a glass of lemonade.

Anna took a sip. It was dry, strong and almost pleasant. She reached for some bread. She'd eaten very little all day and was still feeling light-headed after the wine.

Celia appeared at her side, wearing a gingham shirt and an ankle-length navy skirt. 'You look lovely,' said Anna, surprised, wishing that she had chosen something more elegant to wear.

'Thanks. Jenny's been helping me sort out my wardrobe. Putting me on the right track. We took two black bags in to her charity shop this week.'

Had the beautiful green jacket passed the Jenny test? Anna was tiring of Celia's Jenny-adulation. 'Has Judith had any more thoughts?' That should jolt her out of it.

Celia smiled bravely, explaining that her daughter had decided to start the procedure to make contact with her birth mother. 'They've told her it might take quite a while.'

Anna, immediately penitent, backtracked. 'Kids.' She shook her head. 'It never stops, does it? Emily, Maddy, Judith…'

'…Christopher Redwood,' added Celia, then covered her mouth with her hand. 'Oh dear. I really shouldn't drink.'

'What's happened to Christopher?'

Celia tried to convince her that it had been a slip of the tongue but soon gave up. 'He's in a bit of trouble at school. Something to do with pornography.'

'Gosh. Selling it? Buying it? What?'

'I don't think I should say any more.'

'You can't stop there, Cee.'

Celia shrugged her shoulders. 'Selling it. Magazines. Videos. That sort of thing.'

'He hasn't been expelled?'

'No. Peter sorted it out. The school wants it hushed up. Please don't say anything, Anna. She'll know it was me.'

Their conversation was cut short when Bill joined them. 'You two lovely ladies are looking distinctly cons … conspar … conspiratorial.' He stood, swaying and grinning, feet apart for increased stability.

If, as Anna suspected, the Davises had fallen out, Bill might be in a reckless mood. Drunk and without Sally to keep him under control, he was a loose cannon. Was it safer to keep Celia with her as chaperone, or get rid of her, in case Bill said something suggestive?

Her dilemma was resolved when Mark appeared and began tuning his guitar. He beckoned his wife to his side and, without any preamble, Celia started to sing. In the space of a few chords she became a star, her pure, sharp voice hitting each note dead centre like a metal rod striking a crystal goblet. Mark's guitar playing was unexceptional but there was a touching empathy between them as they ran through their repertoire. Although she had heard them sing many times, they never failed to touch her, these old songs of love, partings and death. Tears welled. She wanted Tom to put his arm around her and claim her for his own, but he wasn't anywhere to be seen.

Had Tom dreamed up some ridiculous task that couldn't wait? He should be here with her, not off somewhere, messing about with the car or watching rubbish on the television. In the time it takes to sing one maudlin sea-shanty, she'd fallen out with him. How dare he abandon her? Bill was still swaying at her side and she looped her arm through his. It took him a moment to register what had happened, then he turned and gave her a child-like grin of utter happiness.

When the music stopped, she disengaged her arm. 'I must go and find Tom. And perhaps you ought to see if Sally's feeling better.' Bill's smile faded, his face sagging like a deflating balloon.

It was dark now and the evening air felt chill so Mark and Peter decided to light the stove. Jenny and Celia, curled up on the sofa near the fire, were engrossed in conversation and from the hand waving and pointing Anna guessed they were planning the next phase of Celia's transformation. Feeling excluded Anna left, aware that Bill was following a few paces behind her, impossible to ignore as he stomped along. The path back to the house skirted the outbuildings but, still cross with Tom and more than a little disgruntled, she chose to take the shorter route, through her studio. After the glow of the moonlight it was inky black in here and Bill, fuddled from the cider and intoxicated with the remembrance of her arm in his, bumped into the door frame. 'Oops. Sorry,' he apologised.

She turned and took his hot, damp hand, guiding him

into her studio. He put his arms around her, pulling her to him, kissing her on the lips. She knew that this shouldn't be happening, but if Tom hadn't abandoned her she wouldn't be here in the dark with Bill.

She felt horribly nervous but almost faint with excitement. Would she know what to do? It was a long time since she'd kissed anyone else but she needn't have worried. Bill was a truly accomplished kisser and took the lead. How gentle he was for such a big man. The second kiss was less tentative. The last time she'd felt anyone's tongue on hers, apart from Tom's, was at their wedding reception when Tom's college friend, Robin, had claimed best man's rights. Tom had thrown Robin down the hotel stairs.

She detached herself, floating above this kissing couple, an airborne voyeur. Experiencing the kiss and watching it at the same time made it doubly intoxicating. For the second time that day she felt aroused. Bill's hand came up inside her t-shirt – Tom's t-shirt – his thumb slowly fondling her nipples, first one then the other. They engorged and tingled with the exquisite pain. She pushed against him with all the anger she was feeling for Tom, proud that she was the cause of his erection. Now he was moving his hand inside the waistband of her trousers, moving it from side to side across her belly. A memory of Arthur standing on the tree-stump, waving his Excalibur-stick, came into clear focus. She shoved Bill away and ran out into the yard. They had not exchanged one single word.

The doors to the summerhouse were shut and she stood in the pool of light cast on the grass, peering in. Jenny and Celia were still talking. Mark, Peter and Tom were over at the table, picking at the leftovers. When her breathing had returned to normal and the damp air had cooled her cheeks, she tapped on the glass, as if needing permission to rejoin the real world. Five faces turned towards her and Jenny put her hand on her heart, startled by the noise.

Tom smiled. 'Where *have* you been?'

'I came to look for you. You missed the singing.'

'Not quite. I could hear it.' He lowered his voice. 'I didn't want to scare anyone but I'm sure there was someone skulking around. Just before Celia sang. I went to check but I couldn't see anyone.'

'Where did you go?' Anna held her breath.

'Across the garden and up the field. Did you notice the fantastic moon? It's bright enough to see without a torch. I had a bit of a mooch around. When I got back, you'd disappeared.'

They started to clear up the party things, only then noticing that Bill wasn't there. The men remarked, again, that he'd not been himself all day but admitted that they hadn't pressed him for an explanation.

'I think they're both more concerned about Emily than they want to admit,' said Anna, eager to suggest a reason for the Davises' behaviour. 'I was talking to Sal about it earlier. Cee and I were only saying this evening, you never stop worrying about your children.' She looked to Celia for confirmation.

It was the perfect opening for the Redwoods to tell them about Christopher and share any problems they might be having, but instead they were quick to criticise. 'You fuss too much, Anna. We've made it quite clear to ours that, once they're eighteen, they're on their own.'

It was getting on for midnight by the time they locked up, following each other single file back to the house. When Anna looked across the Davises' house was in darkness.

Although it was late, she ran a bath, only remembering as she climbed in that she'd already had a bath that day. She took the sponge and scrubbed herself all over, as if it were possible to remove every trace of Bill Davis from her skin. Then she cleaned her teeth, scouring her tongue with her toothbrush, and only then did she feel ready for Tom to reclaim her.

The bedroom was in darkness and Tom was already in bed. She slid under the quilt and put her leg across his. He was wearing pyjamas. He started from his sleep and, touching her naked thigh, muttered, 'Too hot?'

She rolled and pressed against him but the early start and the cider had combined to thwart her and he lay at her side, a sack of warm sand. Turning away, she willed sleep to end this horrid day.

Tom's steady breathing slowed and he started a gentle snore. While he escaped into his dreams, the drink and the food and the kiss in the outhouse ganged up to deny her rest. Every time she closed her eyes she was in Bill's arms, his hands touching her. Eventually, instead of resisting she allowed her imagination to run on, hoping that way to exorcise the encounter.

At two o'clock she gave up and went down to the kitchen. She made herself a cup of tea, although she wasn't thirsty. Outside the back door she perched on the wall, hands cupped around the mug. The big old house was in darkness. Moon shadows, blue and soft, reached across the yard towards her. The night air on her sunburnt arms made her shiver. She could smell damp grass and hear a cow, bellowing for a lost calf.

14

Anna heard that Sally had gone to stay with her sister, Carol, in Gloucester. Jenny had spotted her, loading several large suitcases into the back of her car the morning after the party. When she went to find out what was going on, Sally had been vague, saying that Carol was 'a bit down'. Jenny reported all this to Anna and Celia when they met for coffee at 'High Trees'.

'She was taking enough luggage for three months.' Jenny rolled her eyes.

'Has anyone asked Bill what's going on?' Celia said.

They agreed that it might be best if one of the men took him aside and tried to get some information. 'On second thoughts, no. They'll go all round the houses and end up talking cars or football,' said Jenny. 'I think it has to be one of us. Anna, you've always been the closest to them.'

Anna shook her head. 'Aren't we jumping to conclusions? Perhaps she has gone to help her sister. Carol's always been a bit unstable. Remember the time she was sure someone was stalking her?'

They reached no conclusion on a strategy for tackling the delicate situation and went away to tell their spouses and to keep an eye open for any clues.

Anna had almost convinced herself that nothing had taken

place that night. Surely heavy petting (such an ugly phrase) with your best friend's husband brought repercussions, and there had been absolutely none. Nothing had changed. She and Tom had made tender, unremarkable love the afternoon after the party and she'd hardly seen Bill. But suddenly Sally had left, which did look horribly like a repercussion.

Tom was finishing a scheme for the refurbishment of a friend's house in Devon. He'd lost a day's work because of the Machynlleth trip and was ensconced in his office, catching up. She busied herself with humdrum chores. Two days of steady rain gave her the perfect excuse to stay in the house, on safe territory. Tom had his favourite meals, regular deliveries of coffee and biscuits at his drawing board and his choice of TV programmes. He'd never once asked why.

Housework, though, made no demands on her mind, leaving it free to wander. While she ironed a shirt she pictured Bill moping around, getting drunk or not bothering to eat properly and she vacillated between sorrow and delight. He and Sally were always having rows which invariably followed the same course. Bill did something which Sally considered childish or unsuitable. She would give him a good dressing down and he would make his apology, usually accompanied by an expensive gift and 'a good screw afterwards' as Sally put it. No matter how severe the rows had seemed, Sally had never walked out before.

Over lunch she passed on the gossip to Tom. 'Don't you think you should go and see if he's OK?'

'No,' said Tom. 'It's nothing to do with us.'

Wasn't it? What if Sally had spotted what was going on? Of course nothing was going on but might it not look as though it were? What if Bill got overwrought and declared amorous feelings for her? He might be assuming that she felt the same way he did and if Sally had gone for good, he would have nothing to lose.

Washing up after lunch, she gazed at the pin-up area alongside the draining board. On it were essential phone numbers, dental appointment cards, raffle tickets and postcards. She had thinned it out recently but already there wasn't a square inch of free space. Arthur had started sending her pictures drawn with his new crayons and these took pride of place. They arrived with scrawled notes from Maddy, full of promises to write a 'proper letter' soon. In the latest picture, Arthur stood with his father and Maddy, bump clearly visible, in front of a little red house with bright yellow curtains and smoke pouring from the single chimney. The pond was electric blue with three giant orange ducks swimming on it. He was trying out all the colours in the box.

She no longer imagined that the baby would be a girl. It had become a miniature Arthur and she had started to short-list appropriate names. Lancelot was the obvious choice but didn't bode well for brotherly harmony. Merlin was a nice idea but would put enormous pressure on the child to perform. She searched through the boxes of books, hunting for her copy of *The Once And Future King*. This had been a mistake. *Watership Down*, *The Hobbit*, *Emile And The Detectives* were all there, waiting to mug her with the blunt instrument of nostalgia. Tom had come up to the spare room only to find her in tears, reading a tattered copy of *Barbar the Elephant*.

The weather report promised an improvement and Anna had a yearning to see the sea. She went up to Tom's office. 'How's it going?'

'Almost finished.'

'I've been thinking. Could we have a bit of a break? Just a couple of nights. Maybe go down to Devon or Dorset. We could call and see Flora and Dad on the way back.' She searched Tom's face for a sign.

'Let's see how I get on this afternoon.'

The rain had eased but the sky was a lifeless grey. If they were heading off for a few days, she should devote some time to the garden. A few warm rainy days had brought everything on. Ranks of salad vegetables – lettuce, beetroot and radishes – marched across the damp soil like a green army. The weeds were flourishing, too, but she loosened them with a hoe, dragging them away from the crops. Within minutes of being torn from the soil, they wilted and started to decay. The nights were frost-free now. The next threat would come from caterpillars and drought. The whole thing was such a gamble. Gardening was for optimists.

When she'd finished she headed back to the house, following the path beside the stone wall. The earrings had been playing on her mind. She'd never intended to leave them there this long and each time she passed the spot she felt uncomfortable. The loose stone, smaller than the rest and projecting slightly, was easy to locate. Checking that no one was watching, she pulled it out and slid her hand into the cavity. The package had gone.

She replaced the stone and hurried to her studio to check if it had been returned to its damp nest, but she knew she wouldn't find it there. Of course, during a heavy rain shower, the box had somehow been washed down, into the body of the wall. She went back and removed the stone again, forcing her hand further into the hole, groping this way and that, until she had skinned her knuckles. Soil and stone dust had, over the years, formed a mortar between the stones. There wasn't room for a pea to fall through, let alone something larger than a match-box.

Through decades of freezing Welsh winters and hot summers the wall had settled, its huge stones tilting and lodging, one against the other. There was no possibility of dismantling the wall without a crowbar or dynamite. If the package had gone, then someone had taken it.

The approaching weekend was Spring Bank Holiday and they decided that it would be wise to book accommodation before they set off. It took several phone calls before she found somewhere, in the small seaside town of Sidmouth. It was a long time since she'd been there and it would be Tom's first visit. Now that they lived in the country, she liked the idea of holidaying in a town. They could forget the car for a couple of days, and enjoy the sensation of tarmac beneath their feet.

When she was a young child, her parents hadn't owned a car. The four of them travelled by bus or, if it was a long journey, train. They took two weeks' holiday a year, usually in Devon or Cornwall. They had once tried Aberystwyth, but the beach was shingle and it had rained every day. Her father would haul the trunk down from the attic and leave it on the landing, ready to receive the freshly laundered clothes. She remembered the thrill of scraping off last year's gummed labels and sticking on the new ones; of placing her bathing costume and her purse, bulging with her ice-cream money, on top of the gaudy beach towels. A lorry came, as if by magic, from the railway station and collected the padlocked trunk a few days before they left home; it would be waiting for them when they arrived. Sometimes they stayed in a guesthouse but she preferred it when they rented a caravan. A caravan was a box of magic tricks. The tabletop flipped and swivelled and – hey presto – it turned into a bed. There were tiny cupboards under the seats and above the gas rings. A plastic door concertina-ed across to delineate the bedroom. It was only when she and Tom took the girls on a caravan holiday that she appreciated what hard work it had been for her mother.

They left a contact address and Celia offered to water the houseplants. As they were leaving, Tom popped across to tell Bill their plans. 'It's funny to think of him there on his own,' he said. 'I'll just fill him in so he doesn't feel like a complete pariah, poor sod.'

She waited, fingers crossed, in case Tom invited him to come with them but he returned alone. 'Did he say anything?'

'Not really. But it's a shambles in the kitchen. By Sally's standards, anyway. He looked a bit rough, too.'

Tom was in good form. Having posted off the drawings the previous afternoon, he was like a child who'd handed in a school project. It was the first time they'd been away, apart from duty visits, since the move. Now that Tom was freelance he tended to accept all the jobs that he was offered and semi-retirement was proving to be harder work than he'd anticipated. 'It'll settle down soon,' he said, 'and I'll be able to pick and choose.'

They decided to get off the motorway and take a cross-country route. The hedgerows were full of wild flowers. Frothy heads of cow parsley bobbed on the verges in the wake of the car. The sun came out and, immediately, it felt as if they were properly on holiday. They stopped for coffee and then, later, for a pub lunch. Tom was usually keen to reach their destination but today he was happy to meander and, without the pressure of a rigid schedule, Anna's map reading was spot-on.

It was mid-afternoon when they checked in. The small hotel was just what they'd hoped for. Their room was on the top floor and they could catch a glimpse of the sea through the dormer window, if they stood on tip-toe.

Anna lay on the bed. 'Three whole days to ourselves,' she

said. 'Why does that seem such a luxury?'

The town was exactly as she remembered it. She'd put a few snaps from the Hill family album in her bag, to ensure that she revisited the right places. Tom indulged her. 'I'm feeling as if I'm joining in your childhood, forty-odd years on,' he said. She liked that idea. Tom would have been a much nicer brother than Steven.

A 'No Vacancies' sign appeared near the front door, as the town became busier with weekend visitors. Room Six, with its crisp cotton sheets and its kettle on the bedside table, was already their home. They tucked in to huge breakfasts which saw them through to generous evening meals. When they were tired of sitting on the beach or walking the footpaths, they returned to make love and cups of hot chocolate. She hardly thought about earrings or babies or her father and only sent one postcard. The card, picturing a boy flying a huge kite on a deserted beach, she sent to Arthur.

They talked a lot or were happy to sit in silence, making friends with each other again, although they'd never actually fallen out.

On the last evening they decided to treat themselves to a special meal in a fish restaurant recommended by the landlady. Anna spent longer than usual getting ready, washing her hair and tying it back with the dark red scarf that Tom had bought her in the craft shop near the harbour. A white linen blouse accentuated her tan. Why was it easier to tan at the seaside than in the garden? 'Sea breezes,' whispered Tom as he dried her, after their shower.

The tiny restaurant was tucked away and easily missed but, by eight o'clock, all the tables were taken. Tom ordered an expensive bottle of white wine and they drank to many more holidays. The food was slow arriving and the wine went to Anna's head. She held his hand across the table. He looked handsome and boyish. They had connected again and it was time to make a clean breast of it and confess the fumble in the outhouse.

'I need to tell you something.'

For a moment she was confused. Those words, which she'd been about to say, had come from Tom's lips.

He repeated it. 'Anna, I have to tell you something.'

She let go of his hand, feeling sick and frightened. 'Who is it?'

'But you don't know what I'm going to say.'

'I do. Who is it?'

'Oh, God…'

'Tell me. Is it Sally?'

'Christ, no.'

'Who?'

'It … Celia. But it didn't mean anything.'

'Celia? Celia?' She was getting louder. 'When?'

'I don't know. Last month. You'd gone to see your father and we were all a bit drunk.'

She imagined Celia, white and naked, lying across Tom's drawing board. 'Did you fuck her?' It sounded ugly and she was pleased.

'Shhhh…' He put his finger up to his lips.

'Don't 'shush' me. Well, did you?'

The diners nearest them stared at their plates, pretending that nothing was happening. Before he could say anything else, she grabbed her jacket from the back of her chair and left the restaurant, knowing that she would have a head start. Even if the last trumpet were sounding, Tom would stay to pay the bill.

She headed towards the sea. The streets were thronged with holidaymakers, meandering and aimless, all getting in her way. She reached the promenade and went down the steps, onto the beach. The tide was out, the sea flat calm, an orange sun skimming the horizon. She ran along the water's edge until the sea started to soak through her expensive shoes, then she changed direction, making her way up the beach where the sand was dry and powdery. She flopped down, leaning against the sea wall, her forehead touching her knees.

She felt sick, but not with jealousy. What hurt her was that she'd missed picking up on whatever had gone on between Tom and Celia. Had Celia confided in Mark? Did the others know? Were they all laughing at her? She removed her shoes, scraping the sand off with a lolly stick but the salt had already formed a wavy white tide mark around them, spoiling them. 'Shit.'

Tom always stuck up for Celia but that was from pity, wasn't it? Everyone felt sorry for Celia. Poor Celia. She picked up handfuls of sand, trickling the silvery grains through her curled fingers. Couples walked along the beach, hand in hand, as they had done the previous evening. A group of lads pushed and jostled each other while their girlfriends, arms linked, walked a safe distance behind. No one took any notice of her – a middle-aged woman watching the sun set over the sea.

The light faded as the sun dipped below the horizon and she shivered. Her cotton jacket had little warmth to it. A night here, on the beach, was not appealing. Perhaps she could sit in the car. There was a rug on the back seat and she would have the radio for company. But if she didn't go back, Tom would be frantic and call the police.

The effect of the wine had worn off and her stomach rumbled. Her last proper meal had been breakfast. When she stood up her legs were stiff, one foot numb with pins and needles, and she stumbled up the steps, missing some of them in the darkness. The coloured lights strung along the length of the promenade enabled her to see her watch. It was ten o'clock. An old man passed, eating fish and chips, and wished her a cheery 'goodnight'. The smell of the vinegar made her mouth water.

She found a fish and chip shop and stood in the queue. The crowd was full of fun and banter, just as they should be on a Bank Holiday at the seaside. She wondered whether the man behind the vat of boiling fat, in his striped apron and white trilby, was cheating on his wife.

It was her turn. 'Cod and chips, please.'

'Cheer up, m'dear. It may never happen,' he said.

She wanted to tell him that something had happened. Not that Tom had been with Celia but that she had enjoyed those minutes with Bill, in the darkness.

The meal came on a polystyrene tray with a flat wooden fork. She found it awkward to cope with the fish as she walked so she sat on the wall of the little park where the town's coat of arms was depicted in alyssum and lobelia. She cleared the tray down to the last morsel of crunchy batter. Food was a great morale booster.

There was no one in the hotel lobby and the key to their room was not on the hook behind the desk. She'd half expected the place to be teeming with police and was disappointed that Tom hadn't been concerned enough to report her missing.

She paused at their door, knocked and went in.

He was sitting in the armchair, drinking tea, watching the news on the television. He glanced up. 'That was rather melodramatic, wasn't it?'

She went into the bathroom and locked herself in. Her fingers were greasy and she washed them, then she sat on the lavatory, breathing deeply, determined not to cry.

'Anna?' he shouted through the door. 'I'm going out for half an hour. I've left something on the bed for you to read.'

The door banged and she waited for several minutes, in

case it was a childish trick to lure her out. When she was sure that he'd gone, she emerged. A sheet of paper set out like a report, with a bullet-pointed list, was lying on the bedspread.

When you went to see your father, in April, Jenny invited us (Celia, Mark and me) for supper. We had rather a lot to drink. After the meal Mark stayed behind to talk to Peter about something – finances, I think. I walked Celia back to their house.
- *We were drunk*
- *She was upset about something (?Judith) and started to cry*
- *She looked pathetic*
- *I tried to comfort her with a hug*
- *Somehow it turned into a kiss*
- *We haven't spoken about it since*

It meant nothing to me but I do not ever want to keep anything from you.
I love you. You know that.

This was the truth. She'd known that he couldn't have slept with Celia. To begin with, Celia was sexless. Mark was, too, so they made an excellent pair, like two pre-pubescent children in their innocence. If he'd kissed Sally or Jenny, it would have been a very different matter.

She was impressed with the succinctness of his explanation. His thoughts were well organised. There were no crossings-out or added phrases. It came as no surprise, therefore, when she saw his first few attempts lying in the bin, screwed into tight balls.

Her stomach had stopped churning, stabilised by fish and chips. She made herself a cup of tea. One misplaced kiss, in over twenty-five years, wasn't bad, especially set against what had gone on with Bill. She could afford to forgive him this tiny indiscretion. It wasn't pleasant to think of his lips on Celia's but it had been done as an act of charity, not lust.

It was Tom's turn to knock.

'Come in.'

He stood inside the door, his face was expressionless. 'I'm sorry.'

She held out her arms and he came to her as the children had done, when they needed forgiveness. 'It's OK,' she said and hugged him.

They didn't make love but lay in each other's arms, like babes in the wood. His breathing slowed until she knew that he was asleep but she couldn't let go of consciousness. She envied him his quiet mind. There had been the possibility in the restaurant that she might have spoken first. Or, once having heard his confession, matched it with her own. When Tess had disclosed her dreadful secret to Angel Clare, the tragic heroine had assumed that love would overcome everything. Look how that turned out.

15

They needed to make an early start if they were to be in Bristol in time for breakfast with Flora. When Tom woke Anna she pleaded for ten more minutes between the crisp sheets. He was very attentive, organising the packing and paying the bill, while she showered and drank two cups of black coffee. Nothing was said about the previous night but, now and again, he touched her or stroked her cheek.

When they were ready to go and she climbed into the car, she found a small package on the dashboard.

'It's for you,' he said, turning the key in the ignition.

She held the package, staring at it.

'Go on. Open it.' He looked pleased with himself.

The tissue paper concealed a velvet box. *Another* velvet box. She eased the lid off, apprehensive of what she might find. Coiled inside, like a tiny snake, was a necklace - the perfect match for the missing earrings.

'Don't you like it?'

'Where did you get it from?' She played for time.

'That little shop in Ludlow. Where we bought the blue jug.'

She took it from the box and, with the light shining through the beads, they glowed, blue and turquoise.

'I bought the earrings first, then went back for those.' He looked at her, taking his eyes off the straight road.

Tom had bought the earrings. Of course he had.

'Anna?'

'What?'

'You did find them, didn't you? The earrings?'

Trapped in the moving car, there was no escape and no way of side stepping his question. There were several answers she might give but no time to reflect on the repercussions associated with each. Three responses came to mind:

A. No, I did not find any earrings

B. They're lovely but I've mislaid them.

C. They're lovely. I'm keeping them for special occasions.

She chose B. 'Yes. In with my clay. They're beautiful.'

'I was a bit surprised that you didn't mention them.'

'I know. I've been feeling dreadful about it.' That was true, anyway. 'You see … When I found them, I put them in my pocket. But I had to pop back to the garden. I'd left something. My cardigan. Then I got side-tracked and …did a bit of weeding. By the time I got back to the house and remembered them, they'd disappeared. They must have slipped out of my pocket when I bent over.' It wasn't totally inaccurate.

'Why didn't you tell me?'

'I didn't want to upset you. And I was sure they'd turn up. We can have a proper look as soon as we get back.' She fastened the beads around her neck. 'At least these are safe. Thank you, love.' She lent across and kissed his morning-smooth cheek.

They made good time and were pulling up at Flora's door half-an-hour ahead of schedule. They rang the bell and waited.

Tom jiggled the loose change in his trouser pocket. 'Bet she's forgotten we're coming.'

There was the sound of footsteps coming down the hall and Flora opened the door. 'Mum. Dad. You're bright and early. I thought you said about ten-thirty.' They exchanged hugs. 'Nice necklace, Mum.' The sound of running water came from somewhere in the flat. Flora, face flushed, was quick to explain, 'Luke's here. Come on in.'

'Luke. That's nice,' Anna said.

'He wanted to be sure to see you. So he came round really early. Didn't you?' Flora addressed the last sentence to Luke, who emerged from the bathroom, wearing jeans and an old sweatshirt. His feet were bare and he smelled of toothpaste.

'Hi, Auntie Anna. Uncle Tom.' He'd dropped the titles years ago but this morning, for some reason, he reverted to childhood nomenclature.

Tom shook hands with the lanky young man whom they'd known since he was four, and Anna kissed him. Flora, also barefoot, led them through to the kitchen. Remnants of last-night's meal, including an empty champagne bottle, stood on the work-top.

They breakfasted on coffee and croissants which Luke fetched from the bakery a few doors away. They chatted about Sidmouth and then the conversation turned to Pen Craig.

'How's life in the commune?' asked Luke.

'Fine,' said Anna. They'd given up explaining that there was nothing communal about it.

'We're a bit worried about your Dad, though,' said Tom. She kicked him under the table.

'In what way "worried"?' Luke asked.

She glared at Tom. It left her no alternative but to tell them that Sally wasn't at Pen Craig at the moment. 'It's just a tiff that got out of hand. I'm sure they'll work it out.'

'Mmmm. Mum's never actually walked out before. D'you think I should come up?'

'Couldn't you phone Carol and at least check she's OK?' said Flora.

Luke said he would think about it. 'I don't want to involve more people than necessary. It's between the two of them and at least Dad's got plenty of people to keep an eye out for him.'

'And what about you two?' asked Anna, brightly. 'Any news?'

Flora was thinking of redecorating the flat and buying some new furniture. They discussed the pros and cons of stripped floorboards and free-standing wardrobes. 'Oh, and I called to see Grandpa last week. To tell the truth, I was hoping to meet the mysterious Dorothy. But there was no sign of him, so I just pushed a note through the door.'

Attention turned to Luke and his plans for the future. 'I might try and get a place at law school, if I can rustle up the money to fund it.'

'Your mother will be pleased,' said Anna.

'That's probably why I haven't done it already.'

Anna went to the lavatory, taking the opportunity to snoop around the bathroom. There were several toothbrushes in the mug and a pack of disposable razors on the shelf. Inconclusive evidence. Convincing herself that she needed an aspirin, she opened the medicine cabinet. A bottle of aftershave sat at the back of the shelf, behind the shampoo and cough mixture. Up until last Christmas, Flora had been seeing a young man called Angus. Angus had a beard.

After another coffee and some advice from Tom on dealing with a damp patch under the sink, they left.

'Luke's a nice lad,' said Tom, as they pulled away.

'He'd obviously been there all night,' said Anna.

'How do you mean?'

'I think we almost caught them out.'

'Really?'

It was mid-day and the roads had become congested with Bank Holiday traffic. Tom concentrated on driving whilst she pondered.

She started with the earrings. If they recruited everyone to help with the search, it was possible that they might turn up, regardless of the circumstances of their disappearance. She wasn't sure how Tom would take it if they didn't. But he was still making amends for his own fall from grace, so he couldn't afford to be too cross with her for losing them.

On to Flora with her pink cheeks and champagne bottle. If she and Luke had embarked on a liaison, it was odd that they should keep it secret. She and Sally had often talked about the possibility of romance between their older children but had reached the conclusion that the youngsters might consider it tantamount to incest. But there was no doubt about it, Flora's cheeks and the time it had taken to answer the door were pretty conclusive evidence.

'Luke certainly had no idea that Sally had gone,' said Tom.

'She may be there when we get back,' said Anna, without conviction.

Anna had warned her father to expect them for lunch. She'd suggested that they go out to eat but he wasn't keen and offered to provide beans on toast, with ice-cream to follow.

When they reached the house, Steven's car was parked in the drive.

'Steven and Elaine are here,' her father announced when he opened the door. 'We're in the garden.' Her mother had been the demonstrative one and now visitors received little by way of a welcome. Tom might be the same, if he were left to deal with the world on his own.

They followed Frank through the house and out of the

back door. Strange, but today the familiar smell was absent, maybe because all the windows were open. Everything looked spick and span. The tea towels were folded neatly on the rail by the cooker and there was a vase of flowers on the sill.

Steven and Elaine were outside, perched on the upright chairs from the kitchen, and there were four empty chairs. All it needed was a table piled with old magazines and it could have been a doctor's waiting room. What had her father done with the nice set of garden furniture they'd bought him last summer? So many of their gifts disappeared without trace.

'This is a nice surprise,' Anna bent to kiss her brother and then his wife. Elaine's hair was stiff and scratchy as it grazed her forehead. Her sister-in-law was a redhead but, at this proximity, she could detect a tell-tale white root at the base of each hair.

Steven was good-looking in a filmstar-ish way. When they were youngsters, she'd been convinced that they'd been allocated the wrong genders. Whilst Steven had long eyelashes and beautiful teeth, she battled against unruly hair and large feet. His baby-face and mild manners made him appealing and all her teenage friends had mooned around after him. In fact, many of them were friendly with her because they fancied her brother.

During his student days Steven had brought home a string of interesting girlfriends with exotic names – Vivienne, Francesca, Charlotte. The most fascinating to her had been a Danish girl called Dagmar. Dagmar had hairy armpits and smoked but, more exciting than that, she didn't wear a bra. When she wore t-shirts, her erect nipples stood out for all to see. Anna wasn't sure what her mother and father had made of this, but after a few months Dagmar returned to Copenhagen and was replaced by a Scottish girl called Fiona, who was flat-chested.

After such a promising start, her brother's eventual choice of a wife had been a great disappointment. Elaine worked at the bank and had set her cap at Steven when he opened an account there, depositing his first month's salary. She was glamorous but conventional; maybe what Steven needed, to promote his career, was a presentable wife who could make small-talk and shaved her armpits. While all this was going on, Anna slipped away to art college and cultivated her very own underarm hair.

They sat on the dining chairs while Frank went to make coffee. He looked edgy but refused Anna's offer of help. She was glad because it gave her an opportunity for a few minutes alone with Steven, and they wandered around the garden, pretending to inspect the borders. 'What's going on?' she asked.

'I don't know. He phoned yesterday. Invited us to lunch. I persuaded Elaine to come, on condition we only stayed a couple of hours.'

'Something's up. Haven't you noticed how tidy the kitchen is?'

'We'll find out soon enough.'

They rejoined Tom and Elaine, who were sitting in silence. Elaine looked at her watch and gave a theatrical sigh, tapping the toe of her gold and bronze sandal on the crazy paving.

'I'll give Dad a hand,' Anna said, eager to escape.

In the kitchen her father was opening a second tin of baked beans. She imagined him, day after day, there on his own, turning out his modest meals and she rubbed her hand on his back, hoping that he felt the love in her touch.

'We'll have it in here,' he said.

'Fine. I'll tell them to bring their chairs in.'

The kitchen was filled with people and the smell of burning toast. As they were putting the food on the plates, Frank went into the hall and shouted up the stairs. 'Dorothy.

139

Lunch is ready.'

Anna glanced at Steven. He shrugged and shook his head. Tom took an extra set of cutlery from the drawer. Elaine stifled a giggle. Frank came back into the kitchen and, chin raised, glared at them. They heard the slow thud, thud, thud of someone struggling down the stairs. 'What's the matter?' he asked.

They resumed their tasks, adding theatrical embellishments to cover the confusion. Tom whistled. Anna and Steven chatted, noisily, about a family friend. When Dorothy made her entrance they were casual with their greetings, as though she were someone they saw every day of the week.

There was something different about her. She was thinner than Anna had remembered, more frail. Her white hair was pinned back in a bun at the nape of her neck. On this occasion, too, she wore a white shirt and a long cotton skirt, giving her the air of a retired headmistress or perhaps a writer. Frank went to Dorothy's side and put his arm around her, drawing her into the family circle. He was tender with her. Dorothy leaned a cheek against his hand, curled around her shoulder. The gold signet ring on his third finger, as much part of Anna's childhood as the ornaments on the mantelpiece, had been replaced by a wide gold band. A wedding ring, shiny and unscratched. Her eyes darted to Dorothy's left hand but it was hidden in the folds of her skirt.

Her brother was concentrating on a pan of scrambled eggs and, with all of them crowded into the small kitchen, it was impossible to get near him. Her seat was next to Elaine's but Elaine was the last person she would choose to confide in. Tom, spotting her agitation, mouthed 'You OK?' But she should tell Steven, before anyone else, about the ring.

The crush and disorganisation around the table distracted attention from the stranger in their midst. Whilst they ate, Anna took a closer look at Dorothy. It was six weeks since their only meeting and, in the intervening time, she'd often thought about the old lady. She had a good visual memory but was surprised to realise how inaccurately she had fixed Dorothy in her mind. Her face was thinner than she'd remembered and this was not at all the self-confident woman whom she had watched plodding up to the front door.

'That's a very colourful necklace, Anna.' Elaine's voice broke in. 'Just your sort of thing.' She was accustomed to condescension from her sister-in-law. Elaine always managed to make her feel like an inadequate child, needing approval. When she was younger, exhausted with children and work, this tactic had succeeded but now she felt sorry for her sister-in-law, glamour fading and no children to love and worry about. Elaine had always been the centre of her own limited world and self-obsession had become her defining characteristic.

'Yes, it's lovely isn't it? Tom gave it to me this morning.'

Tom, who had been peering at his food, looked up when he heard his name. 'We're going to try and find the matching earrings, aren't we, love?'

The scrambled eggs were overcooked and the toast burnt. For pudding, and despite her father's protestations, Anna opened both tins of fruit salad, serving them with a generous scoop of vanilla ice cream. Throughout, she kept an eye Dorothy's left hand. There were several rings on her third finger, not unusual in a woman who had lived so long.

After they'd finished, they washed up. Anna had given up trying to communicate her suspicions to her brother for the time being and, as she dried the plates, watched Tom through the window, taking rubbish to the dustbin. He turned, conscious of her scrutiny, and mouthed a kiss.

They made coffee and took it into the sitting room. During the manoeuvres, she found herself alone in the kitchen with Steven. 'They're married,' she whispered.

'Who?'

'Dad and Dorothy. He's wearing a new ring.'

'That doesn't mean…'

'I think it does.'

Frank settled Dorothy in his armchair and drew up a dining chair alongside her. He sat, straight-backed, cup balanced on hand, bony knees sharp through his pale cotton trousers. He looked tense. As soon as they were all there, he cleared his throat and tapped his spoon against his cup. Elaine sighed and fluttered her eyes at the ceiling.

'It's not often that I have the pleasure of seeing you all together, so this is probably as good a time as any to make my announcement. Dorothy and I are man and wife.'

As soon as he tapped the cup, Anna had fixed her eyes on Dorothy's face. She spotted the tiniest of smiles, lifting the corners of her new stepmother's mouth. It was a smile not of triumph, but of tender indulgence.

'Congratulations.' Tom was first to break the silence, then the others joined in with their best wishes. Anna, overcome with an emotion she couldn't identify, went across to hug her father and kiss his bride.

'You're a sly one,' said Elaine.

'When did this happen?' demanded Steven.

'Two weeks ago. We know you're all busy people, with far more interesting things to do, so we decided not to bother you with it.' Was there a hint of victory in Frank's voice?

'It all seems a bit…' Steven looked unhappy.

Anna intervened. 'Well I think it's very romantic. I suppose it's a bit like eloping without the bother of going anywhere.'

'We did go away, actually.' Dorothy's voice was quiet but assured. 'We went to Torquay. I expect your father mentioned that we were going away for a few days.'

In fact he hadn't, but neither Anna nor Steven had

attempted to get in touch with him during that time, and his absence went unnoticed.

'Any more questions?' asked Frank, lifting his chin defiantly. 'No? I think we should call it a day then, don't you?'

Steven followed Anna into the kitchen with the dirty cups. 'He's doing it to spite us.'

'Done it. He's done it.'

Steven ignored her. 'Poor Mum must be…'

'Please, Steve. I don't really want to think about Mum. It doesn't help.'

'And I can't make her out at all. What's the attraction?'

Elaine leaned around the door and tapped the face of her watch, then disappeared, without saying a word. Steve grimaced and dried his hands. 'I'll ring you in a few days. You really should get email sorted out.'

'Tom's not keen.'

'Tom's a Luddite.'

'Tom *loves* machinery. He's not enamoured with IT, if that's what you mean.'

They gathered in the drive, all except Dorothy who had remained in the sitting room. Elaine got into the car and shut the door. Anna hugged her father. For a moment, when he looked at her, his face softened and she wished that they were alone and able to talk.

'Perhaps you and Dorothy can come to Pen Craig soon,' she said.

'Perhaps.'

As they drove away she could see them both, waving from the window.

16

Sally had been back at Pen Craig for a few days. Anna, pinning up the latest drawing from Arthur, spotted her heading towards her car. She grabbed a stack of newspapers and hurried outside.

'Hi, stranger.' She dumped the paper in the recycling bin.

Sally looked tired and unusually scruffy. 'I'm just popping down to the village. We've run out of everything but I can't be bothered to go to Tesco. How are you? And your lot?'

'I'm fine. My father managed to get married without anyone noticing.'

'Good for him. But you knew it was on the cards.'

'Yes, but I suppose I imagined I'd be involved, in some way. And the other thing is, I think your son and my daughter may be seeing each other. Dreadful expression.' She explained the reasons for her suspicions. 'Have you spoken to Luke recently?'

'No. It's been … difficult.' Sally paused. 'I assume you're talking about Flora.'

Anna laughed. 'Don't worry, Maddy's still safely attached to Taliesin.' She waited for a second before asking, 'Time for a coffee? Tom's gone to see a client.'

Bill was out too, at the dentist, and they decided to walk down to the village and have a drink at The Lion. All the way to the pub, they talked about Frank Hill or Flora and Luke.

Anna took the lead and, uncharacteristically, Sally seemed happy to listen.

They bought drinks and found a table in the beer garden.

'It's silly coming down here, when we have all that open space at home,' Anna said.

'It's good to be silly now and again, don't you think? At least there's a bit of life here, if you can call it that.' Sally indicated the other customers, mostly farmers on their way home for a mid-day meal. She lit a cigarette, shutting her eyes and dragging the smoke into her lungs. 'Don't look at me like that. It's not illegal.'

'It's such a shame, when you went through all the agony of giving up.'

'I've given up so many times, I'm quite good at it.'

'Well, you're old enough to know what you're doing. How's Carol?'

'Fine, as far as I know. I haven't actually seen her since Christmas.'

'I did wonder. Look if you don't want to talk…'

'God, I've done nothing *but* talk since I've been back but I'm obviously speaking a foreign language. Bill sits there, refusing to understand. I - am - leaving - you. I - have - had - enough. What's difficult about that? I've tried to let him down gently but he just tells me how nice it is to have me home, and how we're going to make a fresh start. How can I make him understand that it's over?'

This didn't come as a surprise but it was distressing to hear it, nevertheless. Anna watched the bubbles rise through the lemonade, her warm fingers damp with the condensation that had formed on the outside of the glass. 'You two always seemed so well-suited.'

'Put on a great performance, didn't we? When I think back, we lost the plot years ago. It was pretty bad before we moved. Stupid to imagine that coming here was going to solve anything. Being stuck in that god-forsaken house, in the middle of nowhere, has just about finished me off. Now the kids have gone, there's no reason to stay together. Bill may be prepared to wind down to a dead stop but I'm not. He's turning into a caricature of himself, and it's getting to the stage where I can't bear to be with him. He irritates the hell out of me.'

'Where did you go? He was in a dreadful state.'

Sally took a drag of her cigarette, expelling the smoke slowly before replying, 'His name's Tim.'

Anna watched an empty crisp packet drift across the stone slabs and lodge in a lavender bush. Had she misunderstood what Sally was saying?

'Don't look at me like that, Anna. I feel crappy enough as it is.'

This was her friend, maybe her *best* friend, and she must not be judgmental. 'Is it serious with … Tim?' It sounded like dialogue from a bad play.

'D'you mean, am I sleeping with him? Yes, I am. And it's fantastic. Bill and I haven't made love since Christmas. It's wonderful to feel that someone fancies me. But no, it's not serious. It's what I need, at the moment, to help me make the break. I'm scared I'll weaken and give in.'

'Maybe you just need to make your point.' From Sally's face she could see she was making a bad job of this. 'Sorry. You must have been over and over it but it's new to me. I don't know what I'm supposed to say. Or do. Or think.'

'I know you want to help, Anna. And you've always been a wonderful listener. But the trouble is, you love happy endings. You want everyone to be friends and live happily ever after. Good luck to you, if you can make your life work like that. I can't. It's reducing me to a zombie.' She lit another cigarette.

Was this how she came across, a lover of happy endings?

Perhaps Sally would be interested to hear about the episode in the outhouse. How her 'caricature of a husband' had been lusting after her best friend. What's more, Bill had obviously been aroused that night. She could vouch for that.

'What about counselling? Relate, or whatever?'

'Anna, I want to leave. I have absolutely no interest in resurrecting our marriage. Everyone will think I'm a bitch but I don't care. I'll miss you and Tom, of course, and perhaps, one day, we'll be able to be in touch again. If Bill stays living here, he'll need all of you. I'm perfectly happy to be cast as the Wicked Witch of the West, if it makes it easier to have someone to blame.'

'What if Flora and Luke get together?'

'Let's worry about that when it happens, shall we? Come on, I've got to pick up my bits of shopping.'

They left the pub and walked along the main street. The heat had driven everyone inside and Cwm Bont had become the deserted village.

Inside the shop, a neat woman wearing a pale blue tabard was tidying the shelves and manning the till. Anna needed stamps and, while Sally loaded her wire basket, she went to the post office section, beyond the groceries and stationery. She was glad to see that it was Mrs Prosser, not her husband, waiting to serve her.

'A book of first class stamps please, Mrs Prosser.' She pushed the money under the glass screen. And that's where she found her earrings. They were dangling from Mrs Prosser's ear lobes. She stared at the blue-green beads.

'Anything else?'

'What?'

'Can I get you anything else, Mrs Wren?'

'No. No thanks.' She had to say something about them. 'Lovely earrings, Mrs Prosser. I've got a necklace just like them.' She tried to sound off-hand. When it brought no response, she ploughed on. 'Did you get them locally?'

'My husband gave them to me. I'm not sure, myself. They're a bit fancy for me but a change is as good as a rest, or so they say.'

They walked back to the house, Sally talking more about her reasons for leaving. Anna tried to make a useful contribution to the conversation but she was distracted.

So *Prosser* had removed the box from the wall. He must have watched her put it there because there was no chance he might have come across it by accident. If he saw her put the box there, he must have been spying on her. And if he'd taken to spying on her, what else might he have seen? It had been dark that night in the outhouse but it didn't require a genius to work out what she and Bill had been up to.

Sally was still talking as they toiled up the drive. 'I don't know what to do about Emily. I don't even have a contact address. She phoned a week ago and we've had a few emails. But, once I leave here, I don't know how I'll stay in touch.'

'Does she have any idea that you and Bill are splitting up?'

'No. It didn't seem right for her to find out by telephone, when she's on the other side of the world.'

'She's got to know sooner or later.'

'I know. I know.' Sally massaged her temples with her fingers. 'The trouble is, Bill's in denial. If she phones and asks to speak to me, he'll tell her I'm at the hairdressers or something.'

'You can't be at the hairdresser's for weeks on end. She's bound to work it out eventually.'

They decided that it would be a good idea for Sally and Bill to compose an email to their children, setting out the essential facts and reassuring them that they were both fine. 'Now all I've got to do is get Bill to face up to these "essential facts".'

'Can I tell Tom?' Anna asked, as they reached the house. 'Or should I wait until Luke and Emily know?'

'Of course you can tell him. It might even persuade Bill to take his head out of the sand, knowing that Tom knows.'

Bill's car was there and Sally kissed her before going inside. 'I'll see you before I leave.'

Anna was losing heart in her project. If Sally went, she could hardly present everyone with mugs and bowls with 'Paradise' emblazoned across them. She looked at the eight mugs sitting on the shelf above her wheel. Sally's was squat and round. Almost hemispherical and decorated with circles in burnt orange, raspberry pink and cream, echoes of her friend's freckled skin and red hair. She pushed it right to the back, where it could hardly be seen.

In the cool of the kitchen, a sadness settled on her. She wished that Tom would come home and she wished she could ignore the earring fiasco. After all, it was insignificant stuff compared with the breakdown of a marriage. What on earth had made her think that Bill had left them for her, anyway? If Tom had come across a packet hidden amongst his tools, would he assume it was from Celia?

She wandered around, gathering a load for the washing machine. While it clicked and whirred in the utility room she took out her sewing. The baby was due in a couple of months and she'd started to make a small patchwork quilt, to fit a cot.

She liked the idea of sewing much more than the reality. Once she had rounded up the scraps of cotton, cut the hexagons and decided on the layout, she was impatient to see it finished. Her stitching, so neat at the outset, became larger and less accurate. 'It's the effect I'm after,' she'd explained to Tom, when he expressed his surprise at the ambitious undertaking. 'After all, the baby will only dribble on it and chew it.' Her secret hope was that it would turn out to be the child's comforter, taking its place in family legend alongside Flora's square of red fur fabric.

She was pegging out the washing when Tom came back. She wanted to kiss him when he climbed out of the car but such a public display of affection might be upsetting to Bill or Sally, if they happened to be looking out of the window. Catching his hot hand, she led him into the house and poured him a drink of barley water. Once she'd checked that the meeting had gone well and that the client had liked what Tom had showed him, she told him about Sally's confession.

'Hasn't Bill said anything? Dropped any hints?' she asked.

'No. Nothing at all, but he'd probably be more likely to discuss it with you.'

'Why d'you say that?'

'You two get on so well and old Bill's a bit of a ladies' man.'

They shared their regrets and speculated on whether Bill would want to stay on at Pen Craig alone. 'He shouldn't make any snap decisions. Sally may change her mind once she's had time to mull it over,' said Tom.

'You didn't hear what she said to me.'

'Well, either way, there's nothing we can do, so we might as well go and have another look for the box. Come on.'

In the few days since their return from Sidmouth, Tom and Anna had spent hours hunting for the earrings. Tom made her re-enact exactly what she had done on the afternoon when she had dropped the box. He made her put on the same clothes and place the empty necklace box in her pocket, to replicate the conditions. She had stomped about, leaning and bending, trying to make the thing fall out and prove that it could have happened. Somehow, she'd been drawn into this and had almost come to believe that this was, indeed, how the earrings had been lost. But it was hard to continue the charade now that she knew exactly where they were.

They went up to the vegetable garden and Tom continued his search. She watched him, full of remorse that he was wasting his time in the scorching sun looking for something which wasn't lost.

'Any chance you dropped it in the compost bin?' he shouted.

They gave up after an hour and started back towards the house, Tom kicking at the grass and peering under bushes.

'Lost something, Mr Wren?' It was Prosser. She wasn't sure where he'd sprung from but he must have been watching them for a while.

'Afternoon,' said Tom. 'Yes. My wife's dropped a little box. Black. Much like this one but smaller.' He held out the second box, to show Prosser.

'Did it contain anything of value?' There was an insolence in his wheedling tone.

'Earrings. They weren't terribly expensive but they were a present.'

'We'd better find them then, hadn't we?' said Prosser. He bent down, peering in the grass at the foot of the wall, exactly where she'd hidden them ten days earlier.

17

'**W**ell I think she'll come back,' said Jenny, 'once she gets whatever it is out of her system. She's got too much to lose.'

Anna knew that she was referring to money and status and shook her head. 'I'm not so sure.'

When she'd watched Sally drive off early that morning, her car crammed with cases and bags, Bill was nowhere to be seen and Sally had asked her to break the news to the others and spare him the embarrassment. They'd agreed that it would be best to be vague about the reasons for her departure, and certainly not mention Tim. Anna had plumped for 'I think the relationship ran out of steam,' when she, Jenny and Celia met for coffee.

'Poor Bill,' Celia shook her head, her pale eyes welling with tears.

'How are things with you, Celia?' The risk of a protracted discussion of Celia's problems was preferable to further conjecture about the Davises' separation.

'Much the same. The doctor's put me on tablets and I think they're helping me to cope.'

Jenny, sitting out of Celia's line of vision, mouthed 'Prozac.'

'And what about the headaches and insomnia?'

'No change. They don't seem to have a clue what it is.'

Celia smiled suddenly. 'Actually Judith's coming home today. Mark's found her a little car. It'll make life a lot easier for her.'

Tom appeared, needing help to net the ripening strawberries before the birds developed a taste for them, and the party broke up.

'Bill's ears must have been red hot this morning, poor sod,' he said as they stretched the netting over the strawberry patch.

'D'you think there's anything we can do? We can't carry on as if nothing's happened, although I have a feeling that's what he'd prefer.'

'She's being very selfish.'

'How?'

'Spoiling it for everyone. I can see us all selling up.'

'That would be ridiculous,' she said. 'Bill might go but…'

'It would put a blight on the whole venture. There might be some excuse if she were going because of a job or something.'

They pegged the netting down and Anna returned to the house, leaving Tom to consider the problem of the two fields of knee-high grass. On the way past she gathered the washing from the line, dropping the bone-dry clothes into the wicker washing basket. It had been ridiculously expensive. A plastic one would have done the job just as well but it delighted her whenever she used it. Its rich colour and the twist of its handles. How it creaked when she lifted it, full of clean washing.

It was only as she unpegged the last garment that she realised something was missing. There should have been two bras and four pairs of knickers hanging on the line with the rest of the things and they were no longer there. She checked the drum of the washing machine, knowing that she wouldn't find them. Nor were they in the laundry basket, on the ground beneath the clothes-line or in the pile of clothes on the bedroom chair. Her skin goose-pimpled at the thought of a stranger coveting her M&S bras and pants. Her fear turned to shame when she remembered the state the garments were in. They were old and discoloured, having more than once found their way in with the coloureds. Finally she felt sick. Knicker thieves were not nice people.

When Tom returned they ate lunch and she listened to his plan to invite the neighbouring farmer to make the hay from the fields. 'He could take half and we could keep the rest as animal fodder.'

There were no animals at Pen Craig but she let it go. 'Someone's stolen my underwear,' she blurted out and told him what she thought was missing.

'We'd better ring the police.' Tom's face was stern.

'That's a bit drastic.'

'There may have been other thefts. It might help them spot a pattern.'

She said she would check with Jenny and Celia, to see if they had lost anything, before involving the police.

They took their library books and sat outside the summerhouse in the afternoon sun. Within minutes Tom was asleep. She watched him like a mother watches a new baby. How precarious it all was. How unlikely that two people could put up with each other for the whole of their adult lives. What was it that kept them together, after the lust and the thrill of the chase had waned? They'd been married for only a year when Flora was born, distracting their attention from each other to the awesome responsibility of child rearing. Then Madeleine had arrived and they had to more than double their efforts. Tom had suffered a few setbacks with his job. There had been bereavements – first his father, then her mother.

Throughout, they had taken the other's love and loyalty for granted. In the Davises' case this bonding agent, whatever it was, had dissolved and they had become disconnected, one stuck in a rut and the other spinning off into the unknown.

She leaned across and touched the back of his hand. Without really waking, he took hers and squeezed it. His hand was hot but perfectly dry. One of the first things that she'd noticed about him was that he never had sweaty hands.

Peter and Jenny joined them inside the summerhouse, where they had retreated from the sun. Peter rarely found the time (or was it the inclination?) to socialise. Jenny was forever boasting about lectures he was giving or papers he had to write. Then there was his endless list of patients. 'Pete's got the perfect job, if he ever fancies philandering,' Sally had bitched. She was a fine one to talk.

'I've just seen Bill,' Peter said. There was currently no other topic of conversation. 'He's in a bit of a daze but I think he's OK. I told him that we're here if he wants to talk.'

'He won't,' said Anna. 'Sally says he's in denial, or whatever the jargon is.'

'I think we should leave him alone. That's what I'd want,' Tom said.

As usual, the Redwoods were dashing off somewhere. They all walked back to the house together and, passing the clothes line, Tom was prompted to ask whether Jenny had lost any underwear.

'I'm not sure I'd notice. Mrs. P. usually sees to the washing. I put it away, of course, but I can't honestly say I keep tabs on every single bra and thong. And Celia finds underwear embarrassing. She always dries hers inside.'

There was a new car parked in the yard and, when they came closer, they could see a pair of legs poking from beneath it. Mark (recognisable by his cavalry twills) was engaged in doing what he most enjoyed – car maintenance. He jumped up, eager to regale them with a blow-by-blow account of his purchase, from the moment he saw it in 'The Advertiser' to the moment he clinched the deal. 'One careful little-old-lady owner. Just the job.'

Anna found car-talk as tedious as golf-talk, and slipped away. Through the kitchen window of Number Two she spotted Celia and Judith and they beckoned her to join them. They were sitting at the table sorting through a pile of photographs, all of which showed Judith at various stages of growing up. Celia gathered them together, shoved them rather furtively into a brown envelope and placed it in the drawer.

As a child, Judith's features had been boyish and too large for her face. Now she was a striking young woman. Handsome, not beautiful, she was dark with a strong nose and full lips. Her hair was thick and jet-black. It had crossed Anna's mind, more than once, that one of her birth parents might be Indian or South American. When her own children were small, people constantly remarked on their resemblance to her and Tom. Celia, with her see-through skin and pale eyes, would never have received such comments.

'Maddy's very excited abut the baby,' said Judith. 'She's told me all about her new home. And the little boy. Arthur, is it?'

It sounded as if Judith were better informed than she was about Maddy's life and plans for the future. She wanted to cross-question her but pride prevented it. 'Yes, Arthur is delightful. He sends me beautiful drawings.' Was that enough to give the impression that she was *au fait* with her daughter's new life?

'Now Dad's found me this car, maybe I can go and visit them. D'you get there often? It can't be far from here.'

Mark saved her from the shameful admission that they

had never visited. He stuck his head round the door, telling them that he and Tom were going to check the grass in the fields. 'We have to make a decision about it. Apparently it's growing.'

'You might ask Bill to go with you,' suggested Celia.

Suddenly Anna longed for her daughters. When the girls first left, this desolation had swept over her several times a day, making her physically ill. As time went by it, happened less frequently but it was just as intense and now, overwhelmed by it, she made her farewells and went home.

She checked the machine but there were no messages. Maddy had given her a phone number, making it clear that it was only to be used in emergencies. This surge of loneliness and loss certainly felt like an emergency and she debated whether she could invent a reason for phoning. She had no idea what the set-up was in the Leighton household. What if Charles Leighton answered? It made her cross to admit that she was intimidated by his celebrity status.

She tried Flora's number but there was no reply. Then she rang Steven. Nothing. When her father didn't answer either, she panicked. It was six-thirty on a Saturday evening. He rarely went out after tea, which he ate at about five o'clock. Of course his routine might have changed since Dorothy Holton – no, she was Dorothy Hill now – took up residence. Where were they all? They must all be out, having a lovely time, while she was on her own. Before she knew it she was sobbing and then, because she'd started crying, she could find no reason to stop.

Arms enclosed her and she turned, clinging to Tom. The smell and the voice were wrong and she pulled away but Bill held her tight, stroking her hair and making soothing noises. 'There, there. Deep breaths.' He leaned his cheek on the top of her head, crushing her face into his shirt. 'My poor Anna. My poor love.'

'Stop it.' She jerked her head back, catching the side of his nose, and he released her, putting his hands up to his face. His nose was bleeding, the blood trickling through his fingers, running down from wrist to elbow, where it soaked into his rolled shirt-sleeve. It kept coming, dripping in dark splats onto the stone floor. He put his head back and staggered towards the sink.

Shaking, she ran upstairs and locked herself in the bathroom. All that crying had exhausted her. Her face was blotchy, her eyelids swollen. The mottled rash which flared up whenever she was agitated was spreading down her neck. She pulled her clothes off and stepped into the shower, scrubbing herself from head to toe. When she had finished she started at the top and did it again, until finally she stood motionless, letting the scalding stream run over her.

She was drying herself when there was a soft knock at the door. It was Tom. 'You OK?'

'Of course. Why?'

'There's something on the floor in the kitchen. It looks like blood. I thought you might have cut yourself.'

'It is. Blood, I mean. From the meat. The beef. For tomorrow.'

'Well, it needs mopping up.'

She listened to his footsteps, retreating down the stairs, and she was alone again.

18

Anna flipped the calendar over. The picture for June was a crop circle near Marlborough. She pencilled in the birthdays for the coming month, without reference to her birthday book. Tom watched her for a while, then accused her of wasting brain capacity. 'What *should* I be using my brain for, then?' she asked.

'Original thought. Logic. Creative things. Not storing stuff that can be written in a book, that's for sure.'

It would be a pity to sulk on such a beautiful morning. 'Anything you want to do today?' She was determined to enthuse about whatever he might suggest.

'If everyone's around, we ought to make a final decision about the grass. We need to call a house-meeting.'

'But what about Bill?'

'He can't hide forever. He's got to come out of there, sooner or later.'

'You could try writing him a note. Tell him you need his opinion. Make him feel important.'

'Good idea.'

Tom hurried off to contact the others and to compose a note to Bill.

She took a cup of tea across to her studio. The shelves in the alcove were full of pieces she'd made for her project but Sally's departure had put paid to all that. There was a chance that she could sell the pottery in one of the local craft shops. 'Paradise' was a satisfying word and it was conceivable that it might apply to someone's life.

She was pounding clay when she heard a voice. 'Hello there. Hello.' She wiped her hands on her smock and went to see who it was. An angel stood in the yard with a rucksack on his back, where his wings should be. He was holding an armful of wild flowers. The tangle of his auburn hair glowed in the sunshine like a fiery halo. His smile revealed the whitest teeth. 'Hi. You must be Anna. There's no mistaking you. I'm Brendan.' He squeezed her hand and she was happy to leave it in his while he explained, 'I'm a friend of Maddy's. I was with the Travellers until just before Christmas. Since then I've been in Ireland. I need to go back there, now and again.'

'You have family there?'

'I have family everywhere.'

They walked towards the house and he told her that on his return to England, he'd discovered that Maddy had moved on. He'd spent the last few days searching for her. 'She talked about you a great deal. It wasn't too difficult to track you down.' He handed her the wild flowers: yarrow, campion, scabious and honeysuckle. She took one of her tall vases and filled it with water. 'Maddy told me you make wonderful pots.' She placed the flowers in water, wondering how this young man knew so much about her, when she'd never heard his name mentioned. They drank tea and she took a closer look at him.

He was a little older than he first appeared. Mid-twenties, perhaps, with the freckled skin of the redhead, wild hair down to his shoulders and silver rings through his ears and one eyebrow. Not a handsome face but soft and open. His grey-green eyes were fringed with dark lashes. Was he wearing a touch of mascara? But it was his voice that did it.

She could never resist the Irish lilt.

He asked about Maddy but something told her to hold back, and she was vague about her daughter's whereabouts. She said nothing about the baby but asked Brendan if he knew Taliesin, adding, 'He was the only one of her traveller friends that we met.'

'I never liked the man myself. Far too gloomy and sensible. I shouldn't think he's Maddy's cup of tea, either. Didn't he have that weird little kid?' He laughed and held out his mug for a refill.

She showed him the garden. He knew a great deal about hedgerow plants and their medicinal properties. He told her how to make a healing poultice from the comfrey that grew in abundance up the lane and pointed out the tiny milkwort lying low in the rough grass. 'In Ireland, the fairies use it as soap,' he said. By the time they found Tom in the vegetable garden, she'd known Brendan all her life.

'But we only have his word for it,' said Tom when Brendan was taking a shower. 'If he's going to stay here tonight, we'd better be sure that nothing's left lying about.'

'I could ring Maddy and check, if you like,' she suggested. 'I'll do it now, before he comes down.' She ignored his sceptical gaze.

While the phone rang and rang, she composed a literate message in case Charles Leighton answered. When she was about to give up, someone lifted the receiver. A child said 'Hello.' It was Arthur. She told him who she was. 'I hoped you'd phone me one day but I expect you want Maddy. I'll get her for you.' Before she could talk to him, he'd gone, his light voice echoing as he shouted. 'Maddy. It's Anna.'

The slap of her daughter's shoes on the floor grew louder and it took an age for her to reach the phone. The Leighton house must be vast. She pictured a Victorian villa, built by an English industrialist for his Welsh mistress.

'Mum? Is everything OK?'

'Yes. We're all fine. Someone's turned up here, looking for you.' She gave the details of Brendan's arrival. 'Was I right to ring?'

'Where is he now?'

'In the shower. What d'you want me to do?' There was silence at the other end. 'Maddy?'

'Hang on, I'm just thinking. Right. I'll phone you in about an hour. Act surprised. Don't tell him you've spoken to me already. And please don't mention that I'm pregnant. You haven't, have you?'

When she returned to the kitchen Tom was sharpening his penknife. He looked up, waiting to hear what his daughter had said, but Anna ignored him.

Brendan had changed his clothes. He was wearing a white collarless shirt and dark green corduroy trousers. His wet hair appeared darker and, where it had already dried, formed tight curls. For some reason, the sight of the pale skin on his bare feet embarrassed her and she glanced away. He looked as if he had walked out of a Hardy novel.

Brendan kept up an easy flow of conversation. His tales were amusing and he told them well but, throughout the meal, she sat stiff with anticipation, her hands gripping her fork, her shoulders hunched. Tom concentrated on his food, answering in monosyllables when a question was addressed to him.

At last, the phone rang and she hurried to answer it, enunciating clearly, as if in an elocution class, 'Hello. Maddy. What a nice surprise. You'll never guess who we've got here. Brendan. Would you like a word?' She raised her voice further. 'Brendan. It's Maddy.'

Brendan took her place and she returned to the kitchen, shutting the door behind her. 'Why did you do that?' asked

Tom.

'What?'

'Shut the door.'

'It seemed polite. I don't know.'

'What could he need to say to her that we shouldn't hear? I think it's asking for trouble. She's just getting her life in some sort of order and now you're pushing this man at her. He doesn't convince me. But, you've made your mind up.'

She carried the plates over to the sink. Tom had a habit of playing Pontius Pilate when things became complicated.

'She'd like a word with you,' said Brendan when he came back into the kitchen.

Maddy told her mother that she was planning to come to Pen Craig the next day, alone. Art would be at school and Taliesin needed to be there to meet him. She might stay a day or two. She'd ring when her bus got in.

Brendan had finished the dishes and Tom was studying a magazine which she knew he'd read, from cover to cover, weeks ago. She told them about Madeleine's visit

'It'll be grand to see her,' said Brendan.

'She shouldn't be bouncing around on a bus.' Tom shook his head.

'What shall we do this afternoon?' she asked. 'Anyone fancy a walk?'

'I've got work to do,' Tom said, heading upstairs.

'Could I be a bit cheeky and ask if I can practise my flute? Only if I won't be a nuisance,' said Brendan.

She took him to the summerhouse and showed him where they kept the key. Once inside, he put his hand on her arm. 'Don't worry about me, Anna. I'm used to it. Animosity. Rejection. Some people are very afraid of the outsider. But others, like yourself and Maddy, are open to new experiences.' He moved his hand along her arm. 'You're tense. Relax.'

She longed to stay but it wasn't an option. 'See you later,' she mumbled and headed towards the garden.

She worked, accompanied by his music. She had assumed he would play jolly jigs and plaintive folk songs but what she was hearing was a concerto, the runs and trills complex and flawlessly executed. No doubt about it, Brendan was an accomplished flautist. The music wafted through the air, drawing her back to the summerhouse. She stood out of sight, behind the bushes, listening.

A car coming up the lane broke the spell. Doors slammed and there were shouts and laughter from the yard. Curiosity overcame her and she found Flora and Luke taking bags from the car. Bill was there, too.

Flora hurried to kiss her. 'Hi, Mum. Surprise, surprise. We're giving Luke's new car a run.' Over Flora's shoulder, she could see Luke and Bill shaking hands. The last time Luke had visited, Sally had been there to fuss her son and have his favourite meal on the table.

'Come on. Let's find Dad and put the kettle on.' Flora craned her ears from side to side. 'Can I hear music?'

'Tell you later,' said Anna, guiding Flora into the kitchen. 'Tom. Come on down. We've got a visitor.'

They were on their second cup of tea when Brendan appeared, carrying his silver flute. Anna made the introductions and invited him to join them. There were very few women who could have resisted the young man's charms and soon Flora was giggling, cheeks pink and eyes flashing.

Tom went back to work and she followed him. 'I don't know what's the matter with all of you. It's painful to watch. I thought Flora, at least, would see through him. He's a con man and you're all falling for it.'

'Don't be silly. A con man's up to something illegal. OK, Brendan's a bit of a charmer but that doesn't make him a criminal.'

Tom took up his pencil and she was dismissed.

This time yesterday, she had been desperate to connect with her children. Now, unbidden, they were gathering around her. Flora and Luke had both taken the following day off work and didn't have to return to Bristol until the next evening. It would be nice for the girls to catch up with each other. They might even manage a few hours together before falling out.

She prepared the spare rooms. One of the biggest wrenches, when they moved, had been leaving the bedrooms where the girls had grown up. Even after they had left home, they remained 'Flora's Room' and 'Madeleine's Room'. She'd prised the ceramic name-plates from the doors, unwilling to leave them for strangers to discard, and they were in one of the many boxes, still waiting to be unpacked.

Bullying and coaxing duvets into clean covers, she remembered that they had another guest. Where would she put Brendan?

She thought back to Flora and Luke's arrival. Did they look like 'a couple'? It was difficult to tell. Bill's gloomy presence had dominated and everyone was trying, too hard, to gloss over Sally's absence. It certainly hadn't been the right moment to announce a liaison.

The house filled with noise. Flora and Brendan were laughing together in the kitchen. Tom was listening to Miles Davis in his office. All these people around and she was on her own once again. In their bedroom she gathered armfuls of dirty clothes. It had been her mother's trick to use a pair of knickers, en route to the washing machine, as a duster. This dual use made perfect sense to her and she began wiping the dust from the sills and the bedside tables with the boxer shorts Tom had worn the previous day. She moved to the chest of drawers and shunted the surface clutter to the one end. The chest was dark mahogany and had belonged to

Tom's grandmother. When she wiped the dust away, it shone like a conker, fresh out of its casing. She pushed the bits and pieces to the other end. Tom's watch, her hairbrush, a bus timetable, some pegs, the beads that Arthur had given her. And the missing black velvet box.

She rattled it, expecting it to be empty but it wasn't and she eased the lid open. They certainly looked like the original earrings. The necklace that Tom had given her was safely stashed in the lower compartment of her wooden jewellery box and she compared them. A perfect match. She inspected the gold wires but they shone, bright and clean. How could she tell whether they had ever been worn – by her or Mrs. Prosser?

There were several ways they could have found their way back to the chest of drawers but it was difficult to juggle the possibilities in her head. She found a piece of paper and jotted down the options:

1. Tom bought a replacement pair – ie. the pair I saw Mrs P. wearing WAS mine.

2. Tom found the original pair somewhere in the garden – ie. The pair Mrs P. wore WAS NOT mine. (But how on earth had they fallen out of the wall?)

3. Tom saw Mrs P. wearing them and persuaded her to give them/sell them to him to replace the missing ones. (If so, did he ask her how she came by them?)

4. Prosser has put them on the chest. When? How? Why did he give them to his wife then take them back?

It was like a game of chess, in which she was attempting to anticipate the response of an invisible opponent. It was all too much so she pushed the wires through her ears and fastened the necklace around her throat. In Machiavellian mode now, she went to her underwear drawer, took a pair of navy blue French knickers, the only item that could be thought even slightly provocative, folded them neatly and placed them at the back of the drawer, behind her sensible M&S briefs. The only time she'd worn them she had felt distinctly unsafe, but now they might help ascertain whether anyone was interfering with her underwear.

She ran downstairs, the earrings swinging heavily from her ears and the beads bouncing on her chest. On her way past Tom's office, she pushed open the door. He wasn't there. There was no one in the kitchen either, but an empty wine bottle stood in the middle of the table. She should start thinking about supper. How many would she be feeding? The three of them, Luke and there was Brendan of course. And they couldn't leave Bill out. If she made plenty of stuffing and added a few sausages, the small chicken should just about go round.

She prepared it quickly and put it in the oven, then went to look for everyone. As soon as she set foot outside she could hear the sound of raised voices and laughter. Disgruntled at being left out, she was about to go back into the house to sulk when Judith ran across the yard, carrying a guitar. 'Come on, Auntie Anna. You're missing the fun.'

In the summerhouse Brendan, cross-legged on the table, was playing his flute, surrounded by his handmaidens. Flora was strumming a guitar and humming. Celia was singing. Jenny, legs curled up, glass in hand, sat on the sofa. Judith was tuning her guitar. The room throbbed with adulation.

Anna knelt close to Jenny and put her mouth to her ear. 'Where are the others? The men.'

Jenny shrugged. 'I think they're in the field. Something to do with grass.'

The song finished and they applauded themselves, gathering around for Brendan's approval. He dropped down from the table and came towards her, raising his glass in her direction. 'Thanks, Anna, for your gracious hospitality.' She blushed. Furious with herself, a second flush coloured her burning cheeks.

The party continued and she watched Brendan apply himself to charming them all. Flora and Judith were behaving like schoolgirls. Jenny flirted. Even Celia became quite skittish. At one point Luke peered through the window and went away again. She was the only one to notice him. She, herself, stuck to water and kept her distance.

Later, Tom came to find her. 'There's an awful smell of burnt chicken in our kitchen.'

19

They were on their own for breakfast. Brendan had slept in the garden room. Luke was with Bill. And Flora was still upstairs.

Anna talked at the top of Tom's head whilst he read a two-day-old newspaper. 'Flora looks well, doesn't she?' Nothing. 'I didn't realise Judith had such a lovely singing voice.' Still nothing. 'How d'you think Bill's doing?' But he wasn't having any of it.

He was right. Brendan was trouble. She'd watched the lad wheedle his way into each female heart, abetted by a liberal supply of white wine. The effect he had on the men was equally marked. As their women succumbed, they slunk off to talk about cars and cricket without even putting up a fight.

'We should get rid of him before Madeleine arrives,' said Tom, when her small talk had petered out. 'I can guarantee, if we tell him she's seven months pregnant we won't see him for dust.'

'That's a horrid thing to say. Anyway, we mustn't organise her life for her.'

'It's never bothered you before.'

To divert him and without much thought of the consequences, she shook her head violently, causing the earrings to bounce off her cheeks. 'Notice anything?' she asked.

'Of course. You were wearing them yesterday. I assumed you would inform me as to the circumstances of their discovery, when you saw fit.'

Why was he being so pompous? She longed slap him across the face but to suddenly start behaving like that, after thirty years of restraint, could have serious repercussions. But despite her irritation she now knew that Tom had nothing to do with the reappearance of the earrings.

'They turned up in our bedroom, when I tidying up,' she said, which was perfectly true.

'I'm surprised more things don't go missing in that chaos.'

Flora was subdued and aimless. She spent a long time tidying up the pinboard. Anna knew she was waiting until they were alone and, at last, Tom went outside. 'Everything OK?' she asked.

'Not really. I've had a row with Luke.'

'About Brendan?'

'I'm not sure what it was about. Brendan was in there somewhere.'

'There'll be lots of rows about Brendan this morning. I've already had mine.'

'With Dad? You two never row.'

'He thinks Brendan is going to upset Maddy in some way.'

Right on cue, the phone rang. It was Madeleine. She was at the bus station in Ludlow.

'Shall I go and pick her up, Mum? It may be the only chance we get for a proper chat.'

Anna handed over the car keys. 'Drive carefully,' she called out, unable to stop herself.

Absorbed in removing any edible meat from yesterday's

burnt chicken, she didn't hear Luke come in and jumped when he spoke.

'Sorry,' he apologised. 'I thought Flora was here.'

Anna told him where she'd gone.

'Did she go … on her own?'

Luke looked like Sally but today she detected Bill in his solemn face. 'Yes. She wanted Maddy to herself for a bit.' He stood, hands in his pockets, tall and troubled. 'How d'you think your Dad's making out? We're not sure what to do. He does know we all want to help?'

'I don't think he realises that he needs help. He thinks Mum's coming back at any moment.'

'And what do you think?'

'I saw her on Friday. That's why we came up. Well, partly why we came up.'

Anna missed Sally and wanted to ask him how and where his mother was. Sally's companionship was one of the main reasons that she'd thought the move here would work but the Davis family was in disarray and it was selfish to consider her own needs.

Luke, like a lighthouse in the centre of the kitchen, revolved to watch her as she bobbed around him. In the end she thrust a handful of cutlery towards him and pointed at the table.

'How did she seem this morning?' he asked.

'Flora? Miserable. She said you'd fallen out. If it's over Brendan, I wouldn't worry.'

'I've never seen her like that. All girlie and flirty.'

'And why should that bother you?'

He slumped down at the table, as if his legs had buckled beneath him. 'Everything's a mess. Mum's gone. Em's gone. Dad's being weird. I thought I could count on Flo.'

'Count on her for what, exactly?' she coaxed, laying her hand on his.

'She'll murder me for telling you. We're going to get married. But I don't know if she still wants to go ahead.'

'You don't imagine she's going to marry Brendan, do you? You must know her better than that. If you don't, you shouldn't even be contemplating marriage. And another thing. You were very silly not to put up a fight, yesterday. Perhaps she thinks you aren't that bothered, if you just walk away when you see another man chatting her up.' She tried to lighten things. 'Forget Brendan. It's Tom you should be worrying about. He thinks he should be the only man in his daughters' lives.'

Luke didn't look at all encouraged by this. 'How would you feel about it, Anna? If we got married?' he asked.

'Luke, I love you dearly but it's nothing to do with me. You two must sort it out, but I promise I'll be suitably surprised when you make your announcement.' She leant across and kissed him.

He gave her a mournful smile and wandered off to look for his father.

Her stomach was fluttery with anticipation and misgivings. They would all be together soon and the pile of unresolved issues was mounting. She hadn't seen Brendan so far today but she no longer felt obliged to play hostess. He already had enough women running around after him.

Judith's car was still parked outside and Mark was cleaning the windscreen with a chamois leather. He waved. 'That what's-his-name's got the gift of the gab, hasn't he? Judith's phoned in sick. Never known her do that before.'

'Brendan,' she supplied the name. 'Is she not well?'

'She's well enough to swan off for a walk with young Brendan.'

Nothing else required her immediate attention and she went into her studio, hoping for some peace and quiet. As her eyes adapted to the gloom, she noticed a shard of pottery on the floor. Then another. She could see better now, and it became apparent that the shelf in the alcove had collapsed, spilling its load onto the floor and the shelf beneath. Crouching, she could see chunks of plates and mugs, scattered all over Tom's beautiful brick flooring. One of the bowls, Jenny's she thought, must have bounced and a section of it lay against the wall on the far side of the room. Every item was broken or chipped, except for two plates which had slipped onto the lower shelf and been wedged against the wall by the falling plank. She picked them up, frightened to inspect them too closely, but they were intact and she hugged them to her chest.

She sat on the clay-spattered stool, sobbing.

Tom, hearing her, rushed in from his workshop, dropping the tools he was carrying. 'Oh, Christ.' Picking his way carefully through the wreckage, as if it were important not to damage it further, he lifted the dangling shelf and inspected the fixings. One of the supporting wooden battens which he had screwed into the return of the alcove had come adrift. The screws were still there, thrust into the red plastic rawlplugs, like tiny swords in their scabbards.

'There's no way this could have come loose,' he said. 'The shelf might have tipped forwards, but the plugs couldn't have come out like this. It doesn't make sense.'

She didn't want an explanation, she wanted to be comforted. The shelf had collapsed and all her pots were broken. What more did she need to know?

But Tom wouldn't let it go. He lifted the shelf and took it to the window. 'Ahhaaa. Look. See these marks? The shelf's been prised away from the wall with a screwdriver or something.'

Did he think that the conclusion that someone had maliciously destroyed her handiwork would make it better? She set the two undamaged plates on the sill and began collecting up the shards, laying them gently in a black plastic bucket as if she were gathering mushrooms for breakfast. Celia's mug, handle gone, rim chipped. Peter's bowl, now in three pieces. Sally's plate, shattered. She inspected the unbroken pieces. They were the plates she'd made for Tom and herself and they'd been stacked, one on top of the other. His black, hers purple, both decorated with dark red lettering.

'It'll be quicker when you make them next time, now you've worked out the designs.' He smiled encouragement.

She raised the plates high above her head, as if they were trophies, and waited until he turned around before she dropped them.

'What on earth …?'

'It was a stupid idea. How can a mug embody a person? I don't know what I thought I was doing.' She tipped the contents of the bucket back on to the floor.

Car tyres crunched on the gravel outside.

'Please don't say anything to the girls about this,' she pleaded.

It was six weeks since she had seen Maddy. As well as the obvious bulge, she'd put weight on her face and arms. She'd always worn loose clothes, smocks and swirling skirts, but now she filled them. Standing next to her, Flora appeared slight and boyish in jeans and white t-shirt.

'Don't say anything. I hate it. It'll go away afterwards, won't it?' They hugged and Anna was surprised how solid the bump dividing them felt. 'Hi, Dad.'

They walked to the house, Tom carrying Madeleine's bags. Either the girls didn't notice, or chose to ignore their mother's tear-stained face and she was slightly disappointed. As they went in she caught a glimpse of someone at the landing window of Number One, watching them.

'Where's Brendan?' asked Maddy, 'Is he upstairs? I'll pop

up and see him.'

'Hang on a minute. I think we need to clear something up straight away. Just what is your relationship with him?' said Tom.

'Tom, please don't.' Anna shook her head.

'What did you say?' said Maddy. 'I can't believe you're going to start this, before I've even had a chance to sit down.' Her voice quavered.

'It's quite simple. All I want to know is, what is this Brendan to you? A friend? A boyfriend? What? He must be pretty important. You've dropped everything and rushed here to see him. You never seem that keen to come and see us.'

'That's not fair, Dad. How often does Flora come? You never criticise her. Think about it and maybe you'll understand why I don't visit more often.' She hurried out of the kitchen and up the stairs.

Flora hugged her mother and, shaking her head, went to find Luke.

Tom began to eat his lunch.

Anna stood at the sink and looked out of the window. A light breeze scarcely stirred the washing on the line

About an hour later Flora reappeared. 'You OK, Mum?'

Anna nodded her head. 'Have you had something to eat?'

'I'm not hungry.'

'Have you and Luke made it up? He was very unhappy this morning.'

'Yes. It was a silly misunderstanding. We're fine now. Where's Maddy?'

'Talking to Brendan, upstairs in the living room. And your father's digging.' She hoped that, by sticking to hard facts, she might avoid taking sides.

'What was all that about? Dad's always pretty blunt but

you'd think he'd be a bit more considerate. Maddy's blood pressure must be sky-high.'

'You'll have to ask him yourself, love. I'm too tired for all this.'

Tom was the only one who had eaten any lunch and Flora helped her clear the food from the table. Her throat was starting to ache with the strain of not crying. She felt both sick and hungry at the same time and her eyes were sore.

Anna had read page fifty-six of her book at least four times. Above she could hear Maddy and Brendan talking, their voices rising and falling. Twice she had crept to the bottom of the stairs but could infer nothing from the tone of their conversation. Eventually she'd poured a cup of tea for Tom but he wasn't in any of his usual bolt-holes and she'd ended up emptying it onto the grass.

She began doodling on a piece of scrap paper. Apart from the abortive search for Tom, she'd been hanging about in the kitchen now for almost three hours and achieved very little. She had failed to make any headway with her library book. She had washed every dirty dish she could lay her hands on and had wiped down all the work surfaces, twice. She'd designated the kitchen as a buffer zone and it was her duty to remain there in order to prevent them all from attacking each other. Tom was her main concern. He was hiding somewhere, wound up and ticking away like a time bomb, but it might be all right if only she could keep him away from Brendan, and probably Maddy too. There was a sound coming from upstairs which could have been crying or laughing. Maddy had already spent hours rattling about on a bus, then been subjected to Tom's outburst. Yes, they needed to know how Brendan figured in all this but there had to be better ways of finding out. Tension wasn't good for a pregnancy.

There was a tap on the back door and Judith appeared. 'Is

Brendan ready?' she asked.

'Ready?'

'Didn't he tell you? I'm giving him a lift back to Nottingham. If you see him, can you tell him I'm rarin' to go?' She waved as she left. 'Catch you next time.' She didn't mention Maddy.

Had she been dreaming or had Luke told her that he and Flora were getting married? How could such a momentous announcement have drifted, unnoticed, through the kitchen, like thistledown caught on the breeze?

When Brendan eventually left, she had deserted her post to use the downstairs cloakroom, emerging in time to see him toss his rucksack into the back of Judith's car before it headed off down the drive.

Madeleine was lying on her bed, eyes closed, her hand stroking the bedspread. From the day she was born this was the sign that she was about to fall asleep.

'OK, love?' Anna whispered.

'He's gone. Dad should be pleased, anyway.' Maddy spoke without opening her eyes.

'You know that Dad behaves this way because he loves you so much.'

'How come I'm supposed to understand that, but he can't see that it makes me feel like shit? I can never live up to his expectations. Can you imagine how that feels?'

'Is Brendan very important to you?'

'He's the father of this baby, if you call that important.' Maddy had always savoured the moment when she dropped her bombshells. She heaved herself up in the bed. 'When I first realised that I was pregnant, I tried to persuade Brendan that what we had was more than a casual thing. And it was. It really was. But I didn't tell him about the baby because I didn't want to use it to blackmail him into staying with me. I wanted him to stay because he wanted to stay, not because I was carrying his child. He didn't see it like that and he took off to Ireland.'

'You poor…'

'Let me finish Mum, or I'll lose my nerve. I didn't know what to do. Taliesin could see the state I was in. He was very sweet. I told him that I'd decided to have a termination. That's when he said he'd stand by me, if I wanted to carry on with the pregnancy. He offered to support me and my baby. He didn't hassle me. I went over and over it and in the end I said yes.'

'Dad and I assumed …'

'Most people did. Tal's taken all the flak.'

'Does his father know the whole story?'

'No. It's got nothing to do with him.'

Anna didn't like to point out that Charles Leighton might not be so ready to accept Maddy if he knew that the baby wasn't Taliesin's, or Rupert's or whatever he called his son. 'I wish I'd never phoned you. Dad told me not to.'

'Come on, Mum. You had to. And I had to come and tell him about the baby. His baby. The thing is, I still feel the same about him. I hoped I wouldn't but, as soon as I saw him, I knew it was still there. You can't decide who you'll fall in love with, can you?'

'How are things between you now?'

'He doesn't want to know. I shan't ever see him again. Brendan's gone and I've blown it with Tal. Dad will be delighted on both scores.'

'What d'you mean?'

'When I told Tal why I was coming here today, he asked me to think really hard about what I wanted. He said that, if I decided to come, I should buy a one-way ticket.'

Anna shook her head. 'It's all my fault.'

'Maybe it's the best thing in the long run. Taliesin and I

don't – didn't – share a bed or anything. He's a wonderful man and he deserves someone who really, really loves him. He was my best friend, though. And I'll miss Art. I've really fucked up this time haven't I?'

Anna and Tom were in bed. 'Oh, Flora rang while you were in the bath. They're safely home.' Tom was bad about messages, sometimes leaving it until she was sick with worry before he remembered to pass on crucial information.

'You're happy about the engagement, aren't you, Tom?' As they were loading up the car, Flora and Luke had, without any fuss, announced that they planned to marry soon.

'I'm relieved that one of our children is capable of making a rational decision, if that's what you mean.'

Anna felt a niggle of regret that Flora might be *settling* for something by accepting the comfortable and familiar. But Maddy, on her own in the room next door, had never settled for *anything*, and was now facing the future without either a lover or a friend. 'We must try and give Maddy some space.'

'What on earth does that mean?' Tom huffed, turning away from her and within minutes he was asleep.

She listened to the night sounds. A ewe kept up a steady bleating. A motorbike revved somewhere down on the main road. Tomorrow she would ring her father. It was a couple of weeks since she had spoken to him. They must go down to the surgery and register Madeleine with the doctor. She ought to get rid of the smashed pottery and tidy up her studio. How could she get in touch with Sally? And then there were the earrings. And Bill Davis. Should she tell Celia to warn Judith about Brendan? It hurt to think that she might never see Arthur again. Was Prosser up to something? And when were her library books due back?

20

Anna stooped for a handful of pegs. Seren was grizzling herself to sleep. It was another cloudless day and Maddy had left the carrycot in the shade of the trees, near the back door. The pink bootees, hanging next to Tom's socks, made her smile. They had been a gift from Celia and wouldn't have been Madeleine's choice, but a few weeks of motherhood had made her more prepared to compromise. Perhaps sleep deprivation had taken the fight out of her. Whatever it was, the arrival of the baby had altered lots of things.

For a start, she and Tom were now grandparents. To be honest, the prospect of being a grandmother hadn't appealed to her. It advanced her to the front line in the battle of life, as it were. It held connotations of passivity and servitude. Grandparents dropped everything to be unpaid babysitters and child carers. They organised their lives around grandchildren. Her neighbour in Bristol was constantly getting lumbered with her daughter's two sons, freeing the parents to go off skiing or sunning themselves, without the inconvenience of small children. Cafés and shopping malls were full of anxious senior citizens, run ragged with the responsibility of boisterous grandchildren. No, it hadn't been at all appealing.

She hadn't taken into account what would happen when she held her one-hour-old granddaughter in her arms. It was love at first sight and she was lost. This scrap of life was her direct connection to the past and the future.

She continued pegging out the wet clothes. The tiny tie-dyed smock, overprinted with stars, had been one of her gifts to the new baby. Seren was Welsh for 'star'. She had been overcome with emotion when Maddy announced the name she'd chosen for her daughter. Seren Anna Wren.

Tom had changed too, and she was slightly concerned on this score. He was behaving like a proud father. He spent hours and hours walking around, cradling Seren in the crook of his arm. His excuse was that Maddy needed a break to catch up on lost sleep. He meandered around the house and the garden, talking and singing, explaining to the child about the trees and the animals. He recounted the family history and told tales of Maddy and Flora's childhood. Maddy had warned him that there would be nothing left to tell her when she was old enough to understand but Tom had laughed and said he would find plenty to tell his 'little star'. Anna tried, at least once a day, to remind him that the current arrangement was temporary. Maddy would want a place of her own, once she'd had time to get used to motherhood. He nodded but she could see that he didn't believe her.

As well as becoming a grandmother, Anna was a full time mother again. When Maddy had left home, four years ago, it had been sudden and dreadful. A true bereavement. For a while she'd battled on, trying to keep on an even keel for Flora's sake. Then Flora had gone too, leaving her and Tom to face each other across the dinner table, wondering what it had all been about. She began to suffer sinister symptoms. Her heart raced even when she was sitting still. She felt giddy as she walked along a straight street. When she swallowed, it felt as if she had a boiled sweet stuck half way down her throat. This was what had finally sent her to the doctor. He had done a thorough examination and reassured her that she didn't have throat cancer or a heart condition. 'Classic symptoms of anxiety,' he said. 'You've got to stop worrying about things.'

So at least she could stop worrying about the *symptoms* caused by worrying.

She peeped at the baby as she passed. Seren was asleep now, sucking her tiny fist, safe behind the cat net which Tom had draped over the carry cot. She'd forgotten how many things were out there, waiting to harm this innocent, but Mrs Prosser came out of the Redwoods' back door, shaking her yellow duster and interrupting her thoughts. 'She's gorgeous, isn't she? I could eat her up,' she said. 'If I'd had any I wouldn't be able to breastfeed 'em.' She lowered her voice to a whisper. 'Inverted nipples, see.' Anna stared at the ample breasts filling the bleach-splashed t-shirt, sad for this jolly woman's childlessness.

Anna and Mrs Prosser had become quite friendly over the preceding weeks. Jenny kept Mrs P. at arm's length, but Anna was drawn to her for several reasons. There was something undeniably fascinating about a woman who shared her life with Prosser. He continued to crop up all over the place, as a kind of 'brooding presence' (a phrase she remembered from a trailer for *Wuthering Heights*). Jenny told her she was fantasising. 'He comes to give Mrs P. a lift home sometimes but I don't see him as a latter-day Heathcliff.'

Only the other day, Bill had mentioned that Prosser was being a little less obstructive these days. 'He's starting to accept us, I think.'

On the days when Mrs Prosser came to work at the house Anna made sure not to wear the earrings or the necklace. Whenever she bumped into Mrs P. she always checked her ears but since that one occasion in the post office, she'd not seen her wearing anything but plain gold hoops or small studs.

On the underwear front, she'd been quite excited when the French knickers disappeared from her drawer but Maddy admitted to borrowing them, explaining that she'd run out of clean panties.

Tom was in the kitchen, carving something from a piece of beech. He glanced up and smiled at her. 'What time are you off?'

'I'll have a coffee, then go. What's that?' she asked, pointing at the carving.

'A rattle. Remember the ones I made for Flo and Maddy?'

'I feel bad, leaving you two, but I must go down and see them.'

'We'll be fine. Tell your Dad I'm sorry I can't make it this time.'

Between sips of coffee, she gathered together the things to take to Bath. Dorothy had been bed-bound for several weeks and her father was finding the catering difficult. She'd spent the previous day cooking food with which she hoped to tempt the invalid - a light sponge cake, vegetable soup and a cottage pie, all soft and easy to eat without dentures.

'Don't forget the photos.' Tom waved the latest set of prints at her.

She wasn't sure that her father would be as interested in Seren as he was. Men tend not to be besotted with babies, especially baby girls. When she'd phoned to let him know that Maddy had given birth and he was a great-grandfather, he'd seemed more concerned with getting to the chemist's before it shut. From what Steven told her, it sounded as though Dorothy was very ill and Frank Hill was focussing his attention on his new wife.

Maddy came down with another load for the machine. 'How can one baby generate so much washing?' She was looking tired.

'Are you three going to be OK?' Anna asked.

'Of course we are, aren't we Maddy?' Tom chirped.

Maddy yawned and nodded. 'Give Grandpa Frank my love. And Dorothy, even though we've never met. I promise I'll get down to see them soon.'

Tom helped her carry her things to the car and she ran through the survival instructions. 'And the bread's in the bread bin,' he chanted.

As she drove away, the oddest thought came to her. It was as if Tom, Maddy and Seren were the Wren family and she was the outsider who'd been visiting them. Of course that was ridiculous but, looking in the rear-view mirror, she was reminded of a photo that her mother had taken, showing Tom and her with Maddy, a babe in arms, standing outside their home in Bristol. Flora must have been at nursery school because she wasn't in the picture.

She had originally planned to go by train but Tom persuaded her that a car would be useful. There might be errands to run for her father and it meant that she could take provisions with her. If she had an hour to spare, she could get across to see Flora.

'But *you'll* be stuck,' she said. 'What if you have to get the baby to the hospital in a hurry? Or need some shopping?'

'Someone will give us a lift,' he said. 'Anyway, you're only going for a couple of days.'

The journey to Bath was uneventful. She wondered what she would find when she arrived. Steven had arranged to bring Frank and Dorothy to visit them in late June but they had cancelled at the last minute. She and Tom had gone to Bath instead and found Dorothy ill and her father looking every one of his seventy-eight years.

She passed the service station where Bill had confessed that things weren't right between Sally and him. Over the past couple of months Bill had astounded them all. He hadn't cracked up or broken down. He went about being relentlessly cheerful. Because he was in such good spirits, he was no trouble to have around and was included in all the activities, but recently he'd developed a habit of wandering in, unannounced, and making himself at home. Several times she'd come back from somewhere and found him snoozing on the kitchen sofa. He did the same in the other houses, too. 'It's like having a communal pet,' said Jenny.

But for her it was no joke. At every opportunity, his hand would stray onto her knee or his foot would touch hers. If she pulled away, he would apologise and leave her wondering whether it had been accidental. Her irritation was modified by the knowledge that, no matter how brave he seemed, he must be suffering. Now the baby had arrived, he had an added excuse to come calling. Tom and the others still found it hilarious when he asked, 'What's it like then, sleeping with a granny?' Yes, Bill was not going to give up easily. Except, apparently, on his marriage.

The lawn needed cutting. Weeds were colonising the flowerbeds and springing up between the slabs. Her father watched from the bedroom window as she parked the car. He came down to help her unload.

'How are things, Dad?' She hugged him. He'd never been a big man but she could feel that he had lost weight. It had been a hot, dry summer and her tanned arms made his look pallid and scrawny by comparison.

'Not good. She doesn't complain at all but she's failing.'

They went upstairs. Dorothy looked tiny and frail in the big bed, barely making an indentation in the pillows that propped her up. Her father had set up the old Zed-Bed in the room and he was sleeping there, he explained, in case she needed him during the night.

This was only the fourth time that Anna had met Dorothy. She still had no idea why Frank had married her but at least he'd chosen a gracious and interesting person. It was a pity that she wasn't going to get to know her better, because it was obvious that Dorothy was dying. The old lady lay motionless, breathing gently and watching her through half open eyes. She lifted her hand from the bedcover in greeting, then shut her eyes, as if the effort had been too much.

Anna and Frank talked in the kitchen. The routine here was dictated by illness. The nurse came three times every day to give Dorothy her medication and there was also a carer, Pat, who helped wash her and make her comfortable. 'Pat's wonderful,' said Frank. 'She's so gentle with Dot. She's got no flesh on her at all now. I'm afraid I'll hurt her.'

To Anna's dismay, his eyes filled with tears and he blew his nose on a grubby hanky. She held his hand across the table. 'Do they have any idea how long it will be?'

'No. They make out that she's going to get better. They talk to me as if I'm an idiot. When you get beyond seventy, they assume you're senile.'

'Can you cope, Dad? Have you been in touch with her family? Shouldn't they be doing this?'

'No. I want to do it for her.'

'You look exhausted.'

'I'm OK.'

Steven phoned from work. Frank spoke to him briefly then went back upstairs, passing the phone to Anna.

'How's he looking?' her brother asked.

'Exhausted. But he's determined to go on with it. You know how stubborn he is. Dorothy looks dreadful. She can't last much longer.'

He promised to call on his way home. Elaine had made it clear that she was not prepared to get involved and also that nothing must be allowed to disrupt their normal routine. Not for the first time, Anna wished that her brother had taken that first wage-packet to a different bank. He might be a happy man now with a family of his own.

While Frank sat with Dorothy, she did some ironing and cleaned the kitchen. These chores led her into nooks and crannies of her old home that she hadn't visited for years. Now and again, as she cleaned and polished, she glimpsed her own reflection in a mirror or a window-pane, and saw Nancy Hill looking back at her.

The sun drew her outside to tackle the lawns. Her father insisted on using a push-mower and she had a suspicion it was the very one he'd had when they were children and when it had taken him an hour to cut the grass and another to clean the mower afterwards. 'You should respect your tools,' he'd say, 'and you'll only have to buy them once.'

At the sound of the whirring blades, Frank called to her from the window, 'I'll clean it when you've finished.' He didn't trust her to do a proper job but she forgave him immediately, thinking of the times over the past weeks when she'd done the selfsame thing to Maddy. She would have to watch herself.

She looked for an opportunity to talk to her father but he was keeping a vigil in the sick room and it didn't seem right, chatting in front of Dorothy.

She offered to sit with the invalid for a while so that he could go out in the garden and relax in the sun. He refused. She tried to tempt him with her home-made food but he gave up after a few spoonfuls of soup. He insisted that he needed nothing from the supermarket. He was existing on toast, tinned rice pudding and drinking chocolate.

The nurse was a bustling woman. While she was in the house, loud and cajoling, the place came alive but when she left, it slipped back into limbo. After only six hours, Anna was starting to lose her sense of reality and she understood how isolated her father must be feeling. 'Do any of your friends call? Or the neighbours?' she asked.

'No. And I wouldn't expect them to. It's none of their business.'

Steven let himself in. He looked out of place in his dark suit and shiny black shoes. He certainly wasn't dressed for making himself useful.

She showed him the photographs of Seren. 'Dad's not interested. I can understand why but it's a bit upsetting, all the same.'

'Is Maddy OK? What's the news on the father? It's an expensive business, rearing a child.'

Up until now, Anna had provided the sketchiest details of the circumstances surrounding Madeleine's pregnancy. It was enough for the rest of the family to know that she was living at Pen Craig but it was difficult to avoid Steven's direct question. 'She wants to go it alone.'

He took out his wallet, made from the softest black leather. She imagined that Elaine had given it to him for Christmas, when they were in Italy. He slipped out several notes, fifty pounds, she guessed. 'Give her this and tell her to get the baby...'

'Seren.'

'What?'

'Seren. The baby's called Seren.'

'Tell her to get something for Seren.'

'I'll take it, but I know what she would prefer.'

'What's that?'

'A congratulations card from you and Elaine. Something that you'd chosen specifically for her. Something that you'd bothered to put a stamp on and post. But I'm sure she'll put the money to good use.' She took it from him and folded it into her purse. He didn't reply and she knew that her comment had hit home. Straight away she regretted her attack. 'Sorry, Steve. I'm a bit raw at the moment.'

He nodded. 'It's this house. I wish he'd moved after Mum died. I keep expecting her to come in from the garden.'

There was a tap on the back door. It was Flora, who had come straight from work. 'Hi, Uncle Steve.' She kissed her uncle and mother. 'I wasn't sure how difficult things were here and I wanted to be sure to catch Mum. Haven't seen you for ages,' she said to Steven.

Frank came downstairs when he heard Flora's voice. 'She's dozing,' he said. They sat in the kitchen, talking about anything but what was happening in the room above, perching on the edges of the hard chairs, as if they might need to rush upstairs at any second. 'How's that young man of yours?' Frank asked his granddaughter. Anna was surprised to learn that Luke was a regular caller. 'He's a bit gormless but I have to admit, I like him.' The photos of Seren went around the table but he passed them on without comment.

Anna went up to see if Dorothy needed anything. She was more than a little relieved to discover that seeing another woman in her mother's bed, under the bedspread that her mother had made, didn't upset her at all. Dorothy was awake and she beckoned Anna towards her.

'Can I get you anything?' asked Anna. 'Dad'll be up in a minute.'

The old lady held out her hand. When Anna took it in hers, it felt cold and papery. The lumpy veins and arteries looked like roads on a map, blue motorways and red trunk roads. The old lady's rings clinked together and it was only the swollen knuckles that kept them from slipping off.

She gave a little cough, to clear her throat. 'I think we could have been good friends, you and I.' Each sentence required an enormous effort. 'There's something I must tell you.' She lay with her eyes closed, her hand resting in Anna's. In short phrases, and with many pauses for breath, she unravelled the mystery of her relationship with Frank Hill.

They had come to know each other through a day-class at the library and, over the months, he had confided in her, telling her of the crippling guilt that he'd felt when Nancy had died so suddenly. There had been no warning and he'd had no opportunity to care for her, as she had spent all their married life caring for him and putting his welfare first. He felt he had been denied that final act of love. Dorothy, in return, had revealed to Frank that her cancer had come back and she had only months to live. 'You see, he needed to look after someone. We got on well. I fitted the bill. Does that make sense?'

Anna raised the skeletal hand to her lips. 'Yes. And it's so like him. He's such a stickler for doing things properly. Thank you.'

Frank came up from the garden carrying a vase of cream roses. He put it on the dressing table, where Dorothy could see the near-perfect blooms if she opened her eyes. Their scent almost disguised the stale smell of the sickroom. Anna kissed her father and he signalled that she should leave them.

Steven was getting twitchy. Elaine had tracked him down and phoned to remind him that they were going out to eat. 'Better get off. I'll ring tomorrow. You'll still be here?' She nodded. She wanted time to think about what Dorothy had told her, before sharing it with anyone.

She heated the cottage pie and took some up to her father. Flora stayed for supper and they ate in the kitchen, leaving the back door open to catch the evening breeze after the hot day.

'Poor Flora. We haven't done anything at all to celebrate your engagement. It's been lost in the rush. What with the baby and now this.'

Flora smiled. 'Don't worry, Mum. We don't want to make a big thing of it. Anyway, this business with Sally has made it a bit tricky. I keep meaning to ask, has Brendan been in touch with Maddy, at all?'

'Not as far as I know.'

'And Taliesin?'

'He wrote to me about a week after Madeleine came back to Pen Craig. He wanted to check that she was OK.' Anna paused. 'I've spoken to him a few times since. I had to let him know about Seren.'

'Oh, Mum. Does Maddy know?' Flora shook her head and sighed. 'You mustn't go behind her back, Mum. She'll be furious if she finds out.'

'But I think he really *does* care about her.'

'They'll have to sort it out themselves. This isn't a teenage tiff. It's not something that you can fix.'

'But it's my fault. I was the one who told her that Brendan had come to find her.'

'He'd have found his way to her somehow. And he had to be told about the baby. But you must tell her about Taliesin.'

Luke arrived to collect Flora. Anna enquired about Sally and he gave her a contact number. 'She's staying with someone she knows from the University until she can find a flat. I'm sure she'd love to see you while you're here, if you can spare the time. I warned her that you were pretty tied up here.'

After they'd gone, she had a cool bath and went to bed, lying on top of the covers, listening to her father's voice in the room next door. His words were indistinct but it sounded as if he were reciting poetry.

21

The café hadn't changed much since their last visit a couple of years ago and Sally was waiting for her at the table near the window. They filled the first awkward moments with news of Frank and Dorothy. Anna thought her friend looked tired. Her hair could have done with a wash and there was more than a touch of grey showing at the roots.

'I wasn't sure how you'd feel about meeting.' Sally scraped the froth from the inside of her coffee cup.

'Don't be daft.'

'I don't want to make things difficult for you. Bill's sure to ask if you've seen me.'

'I'll tell him the truth. He knows you're in touch with Luke, doesn't he?'

'Yes. But he knows I'd tell you stuff that I wouldn't tell Luke.'

'Stuff?'

'Stuff. Things.'

'Is there stuff? Are there things?'

'Not really. Not any more. The Tim thing was never going to last.'

Sally's confidence and composure had slipped and her clothes weren't quite right. The linen shirt was more creased than was fashionable, her nail varnish, chipped. She looked defeated.

She'd just moved into a flat near the centre of Bristol. The University had offered her some lecturing work and she had nearly completed her latest book. Most of her savings had gone towards the purchase of Pen Craig but royalties on the other books she'd written provided a steady, if modest, income and she was managing.

'I'm delighted about Luke and Flora, aren't you? Can you believe they've finally got it together? Did they tell you how it started? It was when they couldn't get to us at Christmas and were stuck in that motel. I can't believe we didn't latch on.'

Anna had heard the story several times but didn't interrupt. Sally asked about the baby and, although babies weren't her thing, showed genuine interest in the photographs. 'Why on earth did Maddy leave Taliesin? I only met him that once but he seemed such a nice man. Gentle and interesting. Quite unusual.'

Sally had moved out before Brendan had turned up. She'd missed the Irish charmer. Anna, wanting to divulge a confidence and, in so doing, demonstrate her trust and friendship, revealed that Brendan was Seren's father. Sally's eyes filled with tears when she heard how Taliesin had offered to stand by Maddy. 'Christ. I'm going soft. And I'm the last person to advise her to go for the nice guy and the happy ending, aren't I?'

'It'll be OK if you were to change your mind, Sal. Everyone's allowed to make a mistake. Bill's so unhappy. He's just sitting there, waiting for you to come back.'

Why on earth had she said that? After the first few miserable days, he'd never looked back. He'd reorganised the house to his liking. He'd made the kitchen muddled and cosy and had taken to sleeping in the spare room. His cooking wasn't elaborate but he was enlarging his repertoire. He had plenty of friends on hand to advise him or feed him. Only the week before, he'd cooked quite a presentable meal for them all. In fact Bill was going from strength to strength.

'Is he? He hasn't made much effort to get in touch. There are hundreds of ways he could track me down. Through Luke for a start.'

'He wants to give you time. And space.' That ridiculous phrase again. 'He loves you so much. All he wants is for you to be happy.'

'He's told you that?'

'Not in so many words.' She didn't want to sound as if Bill was confiding his feelings to all and sundry and she changed tack. 'More to the point, how d'you feel about him?'

'Confused. It's hard to imagine spending the rest of my life on my own. But, now I've made the break, it would be crazy to weaken just because I'm feeling a bit lonely. It'll be a lot easier when I get a work rhythm going.'

They discussed the wedding. Flora and Luke were talking about getting married as soon as possible. Having known each other all their lives, there was no need for a long engagement. They wanted the whole affair to be low key and were going to organise it themselves. 'The only snag is that Luke really wants Emily to be there. They spoke last week, so at least she knows what's going on.'

'Where is she now?'

'Nepal. I never thought I'd have to look at an atlas to locate my daughter. She might as well be on the moon but there's no point in worrying, is there?' It was obvious that Sally did not believe her own pronouncement.

'Maddy thinks we ought to throw an engagement party for them, at the house. They could invite as many people as they wanted. We're hardly short of space. The young ones could bring tents. A party might cheer us all up. What d'you think?' She waited but when Sally didn't reply she added, 'But there's absolutely no point if you don't come.'

'It was Maddy's idea, you said?'

'Yes. The engagement got completely overlooked when Seren was born and she probably feels responsible. Mind you, I think she'd like the opportunity to show off her daughter.'

'Let me think about that, will you?' Finally she asked about the others. 'Is Celia still following Jenny round like a dog? Ironic when you think how bitchy Jenny could be about her. Dare I mention the swimming pool?'

They said their goodbyes, promising to speak before the week was out.

Anna left the car park and joined the Friday afternoon crawl of traffic back to Bath. What sort of an evening would Sally have? Was she in touch with any of her old workmates? Now that term had finished, the academics would all be heading off for extended holidays. Sally could be in for a miserable summer.

The house was cool and quiet. Her father was in the kitchen, listening to the Test Match on the radio and staring out of the window, as if the teams were playing on the back lawn. When they'd put it to him that he should buy a small television set for the kitchen, they might have been suggesting that he take drugs. And the notion of installing a satellite dish, to increase his choice of programmes, was unthinkable. 'It's the thin end of the wedge,' he protested.

Anna wasn't sure if he was aware of her arrival and spoke gently, not to startle him. 'How are we doing?'

'Losing.'

'And how's Dorothy?'

'Losing, too. She was sleeping when I went up five minutes ago.'

'You go and put your feet up, Dad, and I'll bring you a sandwich. You look exhausted.'

By the time she took a tray into the sitting room, he was asleep, the radio still on.

There wasn't much for her to do around the house. The nurse, the carer and the cleaner were all efficient. The garden was a little neglected but Frank's gardener was due back from his holiday and was going to put in a full day next week.

When she phoned Tom, he assured her that everything was running smoothly at home, too, 'So stay as long as you need to. No point in rushing back. We're managing fine.'

By the following afternoon, she'd more or less run out of things to do. Frank had everything he needed and it was clear that he would not allow the burden of care to be taken from him. Flora and Luke were in London visiting friends. Steven and Elaine were unavailable. There was no real reason for her to stay.

When she was ready to leave, Frank was up in the bedroom. Dorothy's eyes were shut and he was holding her hand, squeezing it gently, and reading the paper.

'Thanks for coming, love.'

'I'll be back again soon.'

'Best not make any promises.'

She ran through a reminder, 'I've left some portions of casserole in the freezer and the rest of the cakes…'

'…are in the cake tin.' He smiled.

The traffic was remarkably quiet for a summer Saturday. All the caravans and camper vans were on the other carriageway, heading south to Devon and Cornwall. She switched on the car radio and drove twenty miles without absorbing a single word, still thinking about her father, steadfastly doing what he had set out to do. She was a little unnerved when she noticed that the petrol gauge was entering the red zone, something she'd forgotten to check before leaving Bath. She was relieved, therefore, when, almost immediately, she saw the sign for the service station and took the slip lane off the motorway.

She filled the tank, then decided a black coffee was what she needed. Was she hungry or not? And if she were, did she fancy something sweet or savoury? Everything in the stainless steel trays smelled the same, the food sitting either in a pool of fat or a puddle of water. Although the cafeteria wasn't busy, a queue of people had formed behind her, panicking her into ordering sausage and chips and a cup of coffee.

The service station felt like a calm backwater and she had drifted in here to escape the concealed currents and treacherous rocks that were tossing her around. Everyone else appeared to be sailing along merrily. Tom was as happy as Larry, protecting Maddy and Seren from … whatever. Flora and Luke were having a whale of a time in London, planning their future together. Her father was assuaging his guilt and helping Dorothy through the process of death. And here she was, eating sausage and chips just off the northbound carriageway of the M5.

On the way back to the car she passed the entrance to the Travel Lodge. The banners festooned along the fence proclaimed that rooms were only £42.50 a night. Something (she would never be able to explain what it was) drew her through the automatic doors and, before she knew it, a pleasant young woman behind the featureless reception desk was swiping her card and booking her in.

It was the first time that she had ever been in a hotel room on her own. This one was clean, blue and anonymous, air-freshener tainting the lifeless air. Without question, every one of the eighty rooms would be exactly the same. The window overlooked the petrol filling station and, despite double-glazing, she could hear the grumble of the traffic on the motorway beyond. The double bed looked suggestive, almost pornographic, in its threadbare anonymity.

The digital readout on the television showed seven thirty-four. At home Tom and Maddy would be preparing supper. Seren should be asleep in her carrycot after her bath. The setting sun would be glancing in through their bedroom window, striking the wall above the head of their bed.

She sat on the edge of the bath and removed the flimsy plastic beaker from its hygienic packaging. The tap water tasted of chlorine but she was desperate for a drink after the salty sausages. Was she having some kind of a breakdown? Didn't things like that come on gradually, over weeks and months? She'd been fine when she left Bath, less than three hours ago. Was she showing off? Attention seeking? That sort of thing was for delinquent teenagers, not grandmothers.

She stripped off her clothes, tossing them out of the bathroom onto the worn carpet. Taking the miniature bottle of bath foam, she stepped under the shower and pulled the curtain around. Once she had mastered the controls, she let the steaming water cascade over her. The stream of water straightened her curls and her wet hair stuck to her back, stretching down to her shoulder blades. She turned this way and that, letting the hot water run across her shoulders and down her body, the warmth and the sound of it inducing a state of near trance. It was five past eight when she switched the water off.

Four white towels hung over the chrome rail. They were harsh from constant laundering but she liked the sensation as they sand-papered her skin dry. She used all four, abandoning them in a damp heap on the slippery tiles. She left the bathroom and sat naked, absolutely motionless, on the edge of the bed, until droplets of water, now cold, dripped from her hair onto her warm thighs and startled her.

She sorted out a change of clothes and repacked her bag then she pulled back the bedcover and rumpled the bed, punching her fists into the pillows. Finally she wrote 'Fuck Fuck Fuck' in the condensation on the bathroom mirror, watching droplets of water from the multiple obscenity racing down the glass.

There was a pay phone in the foyer of the Travel Lodge and Tom answered after the third ring. She explained that she was on her way home and had stopped for a rest and something to eat.

'Take your time, love. No rush. I thought you might stay another night,' he said. 'How is she?'

'Slipping away. Dad's amazing. There wasn't much I could do.'

She rejoined the motorway.

There was still a trace of blue-green in the night sky as she drove up the lane. Tom was sitting on the wall outside the back door, softly strumming his guitar. The sound of laughter and music came from the summerhouse. 'Another party?' she asked, kissing his cheek.

'Christopher's got some friends staying. They were getting a bit loud, so Peter chucked them out of the house.'

'Everything OK here?'

'Fine. Fine. How about you? You look tired.'

'I am. Where's Madeleine? In bed?'

'With that lot.' He pointed towards the summerhouse. 'I knew it wouldn't last.'

'What?'

'The devoted mother thing.'

'She deserves an hour or two off, don't you think?'

'Hmmm.' He didn't sound convinced. 'Why's your hair damp?'

'Sweat. It's stifling in the car.' The lie came easily.

22

Tom had replaced the collapsed shelf and made sure that the others were firmly fixed. Everything was set for her to start again but her enthusiasm for the project had evaporated and she had lost direction. When she thought about it now, the whole scheme was embarrassingly simplistic, like something a child might dream up. How could a few pots affect the way people behaved? They would all have thanked her politely for their crockery sets, then pushed them to the back of a cupboard. Or, after a decent interval, sneaked them into the charity bag.

Flying ants swarmed in the sticky heat. Eric, working on the border near the Redwoods' front door, had cast aside his cap (something he rarely did) and his pale scalp looked like the top of a boiled egg, shell removed and ready for tea. Every window was open but the curtains hung limp and still. The baby had been fractious all morning, her spikey black hair damp with perspiration. They were all on edge and Maddy had ended up in tears of confusion and exhaustion. 'I hate it,' she screamed. Anna dared not ask exactly what it was that she hated. When Tom, anxious that Maddy should do everything properly, had offered to take her and Seren to Cwm Bont for their first visit to the baby clinic, the silence that fell on the house had been a great relief. Anna had forgotten the tension that one crying baby could generate.

The day after the shelf crashed down, she had swept the broken pottery into a dark corner and it had been some weeks before she could face up to disposing of it. Eventually she struck on the fanciful notion of digging a hole outside the outhouse and burying it. One day, hundreds of years hence, an archaeologist might dig it up and wonder what had gone on here. Was that enough to guarantee her immortality?

She perched on the spattered chair and took a gobbet of clay from its plastic wrapping, rolling it back and forth between her hands. It cooled her hot palms and the surface of the clay took on the texture of her skin. Something about the fat roll made her think of a pig and she extended it here and there to form snout and legs. She made a second pig and placed them, side by side, on the trestle table. Next she moulded a pair of cats. The cats were more convincing than the pigs, which she rolled back into a ball. Her sketchbook was on the sill and she started drawing until, soon, she had filled a whole page with pigs. Standing, sitting, lying. Giraffes and elephants came next. The necks and trunks would be a challenge. The idea for a new project began to firm up. She would make an ark for Seren, complete with animals and the whole Noah family. What's more, she would allow the child to play with it, not keep it on a high shelf as an untouchable ornament. She pictured a sturdy little girl setting out the menagerie, two by two.

Taking her sketchpad and pencil case, she walked up to the wood. The contentious fields had both been cut for silage and Stan Roberts, whose farm ran up to Pen Craig, was grazing sheep in the upper field. In exchange for the fodder and the grass keep, he had agreed to maintain the hedges and fences. Tom was delighted with this arrangement. He saw bartering of goods and services as the way forward. No one else had shown much interest but Jenny had commented that the animals added a picturesque-ness to the view.

Finding a comfortable spot in the top corner of the field, she sat on the grass and sketched the sheep. At first they kept a wary distance from her but soon, sensing that she meant them no harm, they nibbled the grass around her outstretched legs.

The sheep heard the sound before she did. As one, they raised their heads and looked beyond her, towards the wood. First one took flight then the rest followed, spilling across the sloping ground to the other side of the field, where they stood alert, staring back in her direction. She froze, pencil in hand, hearing the sound of snapping twigs, as someone walked along the footpath that lay on the other side of the stone wall. Quickly, she drew her knees up and clasped her arms around them, making herself as small as she could. Hidden amongst the fronds of bracken she glanced to her left, along the undulating face of the wall, and caught sight of a man holding binoculars up to his eyes. It was Prosser and he was spying on the house. After a few minutes he slipped back into the wood.

When she told Tom about it later, he asked her why she hadn't gone across and spoken to him. 'Anyway, lots of people use that footpath and I expect most of them look at Pen Craig through binoculars. Normal human curiosity, to take a look at landmarks in the countryside. If anything, I'd say you were the one behaving strangely.'

'But that's the point. He's not a passing rambler, is he?'

He smiled, indulgently.

By late afternoon, a bank of indigo thunderclouds had built up and the sky over the valley resembled a day-old bruise. Seren, exhausted from her crying jag, had fallen asleep, giving Anna and Maddy time to relax with a cup of tea. 'It was a nightmare at the clinic. She screamed the place down. All the other babies slept through the whole thing. Dad was so embarrassed he went out and waited in the car.'

'They're pleased with her?'

'I don't know. I couldn't really hear what the woman was saying. But she's gained half a kilo.' Maddy showed her the clinic card.

Why was weight used as an indicator of success? Babies were supposed to put it on. Children shouldn't put on too much. Women always needed to lose it and men could ignore it. 'Did she ask how you were coping? Offer any tips?'

'She asked if I was getting back to my normal weight.' There it was again. 'It was all a bit of a waste of time.'

A breeze swept through the place, slamming a bedroom door and chilling the air, and she went around the house, shutting all the windows, billowing curtains flapping across her face. From the landing she could see the first huge raindrops, hitting the roofs of the cars below, darkening the stone surface of the yard to a blue-ish grey. Tom dashed across from the shed as the first zig-zag of lightning lit up the sky. She counted. One, two, three and then the thunder cracked. Tom, panting and dishevelled, rushed past her, on his way to disconnect the television set.

The baby slept on past her feed time, as if comforted by the storm. Maddy dithered. 'I should wake her. She'll be all out of synch. And she needs changing.'

'Leave her,' said Anna, 'She'll wake up if she's hungry. Perhaps we should have something to eat, while we have the chance.'

The storm flashed and rumbled overhead and the rain beat on the windows. It wasn't yet six o'clock but they needed to switch the lights on. They sat together around the kitchen table, secure in the solid old house. 'Flo and I stayed with Grandma and Grandpa once – I think you'd gone to a wedding – and there was a thunderstorm. Grandma read us poetry, to take our minds off it. We weren't at all scared but we pretended we were, so she'd keep reading. It was The Rhyme of Ancient Mariner. I can see the book now, it had a green cover.'

Anna remembered her mother had read to her and Steven from the same book. There had been an inscription on the fly-leaf. Something to do with attendance at Sunday school. Was it still on her father's bookshelf? She must find it next time she went.

'Oh, I knew there was something I'd forgotten to tell you.' The food and an hour of peace and quiet had brought the colour back to Maddy's cheeks. 'I was coming back from the summerhouse yesterday and you'll never guess who I saw.' She rolled her eyes. 'Uncle Bill and Auntie Celia. Together.'

'How d'you mean, together?' asked Tom.

'*Together* together.'

'You can't have,' said Anna. 'Well, you might have seen them with each other.'

'It was more than that, Mum. They were kissing. I wanted to laugh. Can you imagine anyone getting worked up about Auntie Celia? It'd be like making love to a blancmange. All pink and damp.'

'Don't be unkind. She's a very nice woman,' said Tom.

'Whatever. But she was certainly going at it with Uncle Bill.'

'Where were they?' asked Anna, as if the location might excuse their behaviour.

'Behind the outbuildings, out of sight. It seemed a shame to interrupt them, so I sneaked around the other way.'

What on earth did Bill think he was playing at? No wonder Sally had left him. The man was insatiable. Anyway, Bill was in love with *her*, not Celia. His favourite colour was purple, not pink. And why couldn't Mark satisfy his pathetic little wife? First she'd come sniffing round Tom, now she had her claws into poor Bill. Judith was taking after her, too. Look how quick she'd been to jump in a car and drive off with Maddy's boyfriend. What a mess.

'Good luck to you all, I say,' said Maddy. 'To think that we were worried you'd all be vegetating out here in rural Wales.'

'What are you talking about?' Tom's voice was sharp.

'Little did we think you'd be reliving the sixties. Free love, wife swapping and all that.'

'We were schoolchildren in the sixties,' said Anna. 'And who's "we"?'

Maddy, the bit between her teeth, continued, 'Wait 'til I tell the others.'

'Madeleine.' Tom shouted. The baby, who had slept through the thunder, woke with a start and began to wail. Maddy lifted her from the carrycot and marched out of the kitchen, her footsteps thudding on the stairs as she stomped to the top of the house.

'Look what you've done now, Tom.'

'Don't blame me. She can't go round causing mischief like that.'

'*She's* not the one causing mischief. God, you men stick together, don't you?'

'Bill's stressed at the moment. He's not totally responsible for his actions.'

'You mean he doesn't know it's wrong to snog Celia?' The word sounded juvenile.

'No. Of course not. But a man can get frustrated.'

'Is that why *you* kissed her?'

'Ah-haa. Now we have it. I knew you'd throw that back in my face sooner or later.'

'That's not fair. Besides, you don't know the half of it,' she taunted, without really knowing what she meant. The rain lashed and the baby cried. The lights dipped as the power surged.

There was a clatter at the back door. Happy to have the excuse to stop the exchange before it veered into dangerous territory, she went to see who it was. Two figures, one tall and one very small, were standing in the driving rain, unrecognisable in waterproof jackets, hoods drawn around their faces.

'Hello, Anna.' It was Arthur.

'Good gracious. Come in, quick.' She pulled them into the utility room.

'You don't mind, do you? We were passing.' Taliesin offered the implausible explanation. No one *passed* Pen Craig.

She helped them off with their dripping coats and sodden shoes, then took them into the kitchen. Tom had disappeared. 'You're soaked through,' she said to the child. 'Let's get these off.' Without complaint, he allowed her to peel off his trousers. His skinny legs were blue and covered with goose bumps. One of the baby's blankets lay on the back of the chair and Anna wrapped it round his shivering legs. 'There. Very dashing.' He smiled and put his cold hand in hers.

'Sorry about the dramatic arrival. The weather overtook us.' Taliesin looked different. Less biblical. He'd shaved off his beard and his hair was neater. 'I should have phoned but I knew she'd make some excuse not to see us. How are they?'

'Fine. Seren's doing really well.' She filled the kettle. 'Have you eaten?'

'Look. I don't want to make things difficult for you. I think it might be best if you told her we're here. We'll go if she wants us to.'

He was right. It wasn't a good idea to make them too welcome but she couldn't help hugging Arthur. 'Come on.' She led him, blanket wrapped sarong-style round his narrow waist, up the stairs and knocked on Maddy's door. 'Can we come in?'

Maddy was sitting in the rocking chair near the window, Seren feeding at her breast. As if it were the most natural thing in the world, Arthur walked across to them and kissed Maddy on the cheek. 'Does it feel funny?' he asked. 'I think it must tickle.' He stood close, watching the baby working hard, grunting as she sucked. 'She's nice.'

Maddy looked at her mother, questioning her with raised eyebrows.

'Honestly, I had no idea they were coming. Taliesin wants to know if you'll see him.'

'Do I have a choice?'

'Yes, I think you do. He's waiting downstairs for an answer.'

'Please, Maddy. He just wants to make sure that you're OK,' Arthur's little voice pleaded. She had forgotten how perceptive he was.

'Where's Dad?'

'I haven't a clue. Why?'

'He won't be horrid to Tal will he?'

'Of course not.' She wasn't so sure.

'OK. Tell him to come up. Art, can you bring me that box of tissues?' The boy smiled and pottered about the room, charmingly oriental in his wrap-around garment.

Tom was in his office, apparently absorbed in whatever was on his drawing board. 'Who was that?'

'Taliesin and Arthur. They were passing. Don't look at me like that, Tom. They just called to see the baby.' She closed the door before he had time to say anything, and ran on down to the kitchen.

The storm rumbled away into the next valley and a calm descended on the house. After the stickiness of the day, the evening was fresh and invigorating. The honeysuckle near the back door scented the air with twice its normal fragrance and the swallows swooped up the lane, gathering insects beneath the dripping trees.

Arthur came down to join Anna and Tom. 'Maddy told me to tell you that we're staying for supper. What are we going to have?'

Taliesin and Arthur had been upstairs for almost an hour and she'd spent much of that time planning a meal. 'New potatoes and peas from the garden, and boiled ham. Come on. I need some help. You can shell the peas for me.'

'Yummy'. The boy concentrated hard, splitting the pods and dropping the peas into the colander. 'Can I eat one?'

'You can eat as many as you like.'

From then on, for every pea that made it into the pot, one found its way into his mouth. 'When I was a little girl,' she leaned across to confide to him, 'my Mum used to buy us fresh peas instead of sweets.'

'Who was your Mum?'

'A nice lady called Nancy. She was Maddy's grandmother.'

'Is she dead, too?'

She looked at the child, painstakingly removing the tiniest pea from the end of the pod. It was heartbreaking to think that he had no mother to create kitchen rituals and enrich his life. There must be a maternal grandmother somewhere and maybe Charles Leighton had a wife, although Maddy had never mentioned another woman in the house at Brecon. She was sure that he would tell her, if she asked, but she didn't want to interrogate him.

When he'd finished his task, he edged around the table to where Tom was peering at a roll of drawings. She was at the sink, scrubbing the potatoes and held her breath. Please Tom, don't take it out on this child. Arthur moved nearer and nearer, as if he were creeping up on a wild beast. His caution paid off. Tom put his arm around the small shoulder and pulled the boy closer to him. 'Can you see what this is?' He spoke in a school masterly voice.

Arthur studied the drawings, giving them his full consideration. 'A windmill, I think.'

'Correct.'

'Are you going to build one? I've seen lots of them in Wales. It's an excellent way to have free electricity. And it's better for the environment.'

Tom, delighted, slapped his hand on the table. 'Exactly. I only wish our neighbours were half as clever as you are, Art.'

From that moment on, Arthur didn't leave Tom's side and, when they set the table, he asked Anna if he could sit next to him.

They ate supper in the kitchen, Seren sleeping contentedly, reassured by voices and the chink of cutlery on plates. They discussed the violence of the storm. Taliesin complimented Anna on the flavour of her vegetables. Arthur and Tom talked about windmills and the best design for a go-cart. Maddy was relaxed and ate a huge meal. Despite the calm, Anna couldn't help feeling that she was balancing on one leg, on a very narrow ledge.

23

A jangling telephone shattered her dream and she was out of bed before she had opened her eyes. A call this early in the morning could only signal an emergency and she grabbed the receiver. 'Hello?'

It was a relief to hear that it was Steven. 'Hi. Sorry about this but Dad's getting a bit steamed up. The thing is, Dorothy died in the night.'

'At the house?'

'No. The Infirmary. They took her in yesterday. I've just brought Dad back. Would you believe he's putting a new washer on the kitchen tap?'

'Why didn't you phone yesterday?'

'Because I didn't know about it myself until late last night. I came round to find out why he wasn't answering the phone. The woman next door told me where they'd gone. Thank God for nosey neighbours. There wasn't much point in ringing you earlier. After all, she's nothing to us.'

Typical of Steven to see it this way. His life was ruled by cold logic and, applying his parameters, what he said made sense. Why should they care? Dorothy was little more than a stranger who had, incidentally, been their stepmother for a few months.

She thought of the featherweight figure whom she'd last seen lying in her father's bed, and felt sad. Day after day, death fuelled the media, titillating and entertaining. Once in a while, a particular death touched the national psyche. Fairytale princesses and innocent children topped the list. Strangers felt compelled to weep. They placed teddy bears and flowers along railings and grass verges in newly devised rituals. Were they displays of regret or pagan offerings, ensuring that their own loved ones escaped similar harrowing fates? Who would be touched by Dorothy Holton's unnewsworthy death?

Her brother's voice was demanding a response. 'Sorry, Steve. What did you say?'

'How soon can you get here? I'm snowed under at work. It's not a good time for me.' How quickly he had claimed this as *his* crisis.

It wasn't a good time for her either and it must be a dreadful time for her father. Tom, yawning and scratching, arrived at her side. Covering the mouthpiece with her hand, she whispered the gist of the conversation. 'Hang on, Steve. Give me a few minutes. Can I phone you back? I'll sort something out with Tom.'

Tom held her. 'Poor Frank. Poor Dorothy.' It was a relief to hear these few words of compassion after Steven's coldheartedness and she let the tears come.

When her mother had died, she'd been unable to cry. Crying had seemed a self-indulgence, a pathetic response to the enormity of what had happened. Everyone had warned her that she was storing up trouble for herself. 'Have a good cry. It'll do you good,' they bullied. Once or twice she'd gone to the bathroom and locked herself in, trying to squeeze out those mystical tears, guaranteed to avert disaster. None came. But today she wept for Dorothy and all the old ladies who had slipped away without any fuss.

The rest of the household began to stir. Maddy was singing to the baby as she fed her. Arthur came hopping into the kitchen, his hair sticking up in mousey tussocks. He attached himself to Tom and helped put the breakfast things out.

'Did you sleep well,' Tom asked him.

'Dad snores.'

That should answer Tom's unvoiced question about where the visitors had slept.

Taliesin arrived next, unshaven and in the same clothes that he'd been wearing the previous evening. So, he hadn't been expecting to stay overnight. They told him what the early phone call had been about and, as they ate, they discussed what they should do.

'I'll have to go down today. Dad mustn't be on his own. I get the impression Steven's not going to be much help.'

'I'll come with you,' said Tom.

'What about Maddy?'

'There are plenty of people around.'

'We could stay and keep her company, if that would be helpful,' said Taliesin. 'I could pop home and fetch a few things. It only takes an hour or so from here. It would be up to Maddy to decide, of course.'

Before they made their final plans, Anna phoned her father. He sounded tired but more communicative than he had been of late. 'Steven's gone to work and I'm tidying up a bit. They were very helpful at the hospital. They've given me a list of what has to be done.'

'Tom and I will be there sometime this afternoon.'

'Drive carefully. It'll be good to see you both.'

She went to tell Maddy. 'Poor Grandpa. He must feel like The Ancient Mariner, surviving all the people he loves.'

'Not really,' she said. 'He married Dorothy knowing that this would happen. Maybe he wasn't expecting it to be quite this soon. It sounds as if he'd like us to go down today. How would you feel about that?'

'I'll be absolutely fine.' She talked while she deftly

212

changed the baby. 'No third degree about Taliesin?'

'Not if you don't want to talk about it.'

'He's still just a friend, Mum. I was afraid I'd ruined it, coming back to see Brendan, but we had a long talk last night and we're friends again. Where is he now?'

'Finishing breakfast.'

'And Dad…?'

'Don't worry. They're getting on fine. Arthur's completely won your father over. He is an amazing little boy. And I'd better warn you, Taliesin's offering to stay and keep you company.'

'You sound disapproving.'

'Not at all. But I don't think you should raise his hopes…'

'Hopes of what? He's not in love with me, Mum. He'll never get over Sarah.'

She cuddled the baby while Madeleine showered and dressed. Seren's shock of black hair gave her a gypsy look. Her eyes, open and watchful, were the colour of wet slate. Anna rested her cheek against the warm, sweet-smelling face. 'How can I bear to leave you?' she murmured.

Madeleine was determined to stay on her own.

'Ring if you change your mind.' Taliesin extracted her promise. 'Dad's more or less given me the car, so we can be here in a flash.'

They waved as the car slipped off down the lane, Arthur's serious little face peering out from the back window. This time, Tom had sent the child off with a gift. It was a tiny toffee-hammer which had always lived at the back of the 'useful' drawer. It was just the right size and weight for him and he was delighted. 'I'm going to make something for Seren,' he said.

Anna let Celia and Jenny know that Maddy was going to

be on her own for a day or two and they both assured her that they would be around. Then she packed their overnight bag and made a list of things that Maddy might need to know. 'Get whatever vegetables you want from the garden. There's plenty of meat in the freezer. Can you try Flora again? I don't want her to feel left out. Oh, and Len likes a chocolate biscuit with his coffee. Have I forgotten anything?'

'Give Grandpa my love. Tell him I'll see him soon. And don't worry. We'll be fine.' Maddy stood on the doorstep, the baby asleep in her arms.

As they left, Anna noticed Prosser, sitting on the wall near the Redwoods' back door. He must have been listening as she shouted instructions to Maddy.

Frank Hill had done his best. He'd set the kitchen table with cutlery and crockery. He'd even found a tablecloth, albeit slightly creased. 'I don't know what you want to eat,' he said.

'D'you fancy fish and chips, Dad? Tom'll fetch them.'

'That sounds nice.' He ran his hand back and forth over the orange and red nasturtiums that Nancy Hill had embroidered on the cloth, when they were newly-weds.

Her father had accomplished an amazing amount since she had spoken to him. He'd collected the death certificate from the Registrar, and arranged for an undertaker to call next morning. Undertaker. For most of her life she'd assumed that undertakers were so called because they took people under the ground. The true explanation, which she only learned when her mother died – that they undertook to perform certain duties for the bereaved – wasn't nearly as satisfying and she preferred her original interpretation.

'Is there anyone we should notify?'

Frank pointed to a sheet of blue notepaper, pinned to the cork-board near the phone. 'She wrote everything down.

Funeral arrangements. What to do with her things. She was determined not to cause me any problems.'

The list, in Dorothy's neat, school-girlish writing, brought her up sharp. What a determined woman she must have been, to bother with all of this when she had so little time left. It was a shame that they'd not had a chance to get to know each other. She'd left the names and addresses of a cousin in Bournemouth and a nephew up in Scotland. 'Who's this Richard Holton, Dad. In Canada.'

'Her son.'

'Her *son*. I didn't think...'

'They fell out when her husband died. He took all the money out of the family business and buggered off. She tried to contact him, when she knew how ill she was. He never replied. I expect he'll show up for the will reading and he'll get all her money. Unfortunately I gave my word that I'd be civil to him.'

'Poor Dad.' She held his restless hand. 'She was very lucky to find you.'

'And I, her. I think your mother would have liked her. Down to earth. Intelligent. Didn't dye her hair.'

Tom returned with hot, greasy packages. It would have been the perfect evening to eat outside but she didn't want to undermine her father's efforts. She watched him clear his plate, tucking in as if he hadn't eaten for a week. When they'd finished, Frank and Tom went into the garden to cool off and she phoned Maddy. Nothing had happened in the short time they'd been away. Celia had called and Jenny had phoned. 'I got through to Flora. I think she's planning to come over and see you this evening.'

While the men were talking, she went upstairs, wandering from room to room. She left her parents' room (it would always be that) until last. Everything had been cleared away and the bed stripped. On the bed itself were four bulging items of luggage, ranging from a holdall to a huge suitcase, the mattress sagging beneath their weight. Dorothy's belongings.

She opened the wardrobe. Her father's clothes hung in the left-hand side, as they had always done, his shoes lined up along the shelf beneath. The other side was empty, apart from a bunch of lavender looped over a cup hook. The bedside table and the chest of drawers were empty too. It shocked her. He must have packed everything away that afternoon, because surely he wouldn't have done it while Dorothy was still alive.

She ran her finger over the top of the chest, inspecting the skim of dust that obliterated the whorls of her fingerprint. How much skin did a human being shed in a lifetime? It was one of those spectacular statistics that regularly cropped up in articles about asthma and allergies, and was immediately forgotten. On her fingertip, there was sure to be a speck or two of Dorothy. Probably enough to provide the DNA sequence which had made her different from any other human being.

'I'll pass those to her son, if he turns up.' Her father pointed at the cases. He was wearing his slippers and she hadn't heard his soft steps on the stairs. 'It's everything she brought to this house. Up to him what he does with it.'

She stood with her finger extended, not knowing what to do with the specks of the dead woman. It was unthinkable to wipe them off with a tissue. 'I've just got to tell Tom something.' She ran downstairs, out into the back garden and across to the far corner, where her mother had planted the scented roses. There, beneath the pale fragrance of 'Madame Carrière', she plunged her dusty finger into the warm soil and laid the motes of Dorothy to rest.

While she was still crouching, Tom and Flora came round the corner.

'What are you doing, Mum?'

'Nothing. Weeding.'

'Where's Grandpa? Is he OK? I don't know what to say to him.'

'He's fine. Remember, it's not like when Grandma died. Just go and give him a big hug. He's in the bedroom.'

Flora left them and Tom and Anna discussed what they might usefully do. The funeral would probably not be until the middle of the following week. 'Let's try and sort everything out in the next few days, then go back home for the weekend. We'll take your Dad with us, if he'll come. I'm sure Steven could cope at this end for a few days. Does that sound reasonable?'

'Mmm. We're seeing the undertaker tomorrow and I can't think that there's going to be anything complicated about it. It would be nice to get back to Maddy. I don't like leaving her for too long.'

Although Frank looked tired, he was in good spirits and far more responsive than he had been for a long time. Before she returned to Bristol, he held Flora's hand and talked at length about his first wife, telling stories about their courtship and the early years of their marriage. 'Steven did as he was told but your mother wasn't always an easy child. She'd stand there, as nice as pie, then go off and do exactly what she wanted. And she was very stubborn. She'd rather stay in her room for a week than apologise. We had a few battles, didn't we, Anna?'

Flora squealed with delight. 'Really? I can't imagine Mum being stroppy. So that's where Maddy gets it from.'

Had she been a difficult child? If so, when had all that awkwardness metamorphosed to compliance? 'Nonsense.'

Anna and Tom walked Flora to her car. It was still light and two children leaned out of the window in the house opposite, too hot to sleep. The nicotiana plants, scruffy and unimpressive by day, gave off their spectacular evening scent.

'I know this probably isn't the time to discuss it, but remember you suggested we might have an engagement party? Well, Luke and I think it would be fun. Maybe we could make it more of a general knees-up, for everyone. What d'you think? We've never had enough room for a proper 'do' before and, if people brought tents, it needn't cause too much disruption in the house. It's up to you two.' They agreed that, if they held it in the middle of September, it could double as a celebration of their first year at Pen Craig.

By the time they returned to the house, Frank had gone to bed. He'd been using Anna's old bedroom, leaving the guest-room for them.

'I'll phone Madeleine before we go to bed. Let her know our plans.'

The phone rang and rang, until Anna heard her own voice announce that no one was available to take the call.

24

The funeral was to take place the following Wednesday, a week to the day after Dorothy's death. In truth, there hadn't been a great deal to do once they'd collected the death certificate from the Registrar and engaged the services of Mr Tunley, an obsequious man who seemed able to move around without disturbing the air.

'He gives me the creeps, mincing about with that pseudo-sympathetic look on his face. He must be delighted to hear that "our loved one" has "passed on". The more the merrier as far as he's concerned,' said Anna.

'He can hardly start cracking jokes, love. Be fair,' said Tom.

Seeing the man again, in his morning suit, with his slicked down hair and manicured nails, brought it all back. He'd asked the same questions of them, in the same hushed tones, six years ago. Admittedly, it was completely different this time. Apart from being, more or less, a stranger, Dorothy had left complete instructions with everything clearly spelled out. 'Cremation; "All things bright and beautiful"; cheapest coffin available. NO FUSS.' Everything Anna would want for herself. Now they'd set events in motion, Steven would be on hand, to deal with any queries.

Frank, although he'd been quiet, did not seem to be unhappy. He'd slept for hours on end, placing his deckchair in a shady spot in the garden. A couple of days in the garden and he was as brown as a berry. Peace had settled on him and she recognised how tense and crabby he'd been for quite a long time. 'And I've never seen him eat so much,' she said to Tom, when they went to the supermarket on a cupboard-stocking mission. It delighted her to see him clear his plate, then push it towards her for 'a smidgen more.'

The traffic wasn't too bad and they were home by late morning. The heat had pushed the silver thread of the wall thermometer well over the eighty-degree mark, nevertheless the back door was shut.

'We're back,' shouted Anna, dumping her bag on the cool flagstones of the utility room. 'Maddy?'

While Tom unpacked the car and ushered Frank Hill into the house, she went in search of Madeleine and found her, in the sitting room, feeding the baby. Seren had fallen asleep at her breast, flushed with contentment and the breathless heat. Maddy laid her gently in the carrycot and fastened the substantial nursing bra.

Anna looked down at her granddaughter. 'I'm sure she's grown. Is that silly?'

'You've only been gone three days, Mum.'

'She looks different somehow.' She ran the back of her index finger across the baby's cheek, but Seren was submerged in milky sleep and didn't twitch.

'Everything OK here?'

The pause was fractionally too long before Madeleine replied, 'Of course.'

'What happened? Something happened, didn't it?'

'Nothing... I don't know.' Tears flooded Maddy's eyes. 'Oh, Mum, I was so scared.'

Anna's heart thudded. 'What? What scared you?'

Between sobs, and with stuttering phrases, Maddy

explained. On Thursday, the day after they had gone to Bath, she had put Seren's carrycot, cat-net securely in place, on the wall outside the back door, in the shade of the house. While the baby slept, she washed the kitchen floor. 'I wanted it to be tidy and clean when you came home. After I finished, I put the mop outside. It was awful, Mum.'

Anna held her breath.

'The net was off. Gone. We looked everywhere. Uncle Bill, Auntie Jenny, all of us. It wasn't in the carrycot. Not on the floor. Nowhere.'

She had a vivid picture of the unprotected cot. 'Could the wind…?'

'It was absolutely still. Not a breath of wind. You do understand what I'm saying? It wasn't there.'

'But Seren was alright?'

'Yes. But what if I hadn't gone out? What if Auntie Celia's cat…? She was crying again now.

Nothing had happened. A piece of net had gone missing and nothing had happened to a sleeping baby. Relieved laughter rose in Anna's throat.

But it wasn't just any old sleeping baby. It was Seren. Their baby. Maddy was taking deep breaths, expelling the air slowly. 'I'm getting more and more scared every day. I don't think I can do this. It's too much responsibility. I daren't take my eyes off her, in case something goes wrong. In case she stops breathing or someone steals her. Why didn't you warn me it would be like this?'

Anna had warned her of course, time and time again. It was implicit in all those exhortations. 'Look both ways,' 'Don't take sweets,' 'Stay with the others,' 'Be home before dark.' She had suffered from the day Flora was born and, since that moment, the world had grown more and more threatening.

'Auntie Celia was really sweet. I stayed with them on Thursday and Friday nights. She said they didn't mind the

221

broken sleep.'

So this was why her calls had gone unanswered. The very time she *should* have been concerned, she'd assumed that Maddy was in the bath or fast asleep, not taking refuge in a neighbour's house. But why had her daughter been so terrified? She wasn't one to get hysterical.

Maddy shuddered and shook herself, sloughing off the clinging menace. 'How's Grandpa Frank?' Her voice rang with false brightness.

'Oh, God. I'd forgotten all about him.'

Leaving Maddy with a promise to return shortly, she went in search of Tom. It was likely that he'd gone to check the garden or open his mail – anywhere to escape the pressure to make small-talk with her father. Frank was standing, stoically, in the middle of the kitchen, holdall at his feet, like a refugee in a flickering old newsreel. 'Tea, Dad?'

'Just a glass of water, please. Then I may go and take a stroll around 'the estate', if that's alright with you..' He took the tumbler she offered and drank it slowly, making little gulping noises. 'Adam's ale. That's what my father used to call it.'

Tom started straight in with, 'You *must* have forgotten to put the net on.' The effect was predictable and Maddy accused him of never believing her or taking her seriously. She flounced out but Anna noted that she slammed the door quietly, as the mother of a sleeping baby always does. Tom followed and she heard him apologising for his thoughtlessness. Progress indeed.

The house, suddenly filled with four generations, had become a lot smaller. Every room was cluttered with mounds of baby clothes or caches of her father's belongings. There were several pairs of his spectacles, in labelled cases, on the arm of the sofa and a trail of hankies and sweet wrappers wherever he went.

Tom could use his work as an excuse to escape whenever he needed solitude, but her only haven was her studio. This was fine if she wanted to work but it wasn't the most comfortable place to read or sit daydreaming. Wherever else she went in the house, she got roped in for baby minding or keeping an old man company. It was temporary of course. They would be going back to Bath for the funeral, but she could already see that her father was enjoying the company. She'd spotted him filling in the application for a Senior Coach Card so it looked like he would be visiting them more often from now on.

'I was starting to get the hang of being Anna Wren,' she said to Jenny, who had just finished briefing Eric on his tasks for the coming week. 'I think I must have been a bit depressed when the girls left. I couldn't work out what I was for. My function. Coming here was supposed to help me work that out. Now I've slipped back to being Frank Hill's daughter and Madeleine's mother.'

'And Seren's grandmother. Don't forget that one.'

They moved into the shade of the overhanging hazel trees. The heat shimmered off a field of ripening wheat and Anna had to squint against the glare.

'Will Maddy stay, d'you think?' Jenny asked.

'For a while. She's got no chance of finding a job. Childminders are ridiculously expensive and, anyway, I don't think she'd trust anyone to look after the baby.'

'Well, you make sure you don't get taken advantage of. I certainly don't intend to provide unpaid childcare for any grandchildren I might have.'

It was easy for Jenny to say this but would she be able to refuse Sophie, or her two sons, when they turned up with a baby and were desperate for support? Yes, of course she would. The Redwoods had plenty of money and Jenny would simply pay someone else to do it.

'Watch out,' said Anna, pulling Jenny's arm. They stood aside as Bill's car came up the lane and swept around the corner. He bipped the horn and waved.

'Did you see Sally while you were away?' Jenny asked. 'It's all gone a bit quiet on that front, hasn't it? Any gossip from Luke?'

'No. Nothing at all. I'm really beginning to believe she's gone for good.'

'Well they won't stand a chance of getting back together, if he carries on the way he's going.' She moved closer and lowered her voice. 'I was in the summerhouse the other afternoon, reading, and he wandered in. He gave me a load of guff about being lonely and needing a woman to talk to. He knew perfectly well that Peter was away. We had a couple of glasses of wine and then he had the nerve to tell me that he'd always fancied me.'

'What did you say?'

'I thought he was joking at first, until he tried to grope me.'

'Did you tell Peter about it?'

'Of course. He roared with laughter. Apparently he likes the idea of my being a sex object. Says it turns him on. Don't look so horrified, Anna. I thought he'd probably tried it on with you, too.'

Would Tom have laughed? Wouldn't he have beaten Bill senseless if he'd known about the kiss? She avoided Jenny's implied question. 'Maddy mentioned that she'd seen him with Celia.'

'Really? She hasn't said anything to me and we've spent quite a lot of time together lately. Frankly, I don't think she's very happy.'

'She was very kind to Madeleine, while we were away.'

'Mmmm. Maybe we three should go out for lunch soon. Have a good natter. It's hopeless here, with all the interruptions.'

'When I get back from the funeral, perhaps. I can't abandon Dad at the moment.'

'Of course. Shall we pencil in next Friday? It's sure to be all right with Celia. They never go out. We could pop up to Shrewsbury and do some shopping.'

Anna had imagined that this sort of thing would be happening all the time. Little jaunts with her friends. Good company on tap. But she could count, on the fingers of one hand, the times that they'd been out together. She did miss Sally. Her intelligence and wit more than compensated for her irritating traits. The foursome had divided into pairs and Jenny and Celia had become very palsy. Then Sally's departure and Madeleine's return had altered the balance of everything.

Tom invited his father-in-law to help rationalise the log supply. He was aiming to stock-pile enough wood for the winter and had built a log store against the outhouse wall. He constantly encouraged everyone to drag back a fallen branch whenever they went for a walk up to the wood, but he was the only one who ever bothered to do it.

'Say no if you're too tired, Dad. We want you to do whatever you feel like doing,' said Anna.

'Sounds good to me. I need some fresh air. Tom can do the manhandling and I'll tell him where he's going wrong.'

When he was younger her father had seemed a well-built man, taller than Tom but not as solid. Watching him walking across the yard, she could see that he had shrunk. His neck looked too thin to support his head and he'd had to roll up the legs of Tom's old overalls several times, to keep them from dragging on the floor. She ran after him with a tattered straw hat and, when he turned for her to put it on his head, she kissed his cheek. 'What's that in aid of?'

'To stop you getting sunstroke.' She chose to misunderstand his question.

Back in the kitchen, Maddy was organising the baby in the sling on her chest, fiddling with the straps. 'Judith's home and I thought we might go for a stroll. We could go up to the wood, see if it's cooler up there.'

'D'you want to leave Seren with me and have an hour off?'

'Thanks, Mum, but I'm fine. We'll be back in an hour or so.'

When they'd gone, she phoned Steven at work. He assured her that he had checked with Mr Tunley, only an hour before, and everything was proceeding smoothly. He didn't ask about their father and the call finished abruptly when his secretary called him away to do something that couldn't wait another minute.

There was no question of cooking on such a stifling day and, with nothing to do in the kitchen and everyone engaged elsewhere, she had an hour or two to herself. The August sky was almost colourless and there was no breeze to give relief. The air smelled of hot car oil and she remembered one similarly scorching summer's day when Tom and Bill had attempted to fry an egg on a manhole cover. The girls were young and they were on holiday, with the Davis family, in west Wales. The egg hadn't cooked and had made a terrible mess and they had laughed about it for days. It had been a wonderful holiday, even if Maddy had spent the whole week terrorising Emily with a bucket of crabs.

Gardening was out of the question and she made for the shade of her studio. The thick walls of the old building regulated the temperature. In the winter it was bearable, even when the north-east wind drove the snow up the valley.

And in the summer it was a cool retreat.

It was less than a week since she'd started to model the animals for Noah's Ark but Dorothy's death, and the trip to Bath, had pushed the new project out of her head. This was how she would spend her afternoon, making some more creatures to send in, two by two. But neither her hippos nor her horses would shape up and, after several attempts, she lost patience and abandoned them.

The back door to Number One was open and she could hear Bill whistling in the kitchen. She slammed the studio door and crossed the yard, slapping her flat sandals on the smooth paviers. He looked up and waved to her from the window.

'Hi, Bill,' she shouted, wandering into the kitchen. He stood at the sink, balancing a pile of dirty crockery. His tight khaki shorts and yellow polo-shirt made him look like an overgrown Boy Scout.

'Sorry about the get up. If we have a continuous spell of anything I tend to get caught out. This is my last hot weather outfit. If the temperature doesn't drop tomorrow, I'm done for.' He grinned.

'I think you look rather … stylish.'

'You're very kind. And you look as lovely as ever. Can't think why Tom lets you out of his sight. I wouldn't. Fancy a cold drink? Or something stronger?'

'I don't want to stop you doing that. Come to think of it, why are you doing that?'

'The dishwasher's broken. Well, not broken exactly. Stuck shut.'

'Is it…?'

'Yes, full to bursting. That's why I've been using this stuff.'

Anna could see that 'this stuff' was Sally's exquisite Villeroy and Bosch dinner service, the one she'd bought to commemorate their silver anniversary and which took pride of place in the china cabinet. 'D'you think that's a good idea? Isn't it a bit fragile for every day?'

'No choice. It's this or the old plastic picnic set and I'm buggered if I'm going to eat off plastic plates. Can't see the point of having the stuff, if you can't use it. The chap's coming to have a look at the machine on Monday.' He turned back to the bowl of soapy water and started dunking the plates.

'I'll have a white wine, if you've got a bottle open.' She gave a belated reply to his offer of a drink.

'Oops.' One of the plates slipped from his wet hands, back into the bowl. Fishing it out, he inspected the rim. 'Only a tiny chip. No real damage.'

25

They carried the bottle of wine up to the sitting room, where Bill assured her it would be cooler. 'Catches a through draught up here.'

The Chardonnay was chilled and far too easy to drink. She was thirsty and, after a couple of glasses, it was the most natural thing in the world to slip off her shoes and lie back on the sofa. Bill began massaging her feet, holding each one firmly, gently kneading the flesh and flexing the ligaments. He worked his way up, pushing his thumbs hard enough into her calf muscles to cause a satisfying pain. He took it slowly and, without a word from her apart from the occasional involuntary 'Mmmm', sensed what gave her pleasure. Odd, considering how big and clumsy his hands were, but her eyes were closed and his touch was thoughtful and tender. She drifted.

He had already proved himself to be an accomplished kisser and he confirmed this, as he lowered himself carefully on top of her and opened his lips on hers. As she responded, she heard Tom, calling from the garden, but it didn't sound an urgent summons and he only called her name twice.

Anna had everything under control. They were both fully clothed and, although she could feel that he was aroused, the stout cotton layers of his shorts and underpants separated them. Her skirt had been there, too, when they started but somehow it had ridden up to her waist. He pressed down harder and it became more difficult for her to breathe.

'Thank you, thank you. I'm so happy.' She opened her eyes. There was a soppy look on his face, as he drew his head back, leering at her. His fleshy cheeks wobbled and a thread of saliva hung from his lips. He didn't look like Bill any more.

'What d'you mean, thank you?'

'I love you, Anna.'

She felt his hand groping for the zip on his shorts, pinching the tender skin on the inside of her thighs. 'No. Stop. Stop it.' She heaved herself up and pushed him away, her forehead bumping his slack mouth. He recoiled and slid sideways onto the floor. She pulled her skirt down, grabbed her sandals and ran down the stairs and out of the house.

When the family reconvened in the kitchen at the end of the afternoon, no one asked her how she had spent her time but, by the time she started preparing supper, she felt detached and dizzy. It might have been a touch of heat stroke, or more likely the effect of the white wine. She had a suspicion that they'd finished off a litre over the course of an hour.

Madeleine chatted to Frank, reminiscing about a trip to the seaside one long-ago August day. 'It was hot, like today and, on the way back to the car, we lay in the shade of the bracken, eating jelly babies. Flora, me, you and Grandma. Where would that have been?'

'Three Cliffs. Or Pennard. She loved those Gower beaches.' And he loved to talk about Nancy.

Tom wandered around, singing to the baby cradled in the crook of his arm. Seren was awake but very calm, staring up into his face, her oily blue eyes unblinking. 'You are my sunshine, my only sunshine...' Just like he'd sung to their babies. '...You make me happy when skies are grey.' Here they were, content and peaceful, like any other family on a perfect summer's day.

The lettuce which Tom had picked less than an hour earlier needed washing and, as she pulled the individual leaves away, a fat caterpillar dropped into the water. It had been eating its way out from the centre of the lettuce and the inner leaves were slimy with its dark green excrement. Her stomach churned but she managed to get to the cloakroom before she was sick. Clammy and shaking, she steadied herself, waiting for the next wave of nausea. It came, a trace of wine lingering with the smell of vomit. And again, until she knew that it was over.

'You OK, love?' Tom, baby now over his shoulder, pushed the door open.

She nodded and tried a smile. 'Must be the heat. I'll stay here for a bit, just in case.'

Maddy came and took Seren.

Tom felt the back of her neck. He handed her a towel, to wipe away the sweat, and filled a glass with cold water. 'Rinse your mouth with this.'

'Thanks. I'm sorry.'

'For what? Don't be silly. Here.' He lowered the lavatory seat and she sat down, overcome with a fit of shivering. 'Give it a minute or two and then I think we should get you up to bed.'

'What about supper?'

'We'll sort all that out. Come on.'

He helped her up the stairs. Her head felt tender and her stomach was cramping.

'Would a shower make you feel nice?' He eased her clothes off as if she were a small child, then sponged her down gently in barely-warm water. By the time he dried her, she was almost incapable of moving. He coaxed her across the landing and steered her towards the bed, flipping back

231

the cotton sheet. It was wonderful to lie down and not to fight the swirling giddiness. He drew the curtains to dim the room and, kissing her lightly on her forehead, went out, shutting the door behind him.

'Feeling better, Mum?'

'I think I've been asleep. What's the time?'

'About eight, I think.'

'Did you have something to eat? I don't know what…'

'Yes. Don't worry. Grandpa Frank's gone for a walk and Dad's doing the washing up. I think Seren may be asleep.'

Raising her hand to her forehead, Anna touched the skin, aware of a slight lump where she had collided with Bill's teeth. No one had mentioned it, so perhaps there was nothing much to see.

Maddy stood at the open window, peering down into the yard. 'Bill and Celia look so tiny from here. They haven't a clue anyone's spying on them.' She leaned forward. 'I've always thought Bill was a bit of a dark horse.'

'What?'

'Well, haven't you? He probably needs a secret life to escape from Sally. She can be a bit controlling sometimes.'

'Nonsense. What are they doing?'

'Talking. I can't see their faces but it looks as if it's serious. Hang on, Bill's putting a bag in his car. Is he off somewhere? Yes, he's getting in.'

She wished she could time-travel back twenty-four hours and re-start this horrid day. What in heaven's name had come over her? Could it be the menopause? Mood swings and erratic behaviour were commonly quoted symptoms but, then again, so was a decrease in libido. Was she trying to make up for lost time or something? Tom had been only her second sexual partner and maybe she was feeling a bit short-changed. However she looked at it, it was definitely

Sally's fault. If Sally had accepted comfortable middle age here, with her husband, none of this would have happened.

'… and he's been asking about us … Mum?'

'What?'

'I said Brendan's been in touch with Judith. Remember she gave him a lift that time? He's been asking about the baby and me. He's talking about coming to see his daughter.'

Anna could think of nothing to say but Maddy wasn't prepared for her to remain silent.

'Say something, Mum. Don't lie there looking pained.'

'It's just that … I thought it was over between you. You said he was a big mistake.'

'You'd all love that, wouldn't you? You want me to settle for Tal and for everything to be neat and tidy. Like Flora's going to settle down with boring old Luke and you've settled for boring old Dad. I think you're all jealous that I …'

'How dare you.'

'What?'

'Will you stop behaving as if you're different from the rest of us. You're not. Grown-ups don't always get what they want. Now you've got a child of your own, you've got to put her first. I'm sick and tired of having to listen to everyone's problems, then being shouted at when I tell them what I think. You've obviously made up your mind what you're going to do, so there's little point in discussing it further. Could you go now, please? I feel dreadful.' Anna rolled onto her side, pulling the sheet up over her face. It felt good to let her feelings out. Tom did it all the time. Let him play peacemaker.

She stayed under the cover, waiting for the door to slam but the room was quiet, apart from the summer noises brought in on the freshening breeze. Before she knew it, she was sliding away, down the echoing passageway towards sleep.

She reached across the cool sheet but Tom wasn't there.

She angled her wrist to catch the moonlight on her watch. Almost two. Where could he be? The vomiting had left her with a raging thirst and she went to the bathroom and drank two beakers of water. The house was silent, so they must all be asleep somewhere.

The kitchen was extremely tidy. There was nothing to be washed up, nothing drying in the rack. In the fridge, several plates of supper leftovers lay neatly covered with cling film. The ironing pile had disappeared from the utility room. Her fairy godmother must have flown in while she was sleeping.

Wide-awake and ravenous, she took a raspberry yoghurt from the fridge, condensation forming on the cold plastic under her hand. One tub didn't satisfy her and she took another. Blackcurrant this time. Her empty stomach cramped a little but her head was clear and she couldn't prevent thoughts from rushing in. All those months avoiding the man and then marching in and asking him to…what? What had she been asking him to do? It was essential to fathom it out now, whilst she still remembered exactly how it had been.

Long before Bill had kissed Celia or groped Jenny, he'd chosen her and she'd rather come to count on his admiration. Knowing that Bill's passion was smouldering away had been rather thrilling. Wasn't it selfish, though, expecting him to stay keen, when he received no jot of encouragement? All she'd been trying to do was to offer him a little something in return. But only a little something.

Whoever had worked the miracles in the kitchen had forgotten to lock the back door. She had lost track of her family, where they were sleeping and what they were doing. After the heat, the night air was deliciously refreshing and the moon was a silver-white disc. The stones felt neither hot nor cold beneath her bare feet, as she tip-toed to sit on the low wall opposite the back door. All the houses were in darkness, as she would have expected them to be at this time of night. Bill's car was absent. He hadn't come back. Raising her fingers to her forehead, she pressed the tender spot again, the only evidence that anything had happened.

Footsteps crunched on the gravel path at the side of the outhouse and Tom appeared out of the velvety shadows. 'Hi. Feeling better?'

'Much. I must have had too much sun. Now I've had too much sleep. Where have you been?'

'I started off in the living room. You were sleeping so peacefully I didn't want to disturb you. But I was restless. Your father and I found a badger sett yesterday, up in the wood, and I'd decided to go and take a look.'

'Did you see anything?'

'No. They must have heard me coming or caught my scent. But I'll try again tomorrow, maybe.'

'Can I come?'

'Only if you roll in cow dung to cover up your lovely smell. And you mustn't utter one single word.'

'It's a deal.'

'And we'll have to stay stock still for four or five hours.'

'My idea of a great night out.'

Seren's intermittent cry came from the open window, above. The light went on and she heard Maddy cooing the familiar words of comfort that all mothers whisper to their fretful babies.

26

The weather broke at the end of the week. After the long, dry spell the first giant raindrops unleashed earthy scents from the baked soil and desiccated grass.

'Ideal conditions for the party.' Tom in shorts, wellington boots and waterproof jacket, dripped into the utility room, carrying a bucket of potatoes.

'Come on. It's not for a couple of weeks. And the garden could do with it.'

The house was theirs again. Maddy had stayed on in Bath after the funeral, to keep her grandfather company. He was very positive about the arrangement, readily accepting the disruption that accompanies a four-week-old baby. Transporting Seren, with all her attendant equipment, had necessitated towing the trailer. 'It's like the arrival of the Queen of Sheba,' Frank had commented, cheerfully. They were the only mourners to arrive at the funeral with a trailer but Frank was sure that Dorothy would have been 'tickled pink'.

'You think we should go ahead with this party, do you? Won't it look a bit odd to celebrate an engagement without either of the bridegroom's parents being present?' Tom hadn't been keen on the party but Flora never demanded much of them and he had gone along with it.

'They're Luke's parents. I think he should have the final

say.'

'I can't understand what Bill's playing at, can you? If he needs time to "get his head around things," I would have thought he'd be better off at home than in Aberystwyth.' Tom pulled the postcard off the board, scanning the over-bright picture. 'The Promenade.' He turned it over. '"Trying to get my head around things. Could someone water the plants?" Does that sound like a man who's thinking of hosting a party?'

'He's old enough to decide for himself and it's good to hear he's OK.'

'Why has it taken him this long to crack up? Sally's been gone a couple of months and he was doing fine.'

'I expect he thought she'd come back. Maybe he's not so sure now. Did you go in there today?'

'Yes. It smells funny, but I couldn't find anything obvious. I've opened a few windows. There were some letters, too. Of course Len must have twigged that something's up. It's probably all round the village by now.' He pulled a clutch of wet envelopes from his pocket. 'What d'you think we should do with these?'

The paper was sodden from the rain and already starting to disintegrate. Two were bills, but the third was a pale blue envelope, addressed by hand, to 'Bill Davis'. The ink had run but, nevertheless, Anna recognised the writing. 'It's from Sally. She always uses a fountain pen.'

He peered at the smudged postmark. 'London. Wonder what that means.'

Over lunch they debated what to do with Sally's letter, as they had no forwarding address. They tried to ease open the flap of the envelope with a knife, and would have succeeded had the paper been wetter. In the end, Anna phoned Flora at work. 'We've got a letter from Sally here, addressed to Bill. Can Luke contact him and find out what he wants us to do with it? It could be important.'

'She wrote to Luke, too. From Heathrow. She's gone to India, to meet Emily.'

'Good grief.'

'Exactly. Luke's not very happy about it. He says he feels like a parent with a couple of delinquent children. Uncle Bill's not answering his mobile, just sending text messages that don't really make any sense. It's getting a bit much. I'm beginning to think we'll have to call the party off. At this rate, the whole Davis family will have run away.'

Tom cheered up considerably at the prospect of cancellation. To add to his good humour, the rain stopped and within ten minutes the roofs were steaming in the sunshine.

Peter and Mark emerged from the Redwoods' back door, golf clubs rattling in their bags. They were off to the municipal course and invited Tom to join them. He glanced at Anna for permission. She was planning to do some weeding whilst the soil was damp and, when it was cooler, to pop in to Ludlow for the shopping. 'Off you go. Take as long as you like. We'll have a late supper.'

'Celia and Jenny are in the house, if you want some company,' said Mark.

She shook her head. 'I've got loads of things to do. Don't worry about me.'

The soil, softened by the downpour, responded to her hoe and, in no time at all, she had cleared the encroaching chickweed and couch grass from the bean and pea rows. The rain had revived the flagging spinach and the leaves stood dark and shiny. The moisture would swell the onions, too, and ensure that the cabbage seed germinated quickly. She would be soon be looking for sturdy seedlings to plant out for next spring's crop.

When Bill left Pen Craig, certain possibilities went with

him. There was no chance that she might bump into him in the yard or that he would wander into the summerhouse while she was reading. He wouldn't be watching her through the kitchen window as she did the washing up. He wasn't going to be in the yard with Tom and the others, discussing the swimming pool. Nor lurking in the shadows, waiting to kiss her or make love to her.

She cleaned the tools and let her imagination slip the leash. When Tom was around, she never indulged in such thoughts. Working to rules made things simpler. Besides, the Bill business had nothing to do with what she felt for Tom. It was more as if she had a hoard of memories and feelings, safely hidden away, which she could summon up at will. Shorthand for the phenomenon might be 'fantasy world' but it was more subtle than that. Whatever it was, it was proving to be much more enjoyable now that Bill had gone and she didn't have to deal with the reality of the man, whom she wasn't even sure she liked.

She filled the kettle and wrote a shopping list while she waited for it to boil. Tom's navy linen suit needed to go to the dry cleaners'. He looked very dashing when he wore it and she wanted it to be clean and pressed in case the party did go ahead. Then there were her library books to take back. And she ought to start looking for Jenny's birthday present because it always took longer to find a suitable gift for Jenny, than for any of the others. Finally there was food shopping, although they didn't need so much now that they'd reverted to being a two-person household.

The suit was in Tom's wardrobe and she sang to herself as she ran up the stairs. Madeleine's room was quiet and tidy without its occupants. She missed the baby, but they would be back soon enough and she vowed to make the most of the peace.

Immediately she walked into the bedroom, she knew

that someone was there. Swinging round, she saw him, half hidden by the open door. He wore a tweed suit and his face was shiny with sweat and expressionless, as if it were in neutral, waiting to start a journey. He kicked the door shut.

She had often wondered how she would react in a crisis. Would she turn the steering wheel the right way on the patch of ice? Would she remember the Heimlich manoeuvre or whatever it was called, if someone were choking on food? Could she perform mouth to mouth resuscitation effectively? These were things that she'd rehearsed but she'd never been told what to do if she came upon an intruder in her bedroom. In this case, the intruder wasn't even a stranger which made it, somehow, more shocking. 'Hello, Mr Prosser.' What a ridiculous thing to say.

'Hello, Mrs Wren … Anna.' He rolled her name around his tongue, as if it were an insult.

Was there a helmet, clamped over her ears, distorting sounds and doing something weird to her eardrums? 'Can I … is there … what?' She was finding it impossible to assemble enough words to make even the simplest sentence.

'You're supposed to be in the garden.'

'I was. But. But… Tom? Tom?' She raised her voice, calling for him, although she knew he wouldn't come.

'I'm not stupid, Mrs Wren. Tom's off golfing, isn't he? You told him not to rush back, didn't you?'

Oh God, oh God, he must have been out there in the yard, listening. Her tongue, dry as chalk, felt as if it had swelled inside her mouth. 'Celia and Jenny…'

'…went off together, in the car. To Shrewsbury.'

Why hadn't she done what Mark suggested and gone with them? Right now she could be sitting in a café, drinking coffee and gossiping about Sally. She couldn't speak. Her brain was a tangle of disconnections, incapable of logical thought. Ugly, terrifying words flashed through her mind, like neon signs tearing the darkness. Rape. Torture. Murder. Assault. None of them held any hope or reassurance.

Prosser avoided eye contact and stood, clenched fists at his sides. Something that might have been a bra strap dangled from his jacket pocket. He was acting tough but he must be as scared as she was. Anger bubbled up through the incapacitating fear. How dare he come snooping, especially when the room was in such a mess? Yesterday's knickers lay on the floor next to the laundry basket, and the bed was unmade.

He held something out towards her. 'You never thanked me for bringing them back.' The earrings lay in the palm of his hand. 'Aren't you going to wear them for me? Go on.'

Not knowing what else to do, she took the earrings from him, her fingertips brushing his calloused palm, and fumbled the hooks through her ears. 'I don't think they go with my outfit, do you?' She immediately regretted the puerile attempt at humour. Then, without warning, she was overcome with a need to urinate. 'I really have to go to the bathroom. Please. I can't wait.'

She took a step forwards and, for one second, it appeared that he might stand aside and allow her to pass, but he held up his hand, making her stop and plead some more.

'Please.' It would be humiliating to wet herself and she was near to tears.

He edged the door open, never taking his eyes off her face. 'Go on then.' There was a half-chance to dash down the stairs but she was so desperate to empty her bladder that she could think of nothing else. She ran across to the bathroom and he followed her, standing in the doorway, back against the doorframe, arm stretched across to the form a shoulder-high barrier. He averted his eyes when she pulled down her cotton trousers and sat on the lavatory. While she urinated, she looked around for anything which might help her. The window was open but it was too small and, anyway, they were two storeys above the paved yard. A pair of nail scissors rested on the rim of the bath, where she'd been cutting her toenails that morning. She turned to pull the toilet paper from the roll and tried to snatch up the scissors, but she misjudged it and they clattered into the bath.

'That's it.' He signalled her to stand and she pulled up her clothes, hunching forward to conceal herself. Then he pulled the black leather belt from the loops on his trousers. Was he was going to undo his flies? A scream rose in her throat as he came towards her and she had time to imagine what might come next. He signalled her to turn round, yanking her arms backwards, using the belt to strap her wrists behind her. He pointed across the landing. 'Take it very slow.' He walked behind her, gripping the several twists of leather and guiding her down the stairs. He was breathing noisily, through his nose, like an overwrought animal. Occasionally he pulled on the belt, tweaking her arms, and causing her shoulder joints to shriek with the pain. Unable to use her arms to balance or hold the banister, it was difficult to walk and impossible to run.

Through the open door, the clock in the sitting room showed ten to four. Tom would be starting his round of golf. Flora was at work and Maddy might be strolling in the park at the end of Cliveden Road. It was a beautiful afternoon to be out in the fresh air.

When they reached the kitchen, he made her sit on the sofa. This room was a particularly dangerous place to loiter with a psychopath. (Was it Bill or Mark who had identified Prosser's tendencies?) Every drawer was stuffed with weapons. Knives, scissors, screwdrivers. Tom kept some of his power tools in the utility room and Prosser knew everything that went on here, so he would surely know that, too.

It is a well-documented phenomenon that hostages stand a better chance of survival if they can form a bond with their captors. Anna had been fascinated by an article about it in one of the 'Sundays', following a plane hijacking. She gave it a try. 'Shall we have a cup of tea? Or a drink of lemonade? You look rather hot.'

He ignored her questions, staring around the room. 'Why did you have to change everything? Spoil it.'

Before she could ask what he meant, the phone rang, making them both jump. She wondered how her heart could be pounding so fast, without bursting. The answer-machine cut in and she listened for a familiar voice but whoever it was rang off without leaving a message. Prosser sat at the table, rubbing his hands back and forth across the wooden surface, staring at the wall opposite. Now and again he glanced at her and once he checked that the belt was still tight around her wrists. Her shoulders were aching so much that she wanted to scream. The only way she found to ease the pain was to lean forward, allowing her trussed arms to rest on her lower back.

After about five minutes Prosser stood up. 'OK. Here's what we're going to do. We're going outside now and I need the keys to your car. And don't mess about, because I've got this.' He drew a Sabatier knife from the wooden knife-block and she wished that Flora hadn't bought them such a murderous house-warming present.

A germ of an idea had formed during that five minutes in the kitchen. It was essential to leave a clue. Some indication that she hadn't gone shopping and that something unusual had happened. Her handbag was on the corner of the table. She always took it with her, even on a trip down to Cwm Bont. If Tom came in and saw it, he would be sure to know that she was in trouble.

'I'll bring your handbag. That would be a dead give-away,

wouldn't it?'

He was behind her, tugging the belt again, giving her no opportunity to take anything or leave anything behind. He shut the back door, locking it with the keys from her handbag, leaving the house exactly as she would leave if she'd gone shopping.

The car keys were in the ignition. Prosser pushed her into the driver's seat, her torso thrust forward to accommodate her bound arms, then he hurried around to the passenger's side and climbed in next to her, shutting and locking the doors. He tossed her bag on to the back seat. Finally he untied her wrists. Her shoulders hurt and she gasped as she flexed them, attempting to restore the blood flow and ease the aching. Her wrists, too, throbbed and there were red ruts where the leather had bitten into the flesh.

'Look, Mr Prosser, can't we sort this out? Why don't you go home and we'll forget all about it? It's not too late.' Pathetic, but she had to give it a try.

He still had the knife but now he was holding it vertically, in his left hand, the point resting on the dashboard. His other arm was draped across the back of her seat and she could smell the sweat from his armpit. 'You must think I'm thick.'

While they were inside the house, there had been a glimmer of hope. Now, as he instructed her to start the car and drive away, he had taken command and, from here on, they would be playing by his rules. At that moment and involuntarily, she became detached from her body, hovering somewhere just above her own head. It was interesting and, more to the point, felt much safer up here, as if she were watching a film at the cinema. This had happened once before. On the day that her mother died, she'd spent most of it looking down at Anna Wren as she spoke her lines and went through the motions. Later, when she was ready to talk about it, the doctor had explained that this literal detachment was a common defence strategy and it might well have saved her from suffering a complete breakdown.

27

As they drove down the lane towards the road, she remembered Tom asking her to fill up with petrol at the supermarket. The gauge was into the red sector which gave them about forty miles' driving, a fact they'd established when forced to soft-pedal it home from a day out in petrol-less mid-Wales. If Prosser intended to go far, they would have to stop for fuel. Then she would get her chance.

'Left at the bottom.' They were heading away from the village.

Firmly back inside her body now, rivulets of perspiration trickled down between her breasts and across her back, soaking into the waistband of her trousers. Occasionally, Prosser dragged a sleeve across his crimson face. His left hand was resting on his knee, the knife dangling down between his legs. Deep breaths, deep breaths. Deep breaths did nothing to calm her, and made her throat even drier.

A Land Rover came towards them and she flicked the headlights at the oncoming vehicle, but they must have been invisible in the strong sunlight and there was no response from the driver. 'Naughty, naughty.' Prosser brought the point of the knife round to rest on her thigh. He twisted in the seat, staring at her, then raised the knife, tapping it on her left earring. The noise, so close to her ear, sounded like a cracked bell. 'We've had some fun with these, haven't we?'

At the T-junction, she automatically indicated right, towards Ludlow, the direction she usually took. He reached across, shaking his head, and pushed the indicator the other way. She had imagined that he would want to get as far away from Pen Craig as possible but this road would lead them back on themselves. There was a fair volume of traffic but she had no way of alerting passing vehicles to her predicament. Even if anyone recognised her, they would assume she was giving someone a lift, not being kidnapped by a homicidal maniac.

They had travelled less than a mile when he muttered 'Next left.' Once again his instruction caught her out. They turned up the winding road, past the spot where she and Arthur had waited for Bill to fetch them. After their adventure they had revisited this valley and she knew that the road narrowed, eventually petering out into a muddy track that followed the stream to its source. The sides of this valley were steep and wooded, and it was cooler in the shade.

Then she knew where he was taking her.

'Swing out wide and drop down into first,' he instructed.

She slewed the car into the lane, half-hidden between the high hedges. The wheels spun on the loose gravel but she managed to avoid stalling. The house loomed up, drab and ugly amongst the summer trees. An assortment of animals still dangled from the fence, like bunches of dried seaweed. 'Up through the gate and in there.' He pointed at a corrugated tin shed.

So this was it. She wasn't going to stop for petrol or signal to a passing motorist or scatter a trail behind her, like Hansel and Gretel. When those doors closed, the car would be invisible from the road below and from the footpath that dropped down to the left of the house. Once inside, there would be no trace of her.

Slumped in the seat, sweating and shivering, she waited.

He came round to the driver's side and pulled her out, binding her wrists again. The floor of the shed was uneven, strewn with debris and, as he pushed her towards the house, she caught her leg on a piece of angle-iron, the metal gouging the flesh where it was thinnest, across the ankle bone. The pain was sickening. Unable to use her arms to steady herself, she fell heavily, grazing both knees through her thin trousers.

Everything was hurting. Her arms, tied behind her back, made it impossible for her to push herself up off the ground. Her shoulder and upper arm had taken her weight as she fell across a pile of bricks. Something sharp was sticking into her hip and the wound on her ankle was bleeding, a warm stickiness running across her foot.

He hauled her to her feet and shoved her out of the shed, shutting the doors. The clang of the metal rang out across the valley, lost amongst the noises of a working day in the summer countryside.

The bleeding slowed but her foot was too painful to take her full weight and she used her toes to balance. Her left side was hurting from shoulder to hip. She hobbled down the moss-covered path towards the back door of the wretched house. Reaching it became her immediate objective. In the house at least she would be able to sit down and have a drink of cool water. He must allow her that.

They entered through a corrugated iron lean-to. To the one side there stood a crazed Belfast sink, the inside stained yellowish-brown and criss-crossed with spiders' webs. A few tools and bamboo canes leaned against the wall. Flies buzzed, trapped between window-pane and filthy net curtains. It smelled of rubber and dry rot.

There was a step up into the dingy kitchen beyond. This was a large room but it had only one window, looking on to a dense holly hedge. Net curtains veiled this window, further limiting the daylight. Set back in a recess was a cast iron range, with easy chairs, facing each other on either side. A pine table and four chairs occupied the centre of the room. Against the far wall stood a sideboard, the top crammed with photographs in tarnished frames. A family's history captured behind flyblown glass. One of the pictures showed an elderly woman, with Prosser, easily recognisable, standing stiffly behind her chair. Then, hanging on the wall behind the sideboard, another picture caught her eye. It was faded sepia but the building silhouetted against the sky was unmistakably Pen Craig.

He shoved her roughly and she collapsed onto one of the dining chairs. 'Can I have a drink?' She cleared her throat. It was the first time that she'd spoken since they had left the yard at home and her voice came out cracked and feeble.

There was another sink in this kitchen and a few glasses stood, upside down, on the draining board. The sound of running water brought the saliva to her mouth and made the few seconds that he took to bring the drink to the table unbearable. He sat next to her, tilting the glass against her lips. It was difficult to drink like this and some of the water trickled onto the table. He kept the glass against her mouth until she couldn't drink any more and, gasping, twisted her head away.

She knew she should get angry. Try to regain some authority. Fight or flight. The phrase looped round and round in her brain. She couldn't walk, so flight was certainly out of the question. Fighting words were the only weapons at her disposal.

'This is silly … We both know…' What did they both know? 'We both know that you didn't intend this to happen. It was an accident.' How was she doing? 'In fact it was my fault. I shouldn't have come upstairs.' He didn't interrupt and she kept going. 'You weren't doing any harm, after all, were you? Just having a bit of a look round.'

While she was talking, he pulled her bra from his pocket and laid it out on the table. It was one that had gone in with the coloureds. Pale pink, the elastic wrinkled, it reminded her of a skinned rabbit. He went to the sideboard, took out one of the small cutlery drawers and brought it to the table. It was filled with neatly folded underwear.

'Is it all mine?'

He smirked. 'Don't flatter yourself.' He set the items out in rows, flattening them with his hand. They were mostly bras and knickers, black, white or navy blue. A red thong and a coffee-coloured lacy bra stood out from the rest and he dangled these from his fingers. 'Mrs Redwood has the nicest things.'

He returned to the sideboard and removed another drawer. This one was full of bric-a-brac. Scissors, beads, spectacles, pens, keys. Amongst it she spotted a shard of her shattered pottery. He held it up, turning it between his index finger and thumb. 'I'm a bit of a collector.' He spoke without emotion, as if he were giving a lecture to the Women's Institute. 'Everyone should have a hobby, don't you think?'

He replaced the drawers then wound the clock which took place of honour on the cluttered mantelpiece, checking it against his watch. Of course, he must come here regularly, to add to his collections and to wind the clock. How odd that he hadn't sold the house or come to live here. Judging from the state of it, his wife never set foot in the place. Mrs P. wouldn't have put up with the filthy windows and the dust. Where did she think he was this afternoon? Shouldn't he be at the Post Office? No, of course not. It was Wednesday – half-day closing.

While they'd been in the car, she'd literally been in the driving seat. There was the chance of crashing into another car or swerving into a ditch. She'd done neither because she had assumed that the situation would resolve itself without putting their lives at risk. It hadn't. Prosser had taken one wrong decision after another and made the situation untenable. He wouldn't get away with it but she might be dead by the time he was apprehended. (She was already employing criminal terminology). Dead. Or raped. Or dead and raped.

Her attempts at negotiation were getting nowhere. The mere sound of her voice appeared to irritate him. She could think of nothing to say that might cause him to modify his stance but, in any case, he was in too deep. She was here on his territory and his terms but, for the first time, he looked unsure of himself. When he removed his heavy jacket, his pale blue shirt was darkened with huge sweat patches beneath the arms and across the back. He paced the kitchen, pausing to twitch the curtain aside and peer obliquely out of the window. At one point he went back through the outhouse but she knew he would be standing in the doorway, blocking her escape route.

He returned, catching her beneath her arms and hauling her to her feet. 'Come on.' He guided her to a door in the corner which she had failed to notice, and lifted the latch. The door opened away from him, swinging over a black void. He flicked the light on, illuminating a flight of stone steps, leading down into a cellar.

'Please don't make me go down there.'

'I don't have a choice.'

'At least undo my arms, so I can balance.'

He was behind her and, although she couldn't see his face, she sensed his indecision. He loosened the belt. Her numb hands burned as the blood flowed back into them, the same pain that she'd felt, as a child, when sensation returned to snow-frozen feet. If she bent her knees, it was possible to edge down the irregular stairs, one hand against the rough wall and the other reaching down to steady herself on the

251

steps.

The walls of the cellar were lined with wooden racks, indicating that the place had once been used for food storage. One bay of shelving was stacked with empty jars and bottles, waiting for jam or cider. A few wooden crates were piled in the corner. He stood at the top, looking down on her. 'Cold?' It was the first sign of consideration and she rushed to take advantage of it.

'Yes. And I need the loo. And a drink.'

He shut the door, his boots sounding on the flagstones as he moved around overhead.

The house was set into the slope of the hillside and the cellar appeared to be located beneath the front of it. It was window-less but there were several ventilation bricks, about six inches below ceiling level, giving a hint of daylight and some air movement. She heard pipes vibrating somewhere, as he ran the water, then his returning footsteps.

The door opened again and he tossed down three cushions. They were heavy, covered in threadbare chintz and she guessed they were from a sofa. Next came two grey blankets, the type found in army surplus shops, and a dark brown, hand-knitted cardigan. The cardigan smelled of mothballs but she was shivering and pulled it on over her short-sleeved shirt, her arms stiff and painful. He disappeared again, then came down the steps with a bucket and a grubby polythene container of, what she assumed, was water. He set these down and took a packet of digestive biscuits and a roll of Softmints from his jacket pocket.

'Light on or off? It's up to you. A word of advice, though. Don't waste your energy trying to get out. This'll be locked,' he nodded towards the cellar door, 'And there's no one within earshot. I'll be back sometime tomorrow.'

'On. Leave the light on.'

He left the cellar and pulled the door shut behind him. She

heard a padlock snap on the far side of the door and held her breath until she was sure that the light was going to stay on.

Nothing unspeakable had happened. Her ankle, knees and the bruised muscles in her left arm were accidental injuries. If she hadn't tripped in the shed, all she'd have to worry about would be sore wrists. He hadn't touched her or done anything horrible, apart from kidnap her. He was a pervert but not a murderer. Yet.

Six-thirty. Tom would be home now, waiting for her to get back with the shopping. When would he start to worry? When he was hungry, probably. Another hour? First he'd go and ask Jenny and Celia if they'd seen her. All the shops in Ludlow shut by six o'clock, except the supermarket. Without the car, he'd ask Mark to give him a lift. There was only one route into town and, once there, they'd check the car park at Tesco. When they didn't find the car, they'd drive back home, then he'd ring the police to report her missing and the search would begin.

She lined up four crates and placed the cushions on top, to form a bed. It felt good to be doing something at last. She put the bucket in the far corner and placed the water container, along with the biscuits and mints, on one of the empty shelves. Prosser hadn't brought her a cup but a jar would do. Would he keep his word and return tomorrow? To be on the safe side, she'd better ration the biscuits. She ran her thumb down the packet, counting the ridges. Twenty-four. She and Tom had eaten lunch just after midday, over six hours ago, and, although she didn't feel hungry, she ate one biscuit.

Occasionally, in the press, there were reports of perfectly nice women, who walked out on husband and children, saying that they were going to post a letter or have coffee with a friend. Would Tom have a problem convincing the police that she wasn't the kind of woman to walk out of her life? Then she remembered the Travel Lodge and wondered whether, perhaps, she was.

The biscuit tasted good and she allowed herself a second, hoping it would settle her stomach which had been feeling queasy from the moment she'd encountered Prosser. When she took a sip from the container, to rinse away the crumbs sticking around her teeth, the water smelled of plastic. Never mind. It was vital to keep up the fluids.

Even with the cardigan on, it was chilly down here and the wool already felt slightly damp. She held her hands up to the light, finding comfort in the heat from the bare bulb.

Wrapping a blanket around herself, she lay down on the improvised bed. The light shone straight into her eyes. Even when she closed them, it penetrated her eyelids. The need to urinate made it impossible to relax and she went to the bucket. Squatting over it, she held on to the shelf, steadying herself, trying not to think about the capacity of the bucket. There was no toilet paper but she would have to manage without, for now. Tomorrow she would work out how to clean herself.

Wrapped up in one blanket, the other pulled over her head, she lay on the musty cushions. An earring, forced into her flesh by the unyielding cushion, cut into her cheek and she took them both out, placing them on the floor next to her bed. She was cold and hurting all down her left side. Her right ankle was swelling up. Maybe it was broken. Her scalp itched and she regretted not washing her hair that morning. Her mouth felt disgusting and her knickers were damp. But it wasn't so bad if she squeezed out of her body and sat up on the shelf, amongst the dusty jam jars.

28

She pushed the blanket back from her face. The cellar looked exactly as it had done at eleven o'clock, midnight, one-thirty and quarter to three. Now it was gone seven and search parties would be out, looking for her.

During the night she had shoved her makeshift bed against the shelving, where she felt less vulnerable. The blanket over her head, shielding her eyes from the light, had an unexpected advantage. Her warm breath, contained in the resulting cocoon, helped keep her body temperature up. It also enhanced the mothball smell that permeated the cardigan but that was the least of her worries.

Her prison was roughly six metres by four metres, its brick walls patchy with flaking whitewash. The floor, too, was brickwork but crude and uneven, not at all like the beautiful floor that Tom had made for her. In one corner there was a drain, covered with an iron grid. The floorboards of the room above formed the ceiling and the single light bulb hung, by a twisted flex, from one of the joists.

The arm and shoulder on which she'd fallen were blotched with navy blue and crimson bruises but it was her ankle, swollen and discoloured, that was the most painful. She decided to spare a little water to clean the wound and to wash herself. Surely when Prosser came back he would refill the container. Needing a cloth of some sort and reluctant to sacrifice her clothing, she tugged at one of the cushions. The cover split and she removed it, giving two decent sized squares of fabric and a few narrow strips. She draped one of the larger pieces over the bucket and ripped one of the strips in half.

Her efforts to wipe away the dried blood, revealed a deep gouge below her ankle bone and a triangular flap of skin folded back. It was a mess and needed stitching. She had a feeling that, if she looked hard enough, she might see the bone. Whatever had caused the wound must have been filthy and she regretted failing to get a tetanus jab after she'd cut her foot in the kitchen.

Taking another scrap of fabric, she wiped her face and hands. It did little to remove the grime but the simple act of moistening her skin was invigorating. Without a brush, there was nothing she could do with her tangled hair and she tugged it back, plaiting it to keep it away from her face.

Breakfast consisted of two biscuits and a few gulps of water, swished around in her mouth, to flush out the crumbs. Her teeth felt stale and coated but rubbing them with the cloth helped. Finally she bit one of the mints in half and sucked it, trying to imagine that it was toothpaste.

Thoughts careered around in her head, leaving vapour trails of panic. As soon as she concentrated on one, another cannoned into it, knocking it aside. Who knew that she was missing? Was this a punishment for her behaviour with Bill? Did she want Prosser to come back or not? Her father must be going frantic. How long before the water ran out? At least she had a granddaughter. Is that what was meant by 'life everlasting'? This would ruin Flora's wedding plans. She didn't want to die in this disgusting place. She wished she'd travelled more. Who would nip the side-shoots out of the tomatoes? What were the last words she'd said to Tom? Would she be brave? She did so want to be brave.

The hands on her watch edged forward but temperature, smell, sound, light levels – nothing else in the cellar varied. 'Sensory deprivation, that's what it is.' Putting a name to what she was experiencing made her feel she a chance of dealing with it. It was critical to keep busy, not to start drifting. She picked up her earrings and hooked them over the lip of one of the glass jars. They dangled, colourful and frivolous, in the drabness.

Her joints, especially hips and ankles, were stiff after a night lying rigid and sleepless on the unforgiving cushions. Moving about helped the stiffness and kept her warm. She took off the cardigan and began some of the gentler exercises she'd learned in a long-ago keep-fit class. Jenny had persuaded her to sign up one January, after a particularly indulgent Christmas. They followed each session with coffee and cakes at the patisserie around the corner. Jenny used to be fun then. Sally must have been at work and Celia was never keen to do anything physical. Poor Celia. She wouldn't last five minutes in Prosser's cellar.

The previous day, during the worst moments, she'd struggled to control her bowels. Through the night things had improved but the exercises had re-activated the churning. It was something she had been dreading. Peeing was bad enough but... She had no choice but to use the bucket and she replaced the chintz cover, holding her breath. Demoralised and disgusted, she sat on her bed and sobbed, stopping only when the taste of salty tears alerted her to the waste of body fluids.

Her spirits rose then plummeted. One minute, confident that she would be rescued within hours, the next, convinced that Prosser would return to perform some unspeakable act.

She must formulate a plan. The only way out of the cellar was through the padlocked door. Unable to put much weight on her right foot, she dragged herself to the top of the steps, using the worn handrail. The door was hinged and locked on the kitchen side, giving her nothing to work on, even if she had some tools. For all she knew, Prosser might be on the other side of the wretched door, listening to her crying and talking to herself. 'You bastard.' she shouted. 'You fucking pervert. You prick.' It was exhilarating to curse him but disappointing that her vocabulary of swear words was so limited. Of course he wouldn't be there. It was eleven o'clock on a Thursday morning and he would be stationed behind the Post Office counter, selling stamps and weighing parcels.

What would Tom do, if he were in her position? When she got out of here and could tell him about it, he'd say 'Why on earth didn't you…?' and come out with a simple solution. Was she missing something obvious? She strained to hear his calm voice, giving her some hint, some clue, some comfort.

She'd eaten four biscuits and drunk about a litre of water. People in mortal danger would often recycle liquid. Hadn't she read about miners surviving for weeks underground, drinking their own urine? Should she pee into the jars and use the bucket just for solids?

There were twenty-seven empty jars on the worm-eaten shelves. Some appeared to be old, with lettering and fancy patterns moulded in the glass. Trade names which she recalled from her grandmother's larder. Someone (Prosser's mother?) had brought them down these steps, in a 'waste-not-want-not' era, when everything was used and reused. How old was this house, anyway? The cement render made it difficult to date and could have been applied long after the house was built. The cellar was lined with bricks. When did bricks become readily available? There was so much that she didn't know.

She transferred the jars to the corner near the bucket,

keeping back the one with the earrings and two more, for drinking and washing. Gathering the few items that lay on the shelves, she examined each one, desperate to find something useful. There was a metal clamp-like thing that might be a mole trap; several dozen white ceramic tiles, half of them chipped; a paper bag of assorted nails and screws; a small brush, the sort that accompanies a dustpan, bristles sparse and clogged with cobwebs; and a metal container, empty, with a handle and a screw cap, which might have held motor oil or paraffin. She removed the cap and sniffed the tin, instantly transported to her father's shed, where a tiny paraffin heater kept them warm on frosty days. Nothing amongst this rusting collection offered a solution and, disappointed, she lay down on the bed.

This was undoubtedly the most dangerous situation she had ever been in, but she was finding it incredibly difficult to believe it was happening. Ironic, considering how much of her life she spent dreaming up things to worry about. Admittedly she was experiencing anxiety symptoms – raised heart rate, churning stomach, spells of uncontrollable shaking – but these symptoms were detached from the specific situation. She wasn't scared that she might die, she was just scared.

People who spent long periods in solitary confinement often professed to being blessed with deeper self-awareness. (Assuming they survived, of course). Given that she must be rescued today, or at the very latest tomorrow, when could she expect this blinding revelation? She lay on her back, eyes closed, blanket over her face, trying to address the issues that really mattered. After fifty-one years on the earth she had two healthy daughters and one beautiful granddaughter. Married to a wonderful man for twenty-eight years. A comfortable home. Some good friends. A productive garden. A collection of lovely pots.

It was no more than a smug, self-congratulatory list and

she had another stab at it.

Jobs that she hadn't taken because Tom didn't want to move. Travelling that she'd longed to do but couldn't, because of family responsibilities. The balancing acts. The compromises. The battles with, and about, Madeleine. A more honest list, but she was no nearer enlightenment.

Try again. How had she made her major life-choices? A poem snatched at the hem of her memory. By an American writer. Something about two paths leading through a wood. Out of curiosity or cussedness, the poet had taken the overgrown path, whereas she'd plodded along the highway, taking the easiest way, the softest option, never brave enough to explore the byways. Well, she was definitely off the beaten track at the moment. She must search out the poem on her next visit to the library.

Standing on a crate, she squinted out through a ventilation brick and saw that it was a beautiful day, out there in the wonderful world. Nothing that she had come across in her inventory would pass through the tiny holes in the brick, but perhaps sound waves might and she held the oil-can near the vent, pounding it with a wine bottle. The noise was deafening inside the confined space and she had no idea whether it was carrying beyond the wall. Random tapping might easily be confused with someone hammering nails, so she beat out the universal Morse code signal. Dot-dot-dot, dash-dash-dash, dot-dot-dot. Every now and again she shrieked 'Help'. After a while her throat became sore, so she sucked a Softmint and rationed the SOS activity to five minutes every half-hour or so.

During the afternoon she urinated into one of the jars and proudly placed it on the shelf.

The tapping and shouting provided a structure to the afternoon. Between bouts of tapping, she exercised but, without pencil and paper to note down her schedule, it was easy to lose track of what to do and when to do it. For some reason, none of the things seemed to have any worth when performed randomly and sporadically. During one of the stretching exercises, she felt something in her back trouser pocket. It was an empty seed packet, bearing the exotic name 'Offenham Flower of Spring 2'. A perfect cabbage was pictured on the front, deep green with white veins spreading across the outer leaves, making them look like green elephant ears. Sometimes, when they had a glut of a particular vegetable, she would cook a whole panful and they would devour it with thick wedges of bread and butter. Only yesterday she had scattered these seeds along the shallow drill. They would be lying there now, beneath the soil, waiting for a warm shower to trigger them into life.

She flattened the crumpled envelope and placed it inside the earring jar, pushing it against the glass to display it, like a masterpiece in a curved frame.

By evening, she was feeling sick. During the day she'd eaten six more biscuits, a few mints and drunk another litre or so of water. If Prosser intended to come, it would have to be soon. She'd rehearsed what she would say to him, speaking the words aloud to check their coherence. Her aim was to engage him in conversation, hoping to get an idea of what he planned to do with her and then persuade him to bring more food and water. Above all, she was determined to remain calm and dignified.

Like a hospital patient preparing for visitors, she tidied her bed. Her hair was matted and she re-plaited it, using her splayed fingers as a comb. Would the way she had reorganised the contents of the cellar annoy him? Urine had become crucial to her plan and she pushed the filled jars behind the empty ones. He was vindictive enough to tip it down the drain. She moved the oil can into the shadows and camouflaged the beating-bottle amongst the others.

At ten o'clock she gave up listening for his tread on the floor above, peed into a jar and crawled under the blanket.

The last proper meal she'd eaten was lunch, thirty-six hours ago. They'd eaten cheese and pickle in wholemeal rolls followed by leftovers of an apple pie. Food fantasies came crowding in. If she closed her eyes, plates piled with fish and chips, a thick fillet steak, Christmas dinner with all the trimmings, hovered mirage-like in front of her. She ate four biscuits, one after the other.

When the children had found it hard to sleep, she would encourage them to 'think about your day and all the lovely things you've done.' Her day in the cellar was not a sleep-inducing meditation and, instead, she thought back to her school days, moving from desk to desk, row to row. Gail Lloyd – long plaits falling below her waist. Alan Brace – good at sport. Angela Something, whose sister had died in a car crash. John Christie – wore wellington boots whatever the weather. Their form teacher, a joyless, bitter man, thin, with nicotine-stained fingers. Jenkins. That was it.

College next and Duncan. Her beautiful Duncan. Her first lover. One day they'd fallen out of love and cried together, as if someone had died. They hadn't kept in touch, although they'd promised they would. She'd seen an article about him a few years ago in one of the Sundays. Now a well-respected painter, the picture showed him, a thin, bald stranger, standing in front of some dingy abstracts.

She was unable to keep them out of her thoughts any longer. Flora. Self-possessed and undemanding, so like Tom in looks and temperament. A child who only demanded that things be fair and just. When she was seven or eight she'd asked, 'Is there really a Father Christmas? Promise you'll tell me the truth.' With Christmas a good six months away, Anna had decided that it was the right time. 'No. But don't tell Maddy. She's only a little girl.' Flora had burst into tears, sobbing for hours, not because it spoiled Christmas, but because she felt silly for ever having believed the fairy story.

And beautiful, difficult, unpredictable Madeleine who had caused them so much anxiety over the years, with her wild streak and her refusal to compromise. This daughter had set out on the less trodden path but would she be able to stick to it, with a daughter of her own to rear?

Then there he was, her Tom, calm and constant, smelling of wood smoke and soap. His broad hands with their cared-for nails, competent yet capable of such tenderness. Her best friend in the whole world, he might be undressing now, pulling his shirt over his head as he had done every night of their married life. She would never again complain about those unbuttoned shirts.

29

She curled into a ball in an attempt to ease her cramping stomach. After a wakeful hour, she gave up. There were nine biscuits left. The damp had crept inside the wrapper and softened them but they tasted wonderful. She ate two, hoping that by giving her digestive system something to work on, she might get back to sleep.

Moving about used precious energy and she returned to bed, lying on her front to protect her eyes from the light and comfort her stomach. The sweet aftertaste of biscuits filled her mouth and made her thirsty again.

Would they be asleep now? Tom might. He was hopeless if he got less than his eight hours. And how were they managing for food? Of course everyone would rally round and sort out the practicalities. People love to have something to do in an emergency. It would be best if Maddy and Seren remained in Bath with her father, away from the unpleasantness, because even tiny babies pick up on tension.

It must be the most exciting thing that had ever happened in Cwm Bont and the village would be buzzing with it. Len would be having the time of his life, disseminating gossip straight from the epicentre. In the Post Office, Prosser would be selling newspapers and tins of baked beans, as usual, confident that neither his wife, nor anyone else for that matter, would come to this house. Surely Mrs. Prosser must have an inkling that her husband was up to something. From the number of items in the drawer, it seemed that Prosser had been 'collecting' for a while. She'd know if Tom were stealing underwear. Wouldn't she?

What if Prosser never came back, or came back but didn't visit the cellar? The door could remain shut forever, or at least until someone else moved into the house. He could carry on with his normal day-to-day routine and, in two or three weeks, she would be dead. Alive she was a liability, dead, no problem at all. Obviously the police would question everyone in Cwm Bont but would they suspect him? Was there anything to connect him with her? If he had a criminal record, or had done something unsavoury in the past, wouldn't they have heard about it?

The unwavering light from the sixty-watt bulb gave no indication of passing time. Her watch was her only point of reference and she took it off, placing it carefully on the shelf near her bed. Some stretches of the day dragged and it required enormous self-discipline not to watch the second hand, jerking through the minutes.

Today was Friday the 15th August. She knew the kitchen calendar didn't have it highlighted as an important day, but it might possibly turn out to be the day on which she died. Her death day. Everyone had a death day which they negotiated each year except their last. The family would always think of her on her death day, assuming, of course, that they knew when it was.

Determined to record the passing days, she experimented. Using the longest nail from the paper bag, it was easy to make marks on the wooden shelves but more satisfactory results came from scratching the oil-can. The can was already covered with indentations on the broader sides, where she had been striking it with the bottle, but the narrow sides were perfect for her rudimentary calendar. With the initial letters of the weekdays inscribed, top to bottom, she could make a down-stroke against each at noon every day. It was logical to start with a W for Wednesday, her first day in captivity. The nail slipped across the frictionless surface but she persevered, tracing the strokes over and over, until they combined to form one bold mark. When she'd finished, she held the can at arm's length, twisting it from side to side, the light picking out the W, T and F.

The family would survive without her. They would be distraught for – how long? A year? Six months? Sad too, of course, and it would spoil their lives for a while. They always say that a missing person is more difficult to deal with than a dead one and people might cross the street to avoid them, stuck for appropriate words. Eventually, they would accept that she was gone and 'move on' as the jargon went, slipping naturally into the past tense when they spoke about her. 'Mum was this… Mum used to do that…'

After seven years she could be 'presumed dead'. Tom would be getting on for sixty then. Funnily enough, Jenny had been telling her some tale, only last week, about a woman whose missing husband had returned after sixteen years, only to find that she'd married his best friend. Tom would never marry Sally but what sort of a woman might he choose? A tidy, housewifely one, organised and reliable, who would replace the cap on the toothpaste and fold the newspaper properly. He rarely criticised her but more than once she had caught him watching her, as though observing an alien life form. Then she remembered that her father had chosen Dorothy for his second wife and there was no satisfactory explanation for that.

Flora would marry Luke and lead a worthy, uneventful life. If Sally spent her days wandering round the world and Bill didn't have the nerve to return, Tom would be delighted to overcompensate for a shortfall of grandparents, when babies came along.

Madeleine would, no doubt, continue to get it wrong. But at least she would experience great passion in her roller-coaster life, always drawn to the Brendans of this world while, try as they might, the Taliesins failed to win her.

And they would all make these mistakes whether she were there or not. If truth were told, and for all her efforts, she had exercised little influence on their lives for years. This realisation lifted a great burden from her and she felt giddy with relief.

Her stomach rumbled most of the time, breaking the silence with aquatic gurgles. Occasionally it griped so badly that it took her breath away. A small quantity of water remained but five jars of urine, in varying shades of amber, stood on the shelf. Her ankle was extremely swollen, the skin around the wound red and hot. Even if she could spare some water, the gash needed more than a dab with a grubby cloth. Urine might possibly be a natural antiseptic but, then again, it might not. She trawled her memory for the answer but all she came up with was the image of an enthusiastic young television presenter, collecting droplets of water from a cut he'd made in the trunk of a silver birch. The memory of the clear liquid dripping into the fragile cup, fashioned from the bark of the tree, was too much and she wept into the musty blanket draped around her shoulders.

If Prosser were carrying on in his normal routine, he would only be able to come to the house when the Post Office was closed. During what would be his lunch hour, she sat on the bed, head resting on drawn-up knees, straining for the faintest sound from above – the creak of the back door, the scuff of a foot on the floor, the sound of the water running in the kitchen. She heard nothing but the swoosh of her own blood, pumping through her ears.

Her head ached continuously and she was lethargic. Her ankle was too stiff to contemplate exercising. The swelling and inflammation had crept up half way to her grazed knee. In fact all her joints ached. 'Dehydration.' She began to recite snatches of poetry and chunks of Shakespeare, learned at school. Her English teacher, Miss Brown, a formidable old woman (although probably younger than *she* was now) who employed ridicule to keep her pupils in order, gave them, every week, a poem to commit to memory. Over the years, these words, learned by rote without consideration of form or content, had surfaced at the least expected moments. In labour with Flora, 'The Pied Piper of Hamelin' had run continuously through her brain, with attendant images of cherubic children, dancing towards their disappearance. Today the dirge favoured by lovesick girls flooded back. 'Remember me when I am gone away...blah-de-blah ... Better by far you should forget and smile, than that you should remember and be sad.' How appropriate.

The evening hours passed and by nine o'clock she knew he wasn't coming. There were five biscuits left now and maybe a pint of water and she ate two of them, took a reckless swig from the water bottle and tidied up her bed. This wasn't to be her death day.

The headache hammered behind her eyes, sending pains shooting into her ears. If she leaned forward, it doubled in intensity. Her mouth tasted foul and her saliva had turned to glue, sticking her lips together. Today was Saturday and she scratched a mark beside the 'S' on her metal calendar. Saturdays used to be special. No school or work and a day to squander. When they lived in Bristol, they often went out for breakfast. Or they might take off down to Devon, to walk along winter beaches or sit on tall chrome stools, drinking milkshakes while they watched the waves. Sidmouth.

Earrings. Babies. Bill's wet kisses. What a shame.

She drank the last of the water and ate the remaining biscuits.

Yesterday she'd abandoned the regular can-banging. It was difficult to expend so much effort on what might be a waste of time. Now and again, she put her face near the air-bricks and yelled 'Help. Help.' It sapped her energy and aggravated her headache.

Today when she peered out of the tiny holes, it was in order to catch sight of the sky or feel fresh air moving across her burning cheeks. Alternately sweating and shivering, she was sure that the gash on her leg had become infected and that she was starting to suffer bouts of delirium.

'I close my eyes, draw back the curtain...' She worked her way through 'Joseph,' the songs popping out, one after the other, in the correct sequence. After six weeks of a rainy school holiday, when the girls had played the record non-stop, how could she ever forget?

The breeze cooled her damp forehead. She shut her eyes, savouring the sensation. And then she heard it. A faint voice coming from the side of the house, where she envisioned the mossy footpath dropping down from the ridge. From the intonation, she knew it was someone calling a dog. A pet not a police dog. 'Oh, God. Oh, God. Please hear me.' Grabbing the oilcan and bottle she beat out her SOS, shouting as loud as she could but her voice was feeble and she doubted that it would carry. After a couple of minutes she stopped, straining to hear whether the voice had been a figment.

There it was, closer now. 'Here, girl.' Someone whistled. Thank God for a disobedient dog. She made encouraging noises, dragging air in through her pursed lips hoping to intrigue an inquisitive animal with the seductive squeak. If the dog returned to its owner, she was sunk. They would clip on a leash, stroll on down to the road, and that would be that.

She'd finished the biscuits which might have lured the dog to her prison. Would human female urine be of interest? She held one of the jars against the tiny air vents, tilting it until the yellow fluid lapped the rim. Tipping it further, the liquid trickled back along the outside of the jar and down her arm, soaking into the cardigan. All the while she called to the dog. 'Here, doggy. Good dog.'

A jar of pee was soaking into her clothing and none of it had passed through the holes. Perhaps it was a waste of time and she should concentrate on making a noise. She resumed her morse-coding on the can. But what if this frightened the dog away? Resorting to her original idea, she poured the contents of a second jar into a wine bottle. This might make it easier to direct the flow of pee out, through the holes. She tried again, pushing the neck of the bottle tight against the air-brick. This time the liquid flowed away from her.

Then she heard, close by, the yapping of a small dog. A Jack Russell maybe. It was difficult to gauge how far away it was but, a few seconds later, something obscured the pinpoints of daylight and she heard snuffling and yipping in the urine-soaked grass. All she had to do was hold the dog's interest until the whistling owner came to find it.

30

The dog, a corgi cross, was called Flossy. During the days following Anna's release, the papers fêted their canine heroine. Pictures of the ugly little mongrel sitting, standing, panting, covered the tabloids and broadsheets alike. Accounts of the circumstances surrounding the kidnapping ranged from the vague to the totally inaccurate. Tom tried his utmost to shield Anna from the crassness of the reports, but as soon as her fellow patients had identified her as 'the victim, fifty-one year old Anna Wren', it was hopeless. The old lady from the next ward hobbled down the corridor with several cuttings in the string bag suspended from her walking frame. 'You'll need these for your scrap book, dear,' she said.

The ankle injury, coupled with the effects of shock and dehydration, required her to spend a week under medical surveillance. She had little, apart from heavy bandaging around her ankle, to show for her incarceration. The bruises on her arms and legs had faded, leaving one or two mustard-coloured patches. She longed to be at home, away from the tests and interviews with inscrutable psychiatrists and ponderous policemen. Many of their questions seemed pointless. 'Did he actually say he was going to kill you, in so many words, or did you make that assumption?'

'I can't remember but he had a kitchen knife at my throat, so I don't think I was jumping to conclusions.' Their deadpan stares chastised her flippancy.

Hospitalisation afforded protection from the dozens of journalists who were descending on Cwm Bont. 'You're better off here at the moment, Mum.' Flora did her best to convince her. 'You wouldn't be able to show your nose if you came home.'

Everyone in the family had made their way to Pen Craig when the news of her disappearance leaked out. Even her brother had taken time off work. Taliesin and Arthur came from Brecon to see whether they could do anything to help. When they ran out of space, Luke suggested that they use Bill's empty house, with the summerhouse if they were still short of accommodation. Jenny and Celia had co-ordinated food for visitors. How irritating to think that whilst she was urinating in a jam jar and rationing digestive biscuits, they were having some kind of jamboree.

The medical staff insisted that there should be no more than two people at her bedside at any time, so Tom devised a visiting rota. Visitors brought flowers, fruit and useless things, like scented wipes and soft toys. Celia, looking more robust than Anna had ever seen her, presented her with a crocheted bed jacket, in a violent shade of orange. 'I bought it at the W.I. Craft Fayre. I know you adore bright colours. We thought it would cheer you up.'

'Mmmm. So … orange. Thank you.'

'Oh, and guess what? My test results came through yesterday. They can't seem to find anything at all…'

'That's marvellous…'

'…so they're going to repeat them. I'm definitely not right.' Celia smiled, happy to remain a diagnostic mystery.

The Redwoods popped in, on their way to a Royal College of Surgeons dinner in Birmingham. Peter, out of place in the role of visitor, wandered around the ward, reading charts and hieroglyphics at the ends of the beds.

'You poor thing, I don't know how you survived without hot water. Ghastly.' Jenny gave a mock shudder. 'We thought this might help you relax.' Her exquisitely wrapped parcel contained a triangular hop-filled pillow which could be heated in the microwave.

'You could always have it for breakfast, if you're desperate,' Flora prodded it when she inspected the growing pile of gifts, stashed away in her mother's bedside locker.

When the visitors left, Anna tried to read. It should have been an opportunity to catch up on her backlog of books but it was impossible to concentrate and she found herself flipping back through pages which she'd already read. The only book to grip her was one she found abandoned in the day-room – a grisly tale of serial killings, packed with forensic detail.

In the hospital, where they were under constant scrutiny, it seemed impossible to get anywhere near Tom and her conversations with him were polite and superficial. They might have been no more than acquaintances. 'Dad's feeling terribly guilty because he didn't contact the police straight away.' Madeleine came nearest to broaching the question which Anna was finding it impossible to ask.

Eventually, a perceptive young doctor spotted the anxiety this was causing her. 'I don't think we can do much more for you here, Mrs. Wren. Your ankle's going to heal fine. There'll be a scar, of course. But promise me you'll see your GP, if things are getting on top of you. Counselling can be very beneficial. Don't be too brave, will you?' He shook her hand and discharged her to the care of her family and the district nurse.

'How *are* you feeling?' Tom helped her into Taliesin's car for the drive home. The police had removed theirs from Prosser's shed, on a low loader, and it was still undergoing forensic investigations, as if it could tell them something that she couldn't.

'Fine. OK, I suppose. Confused.'

'Confused?'

'I don't know. I don't feel ill, more sort of disconnected. Restless.'

'You know Prosser can't hurt you? He's in a secure unit while they assess him.'

'I'm not scared of Prosser, if that's what you think. He never planned to kidnap anyone. I happened to walk in on him and the situation got out of hand. He was disgruntled.'

'Disgruntled?'

'Yes. He resented seeing us living in what he considered to be his rightful home. He wanted to rattle us. Steal a few things. Move things. Maybe that's why the previous owners left.'

'How can you be so bloody understanding? The man was going to let you die. If I ever see him, I'll kill him.'

'Great. That would be really helpful.'

He drove on. They sat side-by-side but were a hundred miles apart. He talked about the garden, the girls and Seren, bringing her up to date on domestic events, as if she'd been away on a holiday. 'The Redwoods and the Webbers have been wonderful.' What else would he expect?

'Tom, where did you think I was that night? The only thing that kept me going was believing you had half the police force out, searching for me.' There, it was out in the open. She watched the hedgerows flashing past the car window, determined not to utter another word until he had answered her question.

'I thought you'd left me.'

'What?' She looked at him but he stared ahead, hands tight on the steering wheel.

'I thought you'd gone to Aberystwyth.'

They were approaching a lay-by, set back behind a strip of

grass and shielded from the road by a few dusty hawthorns. He veered into it, the drivers behind honking and gesticulating at his failure to signal. He switched off the engine and they sat in miserable silence. The sky was almost white and there was no breeze to stir the humid air.

'It's stifling in here.' Anna got out and walked towards an open gate. The grass in the field beyond was long enough for a second cut of silage. Tom locked the car and came after her. Keeping close to the hedge, they followed it up the field, away from the road, until the traffic was barely audible. One of the hedgerow trees had grown bigger than the rest and its distorted trunk hung out, offering a place to sit. A swarm of black flies, 'thunder flies' her mother had always called them, whizzed around their heads, attracted by their salty sweat. She waited for him to continue.

'I knew something was wrong between us but I didn't know if it was my fault. Every time I got near to talking about it, asking you about it, I chickened out. Perhaps I didn't want to know. Remember that time in Sidmouth? I thought if I confessed about that silly business with Celia, you might open up and tell me what was troubling you. Then things went back to normal again and I thought I must have been imagining it. Peter kept dropping obscure hints but I didn't know what he was on about and I never quite trust him, anyway. Then I began to notice things myself. The way Bill looked at you. Some of his jokey remarks. How he always managed to sit next to you. It all fell into place.'

'How did you think *I* was feeling? At first I thought I was imagining it, too. What was I supposed to do when your ... our ... best friend started getting ... I don't know what you'd call it. Fresh? Do we say that any more? I didn't want to make a fuss in case it made things awkward. We'd moved here to support each other, not ruin each other's marriages. And when Flora and Luke announced their engagement, how could I spoil it for them?'

'I wondered if Sally left because she'd seen what was going on.'

'Hold on a minute. "Going on." What d'you think was "going on"?'

'I don't know. You tell me.'

To reveal that Bill had kissed her (twice) and touched her breasts, would be an accurate account of events but it had been more than that. How could she explain that she had been excited, aroused and consumed by a desire to experience sex with another man but that it had nothing at all to do with her feelings for *him*? She couldn't understand it herself, so what would Tom make of it?

A jaunty ringing came from Tom's clothing. 'What on earth's that?' she asked.

'Mobile.' He produced a small, silver object from his pocket.

'We haven't got a mobile. You always said you'd never have one.'

'I changed my mind. When you were … missing, I had to be contactable. Mark sorted it out for me. In fact, I was up in the wood when the police rang on Saturday. I couldn't bear to be inside and I couldn't bear to be *with* anyone. They all seemed so … so not you.' He looked down at the number displayed on the tiny screen. 'It's quite clever, really. You can see who's calling.' He put the phone gingerly to his ear and it was lost in his shock of grey hair. 'Flora? Give us an hour or so. We've just stopped for a breather. OK. Yes, she's fine. 'Bye.'

'Please tell me they're not doing a party.'

'I've told them to leave the house to us. Anyway, wouldn't you like a party?'

'Of course I wouldn't. It would be like celebrating a disaster which should never have happened. Like *not* getting run over or *not* getting burgled.'

He closed his eyes then puffed out his cheeks, letting the air escape slowly through his lips. 'I've got something to say, before we get home, and I want you to hear me out. OK?'

'Oh dear.'

'To be perfectly honest, when you didn't come home that evening I wasn't totally surprised. I assumed that you'd gone away. I thought it was likely that you'd gone to Bill. Mind you, I was a bit miffed that you hadn't left a message to let me know you were all right.

'Maybe that's because I *wasn't* all right.'

He raised his hand to silence her. 'That first night, in the house on my own, I tried to work it out. To put myself in your place. To think like you think. But I didn't have a clue.'

'That's me. Enigmatic…'

'Please let me finish, Anna. Then, the next afternoon, when I came back from the police station, I was up in the wood, sawing logs…'

'Sawing logs?'

'…I was sawing logs, when it came to me. You know those bits of music that get you right here?' He pushed his fingers hard into his chest. 'And here?' He touched his throat. 'I don't understand how that works either but I simply accept it and enjoy it. So that's what I've decided to do. Sorry. That sounds a bit wet, doesn't it?'

'Wet, yes, but wonderful too.'

'So, I don't give a flying fuck about Bill Davis, or anything else, as long as you come back with me. Will you?'

'Yes, of course I will. And I'm so sorry I didn't talk to you about it. I wasn't…'

'Ssshhh.' He placed his finger across her lips. 'That's all over and done with.'

She buried her head in his chest and they clung together,

until a spasm of cramp in her calf made her jump up, half crying, half laughing. He stood up, too, and took her in his arms, lifting her slightly to take the weight off her bandaged ankle and they danced an untidy polka, finally dropping to the ground, gasping and laughing.

'All the time I was in the cellar, I kept asking myself 'what would Tom do?' I knew I was missing something obvious and that any idiot would have worked out how to get out.' She lay on her back, staring at the colourless sky, squinting against the brightness. Overhead a kestrel circled lazily, ready to plummet down on any careless field mouse.

'You did brilliantly, love, although I can't understand why you didn't try...'

'No. Please. I don't want to think about it. Not now anyway. It's like finding out the correct answers after you've done an exam. Pointless.'

'You're an amazing woman.' He rolled on to his front, resting his forehead on his folded arms.

She reached out and rubbed her hand across his back then snuggled against him.

They realised afterwards that they'd slept for over an hour.

Hand in hand, they strolled back to the road. An estate car had parked behind theirs, the open back revealing deckchairs and a parasol. Several children were chasing around the oil-stained tarmac, whooping and shrieking.

'I used to despise people who did that.' She nodded towards the family, positioning a white plastic table on the grass verge, within feet of the passing traffic. 'But it's fine isn't it?'

'How d'you mean?'

'What right have I got to tell anyone what they should, or shouldn't, do?'

31

Tom manoeuvred the car through the crush of vehicles in the yard and stopped near the back door. 'Go on in, love. I'll bring everything.'

It had been ten days since Prosser had marched her out of the house, at knife-point, but everything looked the same. Advertising fliers littered the top of the washing machine. Roses in the purple vase, heads dipped, dropped petals on the sill. A cot blanket hung over the back of the dining chair. And the same smell which had filled their kitchens, wherever they lived, told her she was home.

Tom dumped her holdall and several carrier bags of gifts on the kitchen table.

The house was quiet except for its own soothing sounds. Clocks. Flies. The fridge. 'Where is everyone?' she asked.

'In the summerhouse. I'm afraid they've got champagne and stuff. I couldn't stop them. You know what Jenny's like.'

There was no point in berating him. 'They will have to manage without me. I'm going to have a long soak in the bath, then I want to finish my book.'

'But couldn't you just…?'

'I could but I'm not going to. Tomorrow I intend to get up early and check the garden. There's sure to be a glut of beans after the rain. I need to get them picked and in the freezer before they go to waste.'

Tom hovered in the doorway, miserable, waiting for her to reconsider. 'What d'you want me to tell them?'

'Thank them very much and explain that I'm tired and that I'll see them tomorrow. Cheer up, love, they rarely shoot the messenger.'

When he'd gone, she carted her things up to their bedroom. The door was ajar and she peeped in before entering. There were no clothes heaped on the bedside chairs or protruding from half-shut drawers. She drew her finger along the tops of the picture frames but they were free of dust. Sharp creases quartered the pillowcases and washing-powder scented the air. Someone had changed the bedding that morning.

There was a knock on the open door. Arthur, barefoot, stood on the threshold. He smiled and ran across to her open arms. 'I sneaked up 'cos I wanted to make sure you were all right. Tom said you were fine but grownups don't always tell the truth, do they?'

'Some of them don't, but Tom does.'

'D'you tell the truth?'

'Not always.'

'Why?'

'Oh, lots of reasons but usually it's because I don't want to upset anyone. For example, what if I were to ask you whether you think I'm pretty? You *might* think I'm ugly but not want to hurt my feelings by saying so.'

'People shouldn't ask, if they don't want the truth, should they? And, anyway, I think you are beautiful. You've got interesting hair.' He pulled a curl that had escaped the combs, watching it spring back when he released it.

When she unpacked, the stale-disinfectant smell of the hospital still clung to the clothes she'd worn there. Arthur, wrinkling his nose in distaste, helped her dump everything in the laundry basket. One of the carrier bags was full of get-well cards and he arranged them like tiles, on the floor, counting as he went. '...twenty-two, twenty-three,' then stood back to look at his handiwork. 'This one's my favourite.' The card he held up showed purple irises sketched in bold watercolour strokes. 'It just says "Bill". That's funny, there's no message. Not even a kiss.'

When everything had been put away, they sat together on the bed. He took a twist of dark green tissue paper from the pocket of his baggy shorts and held it out to her. 'Open it.' He grinned, his milk teeth white and shining, like square pearls against his tanned face. She made a great show of opening the tiny package, while he bounced up and down. 'It's a fossil,' he said, unable to contain himself any longer. 'I found it on the beach once, when we went to Lyme-something-or-another. Dad says it might be a million years old.'

A split pebble, almost hemispherical, revealed on its inner surface the segmented spiral of an ammonite. She brushed her fingertips across it, awed by the direct connection with prehistory.

'You *do* like it?'

'I love it. But it's yours, Art.'

'Dad says it's magic. It'll keep you safe forever.'

He was standing now, palms resting on her knees, warm through her cotton trousers. She kissed his forehead. 'Thank you. I'll keep it with my most precious things. And shall I tell you what I think we should do? Before the end of the school holidays, I think we should go to the seaside, you and I.'

'And Tom?'

'And Tom, if you like. And we'll look for another ammonite, so that you've got one to keep *you* safe too. How does that sound?'

The little boy smiled and leaned in towards her. 'Can Dad

and Maddy and Seren come with us? We could find fossils for everyone.'

Tom appeared at the door, carrying two mugs of tea. 'I thought you could do with this. Hello, Art. Your dad's looking for you.'

The child skipped off down the stairs, singing as he went.

'How's the party going?'

'It's getting quite lively. To be honest, I think they've forgotten what it's supposed to be for. Maddy and Flora are arguing about whether money's for spending or saving. Your father's gone to sleep. Mark and Celia are singing. Tal's looking after Seren. Pete and I had another set to but I ran out of steam. If he's *that* determined to live in a place with a swimming pool, we might as well go ahead. Life's too short.'

They sat on the bed, drinking tea. She shut her eyes and put her head back on the familiar pillow. 'Home.'

'Is it?' Tom lay beside her.

'I love this little valley and the garden here. It's wonderful to have my own studio. But wherever we've lived, it's always *felt* the same. It's happened again here. I suppose we carry it with us wherever we go. Am I making sense? Home is us.'

'Now who's sounding wet?'

Next morning she was up before seven o'clock. Tom stirred but didn't argue when she kissed him and told him to stay where he was. The party had gone on late and several times during the night she had surfaced from a dream, hearing giggles and thuds as the revellers returned. Once she heard Seren wake for her feed, then fell back to sleep, Maddy's soft lullaby working on granddaughter and grandmother alike. And whenever she reached out, Tom was at her side.

Anxious not to wake the dreamers, she skipped her shower.

She tip-toed downstairs, pausing on the landing to glimpse the valley, perfect in the morning freshness. The sky was forget-me-not blue, criss-crossed with fluffy vapour trails. Where were those planes heading? America? China? Had Sally flown overhead on her way to India, or was that in the other direction? One day she and Sally might meet and compare notes on these strange days.

There were no glasses left in the kitchen cupboard and she poured orange juice into a mug. In her studio the pottery animals waited, two by two, on the shelf. She picked up the pigs. Would a little girl want to play with these hard, cold animals? They should be made of something soft and forgiving, something warm to her touch, like the living creatures they portrayed. She would ask Arthur for his opinion.

The tool shed was in chaos. The girls always teased Tom about the way he fussed with his tools, never failing to return each one to its proper place. 'If I needed a bow-saw one dark night, when the electricity fails and we've run out of candles, I could put my hand right on it.' The girls had shrieked with laughter at the idea of their father sawing away in the pitch darkness. Tom must have been distraught, to have left his things scattered about like this. Eventually she located the hoe and a bucket.

The doors of the summerhouse were shut when she passed. Two lumpy forms curled up in sleeping bags occupied the sofas, recumbent sailors in a sea of bottles, glasses, plates and crisp packets. It had been quite a party.

She opened the wicket gate which led to the vegetable garden. The rattle of the latch alerted several blackbirds feasting on the raspberries, and they shrieked a warning as they made off, beaks laden with fat berries. A nettle caught her unbandaged ankle and she bent to pick a dock leaf, rubbing its juice into the tiny white blisters.

She made her way along the mown path which skirted the gardens. The Webbers had pulled up the scruffy currant bushes inherited with the property, and seeded their plot with grass. The ground undulated gently and now, after months of attention, looked as if it were covered with a gigantic velvet bedspread. A cane, painted with black and white bands and topped with a triangular pennant, pinpointed the hole.

As a result of Eric's expertise, the Redwoods' garden sported a stunning array of vegetables and flowers for cutting. In the corner there was a sturdy compost bin, constructed from slatted boards. She raised the lid an inch or two and saw the spinach and lettuce which had gone straight from garden to compost bin, without going anywhere near the kitchen. Jenny led a busy life and rarely had time to cook.

Anna paused at the bottom of Bill's plot, overgrown with couch grass and dandelions. Here and there, a rhubarb crown or wilting potato vine poked above the weeds. He'd tried hard, in the beginning, but it took no time at all for nature to reclaim lost ground.

Ten days had passed since she was last here. The runner beans, unchecked, had outstripped their framework of bamboo canes and they waved in the light breeze, tendrils searching for something to cling to. Bees homed in on the scarlet flowers, ensuring the next flush. The rough-skinned crop hung in swathes and soon she'd picked enough to fill the bucket.

She moved along the rows of vegetables, sliding the shiny blade of the hoe beneath the surface of the soil, severing the roots of the opportunist chickweed and groundsel. They would all go on the heap to rot down, in time forming crumbly black compost to feed the ground and complete the cycle.

At the bottom corner, nearest the path, she'd worked a small area to a fine tilth. This was the seedbed, where she'd formed the shallow drill and planted the cabbage seed. She crouched down, searching. There it was, a thread of green, breaking through the powdery soil. No more than a tiny pair of leaves, each seed was starting to perform its magic. Under the hedge she found a sturdy twig, driving it into the baked ground to mark the row. She took the empty packet from her shirt pocket and pushed it on to the stick. In a month or so, the seedlings would be big enough to plant out in rows across the garden, and if they survived the pest attacks, the winter frosts and the raging gales, they would be ready to eat in the spring.

ABOUT HONNO

Honno Welsh Women's Press was set up in 1986 by a group of women who felt strongly that women in Wales needed wider opportunities to see their writing in print and to become involved in the publishing process. Our aim is to develop the writing talents of women in Wales, give them new and exciting opportunities to see their work published and often to give them their first 'break' as a writer. We publish any type of writing as long as it meets our quality standards.

Honno is registered as a community co-operative. Any profit that Honno makes goes towards the cost of future publications. Since it was established over 450 women from Wales and around the world have expressed their support for its work by buying shares at £5 each in the co-operative. We hope that many more women will be able to help us in this way. Shareholders' liability is limited to the amount invested, and each shareholder, regardless of the number of shares held, can have her say in the company and a vote at the Annual General Meeting.

To buy shares or to receive further information about forthcoming publications, please write to Honno at the address below, or visit our website: www.honno.co.uk.

Honno
'Ailsa Craig'
Heol y Cawl
Dinas Powys
Bro Morgannwg
CF64 4AH